Anonymous

Life in the Mofussil

or, the Civilian in Lower Bengal by an Ex-Civilian - Vol. 1

Anonymous

Life in the Mofussil
or, the Civilian in Lower Bengal by an Ex-Civilian - Vol. 1

ISBN/EAN: 9783348054140

Printed in Europe, USA, Canada, Australia, Japan

Cover: Foto ©Andreas Hilbeck / pixelio.de

More available books at **www.hansebooks.com**

LIFE IN THE MOFUSSIL;

OR,

THE CIVILIAN IN LOWER BENGAL.

BY

AN EX-CIVILIAN.

VOL. I.

LONDON :

C. KEGAN PAUL & CO., 1, PATERNOSTER SQUARE.

1878.

CONTENTS.

LIFE IN THE MOFUSSIL;

OR; .

THE CIVILIAN IN LOWER BENGAL.

CHAPTER I.

VOYAGE OUT.

THE START FOR INDIA.—THE SIREN.—DEATH ON 'BOARD.—THE
SHARK.—ARRIVAL IN THE HOOGHLY.—THE ARDENT LOVER.—
ON SHORE AT LAST.

HOW well I remember the 4th of October, 186–. It was
a lovely evening, and I was seated, with one or two others
of my own age, smoking the cigar of contentment on the
poop of the good ship *Lady Ellenborough*, now anchored in
the Downs, and waiting for the breeze which should enable
her to make a start independent of tugs and all other such
troublesome and expensive accessories, on her journey to
Calcutta.

It was indeed the cigar of contentment that I smoked ;
for had I not passed the competitive examination for the
Indian Civil Service sufficiently high to enable me to
select Bengal as the field of my future career ? had I not

VOL. I.   B

scraped through the second examination in some mysterious way by the light of nature ? and was I not now fairly
launched in the world, with a prospect of novelty, excitement, and a fair competence before me ?

All my compeers had gone, or were about to go, by the
overland route, and I, in compliance with instructions from
the India Office, had endeavoured to secure a passage
which should enable me to leave England before the end
of November; but the P. and O. officials had informed me
very curtly that they could not supply me with such ; that
they could not let me know if any unforeseen vacancy
should occur ; and when I stated with a certain stiffness
that I must find some other means of getting to my destination, had received the threatening announcement with
the most blank unconcern. The opening of the Suez Canal
has possibly made some alteration in this state of things.

On the whole I was not sorry to be compelled to apply
to Messrs. Green, and was almost disappointed when the
chief mate told me in the docks that the voyage would not
occupy more than three months. Little did I think that
those three months would be stretched into nearly five,
and that long before one-third of the journey had passed I
would have eaten any amount of humble pie to be allowed
any corner on the deck of a P. and O. steamer, with a
chance of a speedy end to the miserable monotony of a
sea voyage.

There were thirty-six of us first-class passengers on
board—eighteen of each sex ; and the agent of the Company, who had come to Gravesend to see us off, had
assured us, with a sort of paternal unction, that we were

a very pleasant party and ought to have an agreeable time of it.

It might be thought that this parity in numbers would have ensured tranquillity ; but it certainly did not, for somehow or other we quarrelled frequently, and with great earnestness.

The placid evening turned into a blustering morning ; the cigar 'of contentment very decidedly disappeared, and for a week or more we tacked from side to side of the Channel, without, as far as I could see, ever getting any further down it, until at length some less unfavourable deity sent us an easterly wind, which froze us all to the marrow, but enabled our pilot to leave us, and carried us well on into the mighty Atlantic.

I think it was about a fortnight after the pilot's departure that I came to the conclusion that woman's society was the greatest bliss upon earth, and, about three weeks later, that woman was the origin of all evil.

There was among us a little lady, a widow, young, decidedly pretty, with golden hair and blue eyes,—one who might have figured as the heroine in one of Miss Braddon's novels,—to whom a gallant lieutenant paid much attention, which attention, according to my inexperienced ideas, appeared to receive marked encouragement. Consequently I envied him much.

One beautiful moonlight evening I was on deck, leaning over the stern, looking at the phosphorescent coruscations in our wake, when I heard the soft rustle of a dress close by me, and on looking round, found the golden-haired siren by my side. We were, of course, on terms of ordinary acquaintance, and made a few commonplace remarks on the beauty of the night. Presently she said,—there was some meal going on in the saloon, and, with the exception of the man at the wheel, we had the poop to ourselves,—

"What a comfort it is to be able to get away, even for a few moments, from the wearisome society of the same individuals day after day."

To which I, thinking of the lieutenant, and inclined to be a little malicious, " Is it all wearisome ? "

" All."

"Without exception ? "

" Without exception."

"That is not very flattering to your fellow-voyagers, myself included."

"You, Mr. Gordon, have not given me much opportunity of ascertaining whether your society is wearisome or the contrary." .

"Would you care to have such opportunity ? "

Hesitatingly, and with an upward glance, " I think I should."

" But," said I, much flattered, " there is an obstacle ; there is "——

" Oh," with a petulant pout, " you mean Lieut. Ogle. His name ought to have been spelt with an ' r,' not an ' l.' He is a bore and a boor. How can you think his society could be any pleasure to me ? "

" Well," I began ; but I thought it better not to say *what* I thought.

She continued, "Don't think me too outspoken ; but

it is such a relief to be able to speak to some one who *perhaps* may sympathize with the dull torture I have endured for the last ten days—*perhaps* would now help to rid me of it."

This with a long, full look of her very pretty blue eyes.

"How?" I asked eagerly.

"Shield me with your companionship," she said ; and her hand stole out towards mine, which grasped it fervently. Just at that moment we heard steps on the companion ladder, and separated.

As I entered the saloon, I saw the lieutenant seated at whist and apparently in high spirits ; but I pitied him— yes, pitied him from the bottom of my heart.

The next morning I finished my breakfast hastily, so as to be early on deck and ready with all those little attentions that male passengers are in the habit of paying to their friends of the other sex on board ship, such as placing chairs, arranging rugs, etc., etc. These were all graciously accepted ; and the lieutenant, on loitering up in the full confidence of possession, was surprised and displeased to find himself forestalled. Still more displeased was he, on offering his services for the usual morning walk on deck, to find mine accepted instead ; and at dinner his brow grew black as thunder when he perceived that the fair one, by some mysterious influence over the captain, had managed to change her seat so as to be near me.

This state of things lasted for some days. The lieutenant ceased to proffer further attentions, and became sulky and moody. He was of a temper not subject to much control, I fancy; but was astounded, as well he might be, at the change in the aspect of affairs, arising from no known fault of his own. To me it was a time of idyllic happiness. My fair companion laid herself out to please me. Her conversation was piquant, she was tolerably well read, and in various respects I began to understand that my society was more congenial to her than that of her former friend. In short, it became gradually a matter of no surprise to me that I was preferred before him.

His demeanour, however, by degrees, became more troublesome to us—to me especially. Puzzled surprise began to give place to an indignant sense of wrong; and as he could not vent his anger on her, it became clear that it would fall on my devoted head. He was sometimes boisterous, sometimes moody, and occasionally made rude remarks about me, intended for my hearing. What was most galling to him probably, was, that in the cramped-up life on board ship it was impossible for him to avoid the sight of the fair cause of all his woe, and his successful rival, for whom, of course, knowing nothing, he could make no excuses. A quarrel might perhaps have been avoided,—for my own wishes were pacific enough,—had it not been for our thus being continually brought in contact with each other. But at length it happened one rough morning, while walking on deck with Mrs. Vivian, I knocked against Ogle and trod hard on his foot. Apart from all previous indignation, it must really have hurt him a little, and he turned round on me like a mad bull. I was prepared to defend myself; but suddenly, with a strong effort, he restrained himself, and saying, "You shall hear more of this," turned away and went below.

I looked at my companion, who appeared composed, but thoughtful.

Presently she said, " Poor fellow ! "

" Who ? " I inquired.

" Lieutenant Ogle."

" Why ? "

" He must have been so fond of me."

This was disconcerting, and I suppose my looks showed it, for she added, that " It was no use, if I could not be fond of him."

That evening, after dinner, a Captain Talbot, a cavalry officer, came to me with a message from Ogle, demanding satisfaction.

" Does he mean me to fight a duel ? " I said.

" Beyond a doubt," said Talbot.

" But it is too absurd. If I trod on his toe, it was purely accidental, and I am quite ready to beg his pardon."

" You have trodden on something else besides his toe. You know very well what I mean. If you don't meet him as he demands, he will assault you ; and as he is physically much stronger than you, you will get the worst of it, and cut rather a sorry figure. You had better refer me to some-body on your part, and possibly matters may hereafter be arranged. You, of course, understand that it is necessary anyhow to keep the matter perfectly secret."

Of course I knew very well what he meant. Naturally, the little episode I have been describing could not go on in our small society without being observed by all our fellow-passengers. Ogle had been the object of some little sym-pathy and a good deal of ridicule. The *causa teterrima* was sincerely hated by all her own sex, and much admired by all the unmarried members of mine, while my apparent good fortune had excited some envy. I began to find myself in anything but a comfortable position. I was under the impression that duelling was a thing of the past, though I had heard of stories of its still occurring occasionally in India. Ogle could certainly thrash me if he chose; but then, was not a thrashing better than possible death? for I knew not how to handle a sword, and my pistol practice was confined to a trial of my new revolver, securely soldered down in a packing-case lined with tin in the hold.

But if I refused to fight I should certainly be branded as a coward, and the fear of the scorn of my fellow-passengers was very terrible to me, a thing not to be escaped from, day after day, for many a weary week. Besides, what would my Helen say? On reflection, it seemed to me there was nothing for it but to fight; so I sought out a young hussar with whom I was on friendly terms, and placed myself in his hands. The next morning he informed me that it was arranged that swords should be the weapons, and the field of battle Talbot's large stern cabin.

Swords had been selected as Ogle was very blood-thirsty and wanted to fight with pistols across a handkerchief. It was thought a combat with swords would probably have a less serious termination, my friend gravely informed me. It also appeared that all available swords were soldered up in tin down in the hold to prevent their being injured by the sea damp; and that until some plausible reason could be assigned to the captain for getting them up, matters must remain in abeyance. Further, the weather was rough, the glass was falling, and until the sea became smooth and the weather fine, no baggage would be got up from the hold.

How fervently I prayed for constant tempest until the voyage's end.

Matters being so far settled, there was no further molestation from Ogle ; indeed, he avoided us as much as possible ; and Mrs. Vivian, with woman's curiosity, was most eager to know what had happened after our deck rencontre. At length I gave way, and told her. She evinced the prettiest consternation, positively lavished tenderness upon me, and actually, I recollect, embroidered my initials in two of my handkerchiefs with her golden hair.

The kindly gale continued for some days ; but even the most welcome storms must come to an end, and after one or two refusals the packing cases had actually been got up from the hold and the swords taken out.

Once or twice during the last two or three days I had found my fair friend in somewhat close conversation with Talbot, and the last time I had remonstrated with her, and told her I thought she had been also a little cold in her manner to me.

" I have been pleading for you," she said, "and trying to get Captain Talbot to put off by some means or other this miserable duel, but without success."

How could I be suspicious after this ?

The dreaded day was at length fixed, and the affair was to come off in the early morning in Talbot's cabin. This was of course a secret from all except the four concerned.

I had bid, as I thought, a specially tender good-night to Mrs. Vivian, and had retired early, intending to make a few memoranda which might be of importance, before turning in. Presently I heard a knock at the door.

"Come in!" I shouted; and there entered, to my intense astonishment, Ogle.

"Shake hands, Gordon," he said, "and permit me to ask if you still insist on our turning out specially early to-morrow morning."

My astonishment was only equalled by a feeling of relief, which for a second or two prevented speech; but I grasped his hand, and at length managed to say, "Most willing to be friends. But why——"

"All right," he interrupted, brusquely. "Good night," and disappeared.

The next day I told Mrs. Vivian of the very unexpected reconciliation that had taken place. To my surprise she got very pale, seemed much agitated, and certainly not pleased, and after one or two vague remarks pleaded a headache, and left me.

That evening Talbot came to me and said: "I have come to you on rather a delicate mission, Gordon. I wish to premise that I have every desire to avoid hurting your feelings in any way; the question whether we are to remain on friendly terms or not must rest with you. Mrs. Vivian has commissioned me to say that your attentions to her have become so marked as to form the subject of remark to her fellow-passengers, and she desires that they may be discontinued."

The sudden and very unexpected nature of this announcement was overwhelming. At length I gasped, "Why are *you* chosen for this communication ? Why has she not told me herself ? "

" I do not know that I am bound to answer that question," he said ; "but I may as well tell you, that possibly the connection between Mrs. Vivian and myself may be of a closer nature than that you at present think likely ; and this mission is a proof of her confidence in me."

I wanted time for reflection. " I will speak to you to-morrow," I said.

That night was a very miserable one for me. My first feeling, I think, was one of intensely mortified vanity. I had been very proud of my selection from among all the other men available, by this very pretty and very desirable creature. My pride had been daily flattered by the consciousness that I was a conspicuous object of envy to my male fellow-passengers ; it would now be daily wounded by the feeling that I was similarly an object of ridicule, the envy being transferred to another. For I felt too certain that nothing I could do would enable the previously existing state of things to continue. I could now fully enter into all poor Ogle's feelings ; but then also I could make excuses for Talbot, for I had had an experience that Ogle had not.

After a sleepless night I came to the conclusion that the only thing to be done was to make the best of what appeared to me then a very unhappy business. Above all things it was desirable to avoid becoming an object of ridicule. The only way to attain this was, if possible, to appear *nonchalant,* to remain friendly both with Talbot and Mrs. Vivian ; and this very difficult line of conduct I set myself resolutely to carry out.

The next morning, therefore, I was able to meet Talbot apparently cheerfully, and to say, " Let us be friends ; and perhaps you will tell Mrs. Vivian I shall obey her instructions, but shall be glad to be on friendly terms with her also, if she will permit it."

He looked at me suspiciously, but he need not have done so, for my only design was to pursue the policy before indicated.

I took care therefore to wish her good morning in the ordinary way, placed her chair, etc., and then left her. She gave me a very curious look, but said nothing.

After this, the tediousness and confinement of the voyage was something almost insupportable. The part I had to play was a very hard one ; and I was exposed to incessant and trying curiosity, and it was difficult to keep one's own counsel. At any rate I had avoided ridicule. Ogle, I think, was astonished at my coolness. He had confided to me unasked, that the night before our proposed combat, he had seen Talbot kissing Mrs. Vivian, and this had convinced him that she was not worth fighting for ; and this explained his sudden desire for a reconciliation and Mrs. Vivian's agitation on hearing of it. On further acquaintance I found him a very good fellow, with high notions of honour, and, though of an impetuous temper, a thorough gentleman.

The weeks wore on, and still we seemed to get no nearer the end of our long journey. The boundless sea around us, no topic of conversation but ourselves. Various other little episodes occurred, but I had been too deeply touched to take much interest in them.

One day I recollect an albatross was caught, and as most ladies on board had expressed a desire for some of the feathers, each man who had some one to please made a dash at the wretched bird as it was drawn on deck, and it was in a dozen pieces almost before it was dead. It had been hauled up by a line, having been caught with a baited hook, like a fish ; and Talbot was so eager in hauling it up that he jerked his watch out of his pocket, and I saw it sink down into the deep, clear sea. I was glad to be out of this proceeding altogether.

I don't think a long voyage is good for characters that have not great powers of self-control. In the first place, it is almost impossible to settle down to any serious pursuit on board ship ; I don't know why this is so, but every one with whom I have travelled has confirmed me in the truth of this statement. After my discomfiture I tried to take up Hindustani with vigour ; but I did very little good, though there was absolutely no other occupation to distract my attention. My thoughts, too, would run on the pleasant companionship I had lost. There was nothing near to replace it, and, indeed, after being so long in daily contact with the same people, without any possibility of change, one began to feel as if all society were limited to one's fellow-passengers, and the most trifling events and feelings assumed undue importance.

I gradually found that, as I had avoided ridicule, so I had obtained a good deal of sympathy ; and more than one fair friend volunteered congratulations on my escape from the chains of the siren ; and this, of course, strengthened me in my line of conduct. For her behaviour I could only account on the old principle of *"Varium et mutabile semper femina."* I think she began to get tired of Talbot. For some time our intercourse had been confined to mere formal salutations, though I occasionally moved her chair or offered some similar attention. One day, when I had done some such thing, no one else being by, she said suddenly, " I did not give you up without a pang."

She looked very pretty, and I was sorely, sorely tempted to give way ; but I mustered all my firmness, and saying merely, " That is an interesting piece of information," moved off.

After this she declined to return my salutations, and we were no longer acquaintances. Occasionally she took the opportunity of making spiteful remarks to Talbot about me in my hearing, and I could see his look of mortified vexation, for he was a fine fellow and a gentleman, and I began to feel that my turn of vengeance had commenced.

Time dragged wearily on. We had crossed the line, and I, with the rest of the male passengers, had undergone the disgusting shaving and ducking that forms part of the ridiculous ceremony on the occasion. I had also induced two credulous and middle-aged women to believe they had actually seen the Equator by stretching a hair across a telescope. We had passed the Cape, and left behind us the friendly and bracing westerly gales which carried us along some 300 miles per day, getting in exchange the calms and heat of the Bay of Bengal. We had buried in the hot blue waves one little child that had been a great

pet on board. The circumstances were very painful, as the
mother was of Asiatic origin and utterly unable to control
her grief. The poor little body had to be taken from her
by force. She swore solemnly that she would throw herself
into the sea when the coffin should be slid overboard; and
it was necessary to confine her to her cabin, with a guard
over her, during the burial ceremony; and all the time her
shrieks, only too audible to all of us, were heartrending.
The coffin, too, was not sufficiently weighted to sink, as it
should have done, and floated within sight until the darkness of night hid it from us.

The only redeeming point was, that before the burial
we caught a shark. It had been seen in our neighbourhood for the last two days, and the sight of it had
been accepted as an evil omen for the fate of the poor
child so dangerously ill. Its pertinacity in following us
certainly appeared to be an instance in support of the
belief that the shark has an instinctive foreknowledge of
the approach of death at sea; but on the other hand, sharks
even more frequently follow ships when there is nobody
dying on board. Several baits of some pounds of pork,
each attached to enormous hooks, had been hung out for
him; but he had treated them all with disdain, until about
2 P.M., or two hours before the hour fixed for the burial,
when he came up to a line held by the second mate, turned
over on his back, displaying his white belly, as sharks are
compelled to do, from the position of their mouth, when
about to seize anything, and wholly gorged the bait.
There ensued a tremendous hauling and pulling, and it
took nearly half an hour to get the monster on deck, and

some further time to despatch him there with a hatchet. He was a most hideous brute; I forget the dimensions now; but on opening him we did not discover in his maw any bracelets or buttons, or such things as are usually described to be found therein. His heart was taken out, and continued to beat strongly. Sailors have a superstition that a shark's heart will not cease to beat until after sunset of the day of its death. I can recollect that I saw his beating fully three hours after the creature was killed, but I cannot remember when it actually became still.

For a month after crossing the line the second time I do not believe we made 100 miles; but at last a southerly breeze sprung up, after a week of which our captain informed us that in another twenty-four hours we should probably sight the pilot brig. He was mistaken, however, for he had taken a wrong course, and for forty-eight hours we were beating about in shoal water on a dangerous coast, the skipper constantly poring over his charts and evidently in a very anxious state of mind. It fell to my lot, many years afterwards, to administer the district to which this coast belongs, and I then better appreciated the dangers we had run during those hours.

On the third morning, just as we were going to breakfast, the man at the masthead shouted, "Brig at anchor," and in another hour we had run down to the vessel, stationed some twenty miles from the mouth of the Hooghly with pilots to convoy vessels up that exceedingly dangerous river; and a little later we saw the first land on which our eyes had rested after passing Madeira.

We were all in the highest spirits. The very smell of the

land appeared sweeter than anything my nostrils had previously experienced; and as the banks of the mighty river narrowed, and I was able to see farther into the country of which I was to be one of the governors, my interest knew no bounds.

We had secured the services of a tug, which before evening towed us as far as Garden Reach, where it was necessary to anchor till the morning.

The joy of us new-comers was a little checked during the night by the attacks of mosquitoes, and in the morning some of our more delicate companions refused to show their faces. It was especially trying for those who had come to join expectant bridegrooms.

One of these was a girl of about six or seven and twenty, frank, unaffected, and honest, though decidedly not good-looking, who had been indulging in the most ardent anticipations of a meeting with her lover, to whom she had been engaged for seven years. It so happened that he was the first to arrive on board, having hastened down on the wings of love (as we supposed) to Garden Reach, and reached the ship before the tug had taken us in tow for the last few miles of our journey in the morning.

How the information got about I don't know, but in less than half an hour it was known to all on board that this ardent lover had thus hurried down to persuade his expectant bride to return to England by the next mail steamer. The reason I never knew. It could not have been mosquito bites, for he had evidently come down determined on this course; and I fear his conduct was only one of

the many refutations of the very untrue statement, that
" absence makes the heart grow fonder."

I felt truly sorry for the poor lady, but at the same time
became convinced of the extreme injudiciousness of such
engagements. However, she was firm, and carried her
point, for some days afterwards I saw their marriage announced in the Calcutta papers ; but it must have taken
some time, at any rate, to efface the recollection of such,
an exceedingly disagreeable episode.

Meantime, with the recalcitrant bridegroom moodily·
leaning over the side, and the disappointed bride surrounded by a phalanx of sympathizing female friends, we
slowly moved up the majestic river, and leaving the luxuriant foliage of Garden Reach behind us, opened out
the stately city of palaces.

The first view of Calcutta is indeed striking—the fine
river, the long line of splendid shipping, the wide
" Maidan" (plain), bounded on two sides by the white
houses with their green Venetian blinds, gleaming under
the bright blue sky of a February morning. It was a
sight welcome to us weary voyagers.

We came to anchor opposite Prinsep's Ghât, an arch
with a flight of steps leading down to the river (all landing places in Bengal are called " ghâts") and were in the
twinkling of an eye surrounded by a multitude of native
boats, the occupants of which were all talking, or rather
screaming, with the full power of their lungs, and making
a noise such as only a native crowd can produce.

I observed among the crowd of dinghies one containing
a number of native commercial agents, or "banians," as

they are called, respectably dressed in long white clothes ; and one young English officer, who had come to meet some one on board, and was making signs of recognition to him. In his eagerness to meet his friend, he sprang from his own "dinghy" on to that next him, and in doing so capsized that from which he sprang, and all the white-clothed baboos were in an instant under the water.

I looked on horror-stricken. The stream was running some six or seven miles an hour, and in half a minute or so I observed that the lightly-clad boatmen had emerged and saved themselves by clinging to boats near them. The unfortunate baboos, however, were too much impeded by their long flowing garments to do this, and I saw once a head with the face perfectly concealed by white linen appear above the muddy waters, and once an arm vainly endeavouring to emancipate itself from the clinging clothes which prevented any effort for life, some hundred yards down the stream. No one seemed to take any notice at first, but after half a minute's precious time lost in jabbering, two out of the fifty boats or more surrounding us did essay to go after the drowning wretches. Meantime the cause of all this catastrophe had climbed up the gangway ladder with a beaming countenance, and did not appear to know that he had consigned to an almost certain death four or five of his fellow creatures ; for, what with under-currents, eddies, sharks, and alligators, a man once committed to the tender mercies of the sacred river is seldom seen again. What became of these baboos I never knew; for I could do nothing to help them, and the bustle of getting on shore soon put all other thoughts out of my head for the time.

At length, with a feeling of really wild delight, after one hundred and forty-two days of imprisonment, I once more put foot on shore.

CHAPTER II.

LIFE AS A STUDENT IN CALCUTTA.

SPENCE'S HOTEL.—FRESH EGGS.—EXAMINATIONS IN NATIVE LAN-
GUAGES.—THE BAITAL PUNSHABINSHATI.—THE "CHUMMERY."—
A CALCUTTA DAY IN THE HOT WEATHER.—THE MALL.—NORTH-
WESTERS.—COMPETITION WALLAHS.—THEATRICALS.—OUR DIN-
NER PARTY.—DISSOLUTION OF "CHUMMERY."—CLUBS.—SNIPE
SHOOTING.—TAKE LEAVE OF CALCUTTA.

A FEW minutes in that curious conveyance, a "palki
gharry" (resembling a palanquin on wheels), sufficed to
convey me to Spence's Hotel ; and I shall not easily forget
the lordly sense of power with which I ordered two fresh
eggs for breakfast. During the last month of our voyage
a hen had confidingly laid an egg, to which each of the
eighteen lady passengers appeared to have some special
claim. But the judicious steward dropped his apple of
discord on deck, and thus avoided a second and very
much exaggerated edition of the Trojan war. But great
was the lamentation over the fall of that egg, and here
was I able to order two at once, and more to follow, if
required.

It was a delightful sense of change and freedom ; and
all the petty strifes and narrow jealousies of the voyage
seemed to have disappeared as if by magic. It was a relief to find that not one of my fellow-passengers had gone
to the same hotel. Indeed, I saw little of them after-

wards. One day I met Mrs. Vivian in Wilson's shop—that great emporium on the ground floor of the hotel now called the Great Eastern. Talbot was following her about like a tame cat. She bowed to me, in the most smiling manner, and on my returning the salutation, informed me that she was now Mrs. Talbot; that they were about to stay a week or two in Calcutta before going up country to join his regiment. Would I come and see them? I offered my congratulations to Talbot; and though I must admit she was nicely dressed and looked well, I felt glad that she was Mrs. Talbot. I never saw them afterwards; but I feel pretty sure that Ogle and myself were well out of it.

A few days saw me fairly launched in Calcutta life, which, for an idle man in the cold weather, is about as pleasant a thing as I know. In those days a young civilian had to pass an examination in Calcutta in two languages before proceeding to any situation in the interior. These languages were Persian and Hindi, if the examinee were appointed to the north-west provinces, Punjaub, or Oudh; and Hindustani and Bengali if his future sphere of action lay in Bengal Proper. The examinations were held monthly, and we were allowed to take up one language only at a time, the second not being commenced upon until the Board of Examiners had certified that we were sufficiently proficient in the first. During this time we were nominally under the control of the said Board, though practically between the intervals of examination they knew nothing about us and did not interfere with our movements. I was, like the rest of my compeers, naturally eager to begin at once upon the administration of the country, and felt much chagrined at being yet again reduced to the status of scholar.

This is all changed now, and young arrivals are sent at once to the district where they may be appointed, and not only have an opportunity of seeing how the official machine works, but of obtaining a practical knowledge of the language. This latter we certainly could not do in Calcutta. The very books we had to study seemed selected with a view to prevent this. Hindustani and Bengali fell to my lot. In the former the " Bagh o Bahar " was our principal text-book, the language being high-flown Persian substantives and adjectives, with here and there a Hindustani verb—the delight of the "moonshees," or tutors appointed by Government, most unpractical of teachers, but useless for us learners.

A thorough knowledge of the above would perhaps help me to appear to advantage in an interview with an educated Mohammedan gentleman, but would be no aid in the conduct of a criminal case or a local inquiry in a Behar village. It would probably be far more useful to civilians who were appointed to the north-west provinces, but for whom it was not prescribed.

The same remarks apply also to the Bengali text-books. The chief was entitled " Baital Punshabinshati ; " or, " The Twenty-five Tales of a Demon "—the vocabulary really Sanscrit, with Bengali terminations and inflections.

It is a weird book, of which the plot may be roughly described as follows :—A very pious Hindoo king is attempting to lay a ghost or demon which has taken up its residence in a tree in a burial ground. To effect this he takes the demon on his back, and the latter consents to go with him on condition that the king gives a correct answer to a problem which he shall propose. The king is unsuccessful in guessing the answer until the twenty-fifth problem is propounded. These problems are in the shape of stories, and are spun out with a multitude of details quite irrelevant to the main issue, but a short abstract of one or two which I recollect will serve to show their nature.

An exceedingly religious king having been blessed with a wife endowed with all good qualities, and a friend of a similar character, determined to make a pilgrimage in their company to a distant shrine. On their way they passed through a dense forest in which they came upon a temple sacred to a goddess (whose name I have forgotten). The king determined to go in and do poojah (say his prayers), leaving his friend and wife outside. After saying his prayers he came to the conclusion that life on the whole is a bore, and that it would be just as well to end it in such a holy place. He therefore drew his sword, cut off his own head, and fell dead at the feet of the image of the goddess. The friend and wife outside wondering at his long absence, the former went into the temple to see what he was about. On discovering the dead body he too was struck with the idea that this is a bad world, and that every one will accuse him of having killed his friend in order to obtain his friend's wife. Deciding therefore to avoid all future trouble by following his friend's example, he cut off his own head, and fell dead by his side. Finally the wife, troubled at the long absence of both her companions, entered the temple to look after them, and on seeing what had happened resolved to kill herself too, as life without her beloved husband was no longer worth having. She was just preparing to despatch herself with her husband's sword when the goddess appeared in person, commended her for her good resolution, and bidding her live, promised to grant her any boon that she might ask. She begged that the two dead bodies might be restored to life. "Very well," said the goddess, "put the heads on to the bodies," and disappeared. The wife, in her agitation, fitted the wrong heads on to the wrong bodies, and when they came to life as promised, they both claimed her as their wife.

"O king," said the demon, after reciting thus far, "whose wife was she?"

The king replied, giving his reasons, that she belonged to that body on which the head of the husband was fastened; but the answer was wrong, for the demon got down from the king's back, and hanged himself up in his tree again.

In another story a king who has performed his religious duties with great ardour all his life, is rewarded by the possession of three of the most delicate wives in the world. One was so delicate that on one occasion when the king was sitting by her side playing with a lotus flower, one of the tendrils fell on her arm and broke it.

The second happened to hear a peasant woman grinding corn in the hand mill (two round stones between which the grain is placed), and the sound broke the drum of her ear.

The third was sitting by the king in the forest one

moonlight evening, when a moonbeam fell on her cheek and burned it.

The demon asked which was the most delicate, and the king, after some pondering, replies, "She on whom the moonbeam fell;" but the answer was not correct. In no case does the demon supply the right solution when the king is wrong; and in all the cases it would be very difficult to do so on satisfactory grounds.

It is easy to conceive that a study of such a work as the above did not conduce to a practical knowledge of the language or of the administration of the laws; and the present system is much better, where young administrators are *compelled* to learn only what is useful, while at the same time inducements in the shape of money prizes are still held out to them to devote what leisure they may have during the early part of their service to the more finished acquisition of Indian languages.

To me, and to many others, the study of Hindustani and Bengali in the above shapes was a very dreary business; and it really was an effort to devote attention to them at all. A little real work would have enabled me to pass the examination in each language in two months, or four months altogether, whereas I lingered in Calcutta for ten, and some of my contemporaries for eighteen.

Eager as I was to rush up country at starting, when the time actually came for my departure from Calcutta I was very loth to go, for I had made many friends whom I was sorry to leave, and I had also heard many things about the dulness of life in the interior.

Spence's Hotel, though cheap, was not the most comfortable residence procurable ; and meeting with some friends of my own age and congenial temperament, we started what is called a " chummery ;" that is, four of us rented a furnished house from a man who had sent his family to the "hills" for the hot weather and rainy season, and thus acquired not only the dignity, but also the responsibilities' and anxieties of the status of householders. The owner was glad to get his house occupied during his absence, and accepted us as tenants at half the rent he himself paid.

Government allowed us in those days 300rs. a month, or about £1 a day, and 30rs. or about £3 a month as moonshee allowance. This latter amount we never saw, as it was paid through the Board of Examiners to the moonshee we had selected from among those licensed by Government, and to whom we granted certificates of regular attendance (with a very liberal interpretation of the word regular) during the month. Our united available monthly income, therefore, from Government was 1200rs., and our actual outgoings for food, wine, house-rent, the wages of some 30 servants, and the keep of six horses were about 850rs. monthly. This would appear, perhaps, more than moderate in the eyes of most old Haileybury civilians ; but the days of the old extravagance had gone by, and the expression, " he's turned his lakh," meaning, " he owes more than £10,000," would be scarcely intelligible to the present generation.

Nevertheless it will be seen that to a man having nothing but his pay, there was not much left for fancy expenditure ; and to such as went out married it was a great struggle to make both ends meet. The purchase, too, of horses and conveyances necessitated an outlay which, in many cases, compelled the resort to a loan at the very start ; and it was not easy, until one had got into the quiet and economy of the "mofussil," or interior, to save anything to pay this off.

My chums, like myself, were all embryo administrators. One of them, Morrison, was a contemporary of mine at Oxford ; Green had been at Harrow, and afterwards at a private tutor's ; while O'Connor was a graduate of Trinity College, Dublin. His brogue denoted most unmistakably the land of his birth.

My long studies on board ship were supposed to have given me a better knowledge of the language than my companions, and to my lot therefore fell the management of the house and the control of the commissariat. To O'Connor was allotted the supervision of the stable, as all Irishmen are supposed to know about horses ; and Green's spirit was too lofty, and Morrison was too dreamy for these insignificant but necessary details.

Our " khansamar," or head table-servant, was supposed to know English, or at any rate the English names of the table necessaries ; and on the morning after we had entered on possession of our house, he came to inform me that it was advisable to lay in a small stock of certain kitchen requisites. " Would I be pleased to make a list, and get them from the European shops ?"

Accordingly I took my pen, while he, standing with his hands clasped in the native attitude of deferential respect, commenced :—

" Makrakurma." " What ?" said I. " Makrakurma," he repeated.

I had never heard of any English eatable of this name; but he assured me it was very common and absolutely ·necessary. "Well," I said, wishing to temporize, "pass on to the next thing." "Burrumchellee," he said. This was no better than the first item; but he insisted that it was equally well known and equally necessary.

This was very disheartening, and I was much puzzled what to do, for I did not like to write down these mystic names and expose my ignorance in an English shop; and further I was unwilling to confess to my chums that I had so utterly failed in my very first attempt at housekeeping. Finally my interlocutor came to the rescue, saying with a condescending smile, "Your highness is a great man, and has probably not paid attention to these matters; but I have a cousin in the bazaar who knows English well, and will, if you approve, write all these things down in English, and only charge eight annas," equal to 1s. English.

I was only too glad to accept this compromise, and get out of my difficulty for one shilling. The next morning therefore the list was brought to me fairly written out; and I discovered that the two mysterious articles were merely maccaroni and vermicelli, articles that possibly a brand-new housekeeper would not think of as heading a list of necessaries. I tried to point out to the khansamar that it was his faulty pronunciation that had necessitated the expenditure of 1s.; but he either could not or would not understand, and my Hindustani being very limited, I was obliged to yield.

Many similar difficulties involved further outlays, until my progress, both in the language and housekeeping experiences, enabled me to do without the assistance of the cousin in the bazaar, whom I afterwards discovered to be no cousin, but an ordinary bazaar writer, and whose real charge I ascertained to be 3*d.* for such documents.

My other difficulty was with the sirdar-bearer. The chief dignitaries among the servants in an Anglo-Bengalee household are the sirdar-bearer and the khansamar. The latter, as may be gathered from the facts related above, supervises the cuisine, the former all matters connected with the internal economy of the house. He has charge of the lamps, the linen, etc., and is responsible that the water-carriers, sweepers, and other subordinate servants do their duty.

At the commencement of each month he brings in an account of his expenditure on account of the house, and also a list of wages due to himself and the servants in his department. These monthly accounts were the bane of my existence. The gross amount was always much more than it ought to have been, and yet it was almost impossible to eliminate or reduce any special item. Each item, too, was so ridiculously small in amount that it seemed scarcely worth while to wrangle about any one in particular. The fact was, the man's whole leisure time, and he had plenty of it, was devoted to making up this bill; and he was prepared with a most elaborate reply to every possible and probable objection. I recollect that he always appeared to have used an enormous amount of string and beeswax, and that the sweepers continually wanted new brooms and baskets. Why the baskets should wear out so was always a puzzle to me. When I became more experienced, I found the wiser plan to be to allow myself to be cheated to a certain extent, and only to pretend to examine the detailed account, and if the total appeared to be too extortionate to make an arbitrary deduction of 10rs. or so.

Such deductions always caused the most heart-rending lamentations, assertions of starvation, and impending death, but they did not last long ; and the bearer, after being driven from the presence with scorn and a certain amount of angry words, would appear at the next interview, half an hour afterwards, as grave and decorous as if nothing had occurred.

The same remarks apply to the khansamar's bill, where, among other things, the number of eggs consumed in a month was always perfectly appalling.

Being inexperienced, and at the same time bound to see that the limited resources of my chums were not extravagantly wasted, the labour of arriving at a satisfactory settlement of these bills was exceedingly irksome, and did not, I think, meet with the gratitude it deserved. It was some consolation, however, to find that O'Connor was just as much bothered with the stable accounts, and occasionally appeared to be suffering from curry-combs and brushes on the brain. The amount of salt; too, that horses consume in India is very astonishing.

Another trouble was the constant bickering of our respective servants.

The servants common to all of us were the derwan, or door-keeper, a very important person, who prevents the ingress and egress of doubtful characters, and examines any suspicious-looking bundles carried out by any servant of the house, the sirdar-bearer, the khansamar, two water-carriers (bheesties), two sweepers, and one cook; but we each had our own bearer, or body-servant, and kitmutgar, or table-servant. It is the custom in India for each person to have his own table-servant; and when dining out, to take him with him to wait behind his chair.

There were, of course, among so many hands, sundry breakages, and many articles, such as spoons, forks, napkins, and towels, mislaid. The khansamar and sirdar-bearer, in their respective departments, were making constant reclamations, which led to vociferous denials and recrimination on the part of the eight servants mentioned above. In our presence they would accuse each other of carelessness or theft; out of it, they abused each other's female relatives. Generally these quarrels blazed hot and fierce for a quarter of an hour or so, and then died away; but occasionally they led to cherished malice and more serious results. A chummery of four inexperienced young Englishmen is not a good school for native servants.

Neither the sirdar-bearer or khansamar would steal anything themselves, or allow, if they could help it, any theft on the part of others in the house. Their profit was made out of their accounts. The bearers, too, would not steal from their own masters, for they too had their private accounts against them; and though their profits were small at present, they hoped they would increase as their masters' salaries increased.

For it is universally the case in Bengal, that as the employer's salary rises, so does the price of everything purchased by his servants rise also. In all the services the servants know exactly what pay their masters receive, and make up their accounts accordingly. It generally happens that on promotion an official changes his district, and the servants are therefore able to assert that prices are higher in the neighbourhood, but it is not so always ; and I recollect a friend who had recently been made a Commissioner in the district in which he had been in the lower office of Collector, found that in his khansamar's account for the succeeding month the price of every article of consumption had considerably increased. On expressing his surprise at this, the man assured him that it was really the case that the bazaar " nerik," or market rate, had so risen. He declined to settle the account until he had made inquiries, and found that all his neighbours had continued to pay the same prices as before. This was pointed out to the khansamar, and he could not deny it, and being driven into a corner, at length said, " But your honour has become a Commissioner Sahib." He did not, of course, get his excess prices on this occasion, but my friend admitted that, though thus at first successful, his monthly bills increased, and he could not keep them down.

People who have not been in India may say, " But why not do your own marketing ?" To this I reply, that it is simply impossible for an English gentleman or lady ; the climate and the customs of the country absolutely prevent it.

But though our bearers would not steal from their own masters, I don't think they had any scruples about taking what they could from the employers of their companions. Fear of detection, and its disagreeable consequences, was

the only deterrent. They watched each other very closely,
however, and hence we were comparatively safe. There
was, I recollect, one serious quarrel between Morrison's and
Green's servants. The latter had been detected by the
former in the act of appropriating some firewood, which he
had collected for the cooking of his mid-day meal. A few
days after, Green missed a gold pencil-case by which he
set much store. A great fuss was made about it, and all
the servants' boxes were searched, without result. Green's
bearer was, of course, suspected; but, on the grounds mentioned above, it was thought improbable that he would
have taken it. Some days afterwards he said to his
master, "Sahib, have you looked in Mr. Morrison's almi-
rah? (wardrobe)."

"No," said Green, "it isn't very likely Mr. Morrison has
committed a theft."

"But," said his bearer, "it is possible that his servant
may have."

So, with Morrison's permission, his wardrobe was
searched, and among his shirts was found the missing
pencil-case. Morrison was naturally indignant, and told
his bearer to leave his service at once. The man in vain
asserted his innocence, and attributed the charge to enmity
about the stolen wood above mentioned. It did not occur
to us that there could be any connection between the two;
but it appeared that he was right, for shortly after his
dismissal the khansamar came to me with an air of important mystery, saying that Jeeboo wished to speak to me.

Jeeboo, I should explain, was the item in the house
which answers to the cat at home. He was a relative of

one of the kitmutgars, who had been admitted to the house
without payment of salary, for the purpose of learning his
duties as a table servant; and all sins of omission and
commission of the table department, such as broken
plates, torn napkins, lost dusters, were in the first instance
laid to his charge—probably, in many cases, with justice;
we had christened him the "Plate-smasher."

I told the khansamar to admit him, and he then informed me that in the morning before the search of Morrison's wardrobe he had been sent upstairs to fetch a cup and
saucer which had been left in Morrison's room, and had
found Green's bearer standing by the wardrobe. Green's
bearer was then confronted with him, and was evidently
taken aback at this unexpected piece of evidence. It was
clear that the boy had no hostility to Green's man, and
further, O'Connor suddenly recollected that he had seen
Green's man coming out of Morrison's room, but had not
thought of it further at the time. This raised such a strong
presumption in favour of the innocence of Morrison's
bearer that messengers were at once sent to recall him,
and Green's servant dismissed with ignominy, and some
very scornful remarks in bad Hindustani from Green,
which, I am bound to admit, did not appear to have very
much effect.

It grieves me to relate that the plate-smasher's connection with us terminated soon after, almost equally disas-
trously. It was the custom at the close of dinner to
remove the lamp just as we were about to leave the table,
and carry it into the drawing-room. The lamp stood in
the centre of the table, under the punkah, a semicircular

space being cut in the fringe of this latter in order to enable it to be pulled without interfering with the former. The punkah is a framework of canvas about a foot and a half in breadth, and of length proportional to the room in which it is suspended. To the framework is attached a fringe of thick holland, about a foot in breadth, and the whole is pulled by a rope attached to its centre and passed through a hole in the wall. The puller (punkah-wallah), stands in the adjoining room, and is of course unable to see what is going on in the room in which the punkah is swinging to and fro. He pulls on mechanically to cool his masters until told to stop. Before removing the lamp, it was necessary to call out to the punkah-wallah to stop. On the evening in question, the "plate-smasher," anxious, I presume, to show himself useful, raised the lamp without taking the precaution previously mentioned. The punkah swung on monotonously, and the result was a crash, total darkness, and a strong smell of castor oil. We sprang to our feet simultaneously, actuated by a common thirst for vengeance; but the "plate-smasher" had disappeared. Our thoughts next turned to the relative who had introduced him; but he also had fled, and we never saw either of them again, though a small amount of wages was due to the latter. Yet, notwithstanding these and similar worries, we had on the whole a sufficiently pleasant time in Calcutta.

In those days it was not thought necessary that the head of the Government should seek the cool fastnesses of Simla during the hot season and rains, and take with him all the fortunate officials attached to the Government of India, the Foreign and Home Offices, and many others.

It is doubtless more pleasant; but beyond this I never could see any reason for the move. In former days the work went on equally well, even though carried on in the climate of Lower Bengal. No one will deny that Lower Bengal civilians have plenty to do, and yet it has never occurred to any one that they require such a change. It seems to me, though perhaps I look at it from a very local point of view, that it is just as though the English Cabinet should go to Malta during the winter months and govern England thence. Some of those who go have admitted to me that great delay and confusion is caused by the transmission of bundles of correspondence. For three weeks before the start from Calcutta, a multitude of matters were at a standstill, because a portion of the correspondence connected with them had "gone on;" and three weeks after the return the result was the same, because the bundles had not come back. However, the fact that delay and confusion must occur in such a case scarcely requires proof.

In those days, then, Calcutta, though badly drained and with no proper water supply, retained a large portion of its European society during the year, and the contrast between the social atmosphere during the winter months and those of the hot and rainy seasons was not so great as it is now. Dinners and even dances went on ; and we waltzed away pluckily at Government House on the 24th May in honour of Her Most Gracious Majesty. It was not cool, I must admit, and artificial complexions would have fared badly.

The description of one day will suffice for most others. Up between 5.30 and 6 a.m., and after " chota haziri," or little breakfast, consisting of coffee and toast, a canter on the "Maidan," the extensive plain, round two sides of which the European portion of Calcutta is built ; back to bathe and breakfast ; after which, moonshees till 12 ; then calls from 12 to 2 p.m., then lunch (if at home) ; sleep, books, or whist, till 5 p.m. ; then a drive to the racket court, where play till 7, at which hour one's riding horse was brought down ; and a gallop across the Maidan to the Eden Gardens, with music and conversation with all the "world," who had turned out to enjoy the cool of the evening, made a pleasant finish to the day.

The Mall, the Rotten Row of Calcutta, is quite unique ; and in its own style, I should say, unsurpassed. The road on which the carriages 'pass up and down runs between the fine river Hooghly on the one side and the Maidan on the other. To the north and east are Government House, the Town Hall, the Esplanade, and the Chowringhee mansions, which have given the place the name of the " City of Palaces," and I think, from the *coup d'œil* afforded, not undeservedly. Close to the road are moored fine ships from all parts of the world, of many thousand tons burden, while the opposite bank is green with foliage throughout the year. The assemblage of vehicles is, it is true, somewhat motley, for there are no exclusive rules here ; and the Governor General's carriage in all its splendour, may be jostled by the hired "palki gharry" with its two wretched ponies, rope harness, nearly naked driver, and wheels whose sinuous motions impress one with the idea that they must come off at the next revolution, and a freight of drunken sailors vociferating sonnets to their sweethearts in a manner anything but harmonious.

Parallel to the carriages, and separated from them only by a wooden railing, figure the riders; and the amount of salutation rendered necessary by this proximity is destructive to the brims of many hats. The fort, of which the Maidan forms the "glacis," is half-way down the drive; officers are obliged to appear in uniform, and this, in conjunction with the varied costumes of the natives of all descriptions, affords a combination of colour which makes the whole scene very striking.

The Eden Gardens border the northern portion of the drive. Though not extensive, they are laid out with considerable horticultural skill; and a large grass plat close to the band-stand is provided for a promenade. Here, as the short twilight fails, it is the custom for the occupants of the various carriages, and the riders, to collect and walk up and down, while listening to good military music. The place is prettily lighted with lamps; and, though decorum reigns supreme, the whole thing brings back a faint flavour of the Château des Fleurs of Paris. I once had occasion to take a young American girl, who had got thus far on a journey round the world from New York *viâ* San Francisco, to this promenade, and she told me it had impressed her more pleasingly than anything, she had hitherto seen.

Here too, on the hot May evenings, all linger to catch the latest breath of the southerly breeze, which comes up from the sea, heedless of the black arched cloud gathering in the west, portending the speedy advent of one of those storms known all over Bengal as nor'-westers. A remarkable feature in these is, that in whatever part of the sky they may gather, they invariably burst from the northwest. The southerly breeze blows steadily, but the black cloud still comes on and on, until there is a sudden lull, and a chill air from the north-west takes the place of the soft sea-born wind. This is the signal for a general run to carriages and horses; there is a perfect stampede of equestrians over the plain. And now comes a mighty rush of wind, every particle of dust on the surface of the thirsty ground seems to be whirled into the air, down comes the rain, in a few minutes the Maidan looks like a lake, the lightning keeps up a continuous flare, and the thunder crashes and roars without one half-second's cessation. The wind is often so strong that it is impossible to raise the hood of buggy or barouche, and ladies' dresses come badly out of this conflict of the elements. Conveyances are occasionally blown completely over; and young horses not rarely bring their riders to grief in the general excitement and confusion.

In one of these storms the wife of one of the highest functionaries in Calcutta was blown positively off her horse into the ditch bythe jail, near the south-east corner of the Maidan. She had separated from her companions in the darkness, and no one at the moment knew what had become of her. The storm, as is usual, passed over in a little more than half an hour; and two men coming by in a buggy became conscious of a lady in riding costume sitting disconsolately in the ditch. They pulled up and offered to assist her home, not knowing who she was;

but her nerves had been so upset by the fright she had undergone that she could not recollect her residence or even her name. At their wits' end what to do, they finally took her to the General Hospital, where, after a couple of hours' rest, her memory returned, and she was able to give directions and be sent home, whither her horse had found its way some time previously, causing much alarm to her husband and family.

In the Eden Gardens O'Connor was in his glory. Personally, I must admit that, meeting the same people day after day, I used to find my powers of conversation somewhat flag. But O'Connor was like the "brook." One objectionable point about him was, that he could not modulate his voice; and some of his tenderest remarks were audible to a great many ears besides that for which they were intended. Some of these appeared to me rather vapid; but there was an Irish absence of bashfulness about him which enabled him to pull through all kinds of awkward situations; and certainly the ladies to whom he addressed his conversation did not seem displeased. My experience teaches me that ladies prefer a talker, however vapid, to a silent man; and on my once asking a middle-aged friend of mine, a keen observer, how it was that girls whom I really thought intelligent could enjoy this kind of conversation, he replied, "Women like being talked to; it is analogous to patting a little dog," and I cannot help thinking he was right. Men, however, were not so complacent; and I heard many remarks that were by no means complimentary to my fluent chum.

Some of these doubtless originated in the strong prejudice that still existed against Competition Wallahs, as we were called, who had obtained our appointments by com- petitive examination.   It was not unnatural that members of old Indian families of either service should look upon us as intruders, who had taken out of the mouths of their children the bread that was their legitimate due.   But this prejudice led them to somewhat unreasonable conclusions.

In their eyes, because a man had not been nominated by a Director and educated at Haileybury, it necessarily followed that he was of low birth and vulgar mind and manners ; that he could not ride or shoot ; in fact, that he was a mere bookworm, devoid of all physical energy. Wallahs are now so numerous that they are quite able to hold their own ; but this general idea still exists, though in a less pronounced form.

From what I have learned of the Haileybury *régime*, it seems to me that the students there were decidedly not likely to be entitled to the *sobriquet* of " bookworms ;" but yet I have never been able to understand why they should, as a necessary consequence, be able to ride and shoot so much better than those educated elsewhere—why they should be so much more refined than the products of Eton and Harrow, Oxford and Cambridge.   But this was only an article of faith with them, and had no more effect on their practice than articles of faith generally exercise. Though they thought of us thus as a class, they treated us well as individuals ; and I received nothing but kindness from members of my own service.   It is true I was often told, as doubtless the majority of my contemporaries have been told, that I was not like an ordinary Wallah ; but this was by way of a compliment. And it must be admitted that some of the new comers, who had not been at a public school or a University, but had scraped through with the aid of crammers, did not possess all the qualities desirable; but were there *no* black sheep among the Haileybury flock?

The knowledge, too, of the existence of this prejudice naturally made Wallahs a little shy on their arrival in Calcutta; but I freely acknowledge that when we did emerge from our reserve, we were kindly and hospitably received.

Calling hours in Calcutta are from 12 to 2 p.m. 2 p.m. is the luncheon hour, and after that ladies not unusually, in the hot weather, divest themselves of all superfluous clothing, and keep as cool and quiet as they can until the time for the evening drive. The male sex, except in the case of such idlers as ourselves and a few military men, were all at office, so there was really not much temptation to keep them in their drawing-rooms.

It is also the Indian custom that the new comers should call on the old residents. The new comers are generally young men and shy; and it is their habit to call in pairs, by way of supporting each other. This is particularly bewildering to the recipients of the visit; for as two cards of two strange men are sent in simultaneously, it is difficult for the hostess to distinguish which is which. I very soon discontinued this custom; for having called at one house in company with Green, I soon after received and accepted an invitation to dine there. My hostess very naïvely expressed surprise at my appearance, stating that she thought my companion had been Mr. Gordon. This was *gauche* on her part, but not the less disagreeable to me.

O'Connor did an immense amount of calling, chiefly alone ; but there was one house to which he generally induced me to accompany him—that of some very pleasant people named Carter—father, mother, and daughter. He held a high civil appointment, and their house was one of the most genial and hospitable in the place. Miss Carter was decidedly pretty and very lively. She seemed to take pleasure in O'Connor's society; at any rate she was amused with him, and I was somehow generally told off to make conversation with Mrs. Carter, not at all an unpleasant task, though perhaps not quite so nice a *rôle* as O'Connor had taken for himself. The whole of our chummery gradually became very intimate there ; and at length, when we were lunching there one day, it was decided that we should get up some private theatricals. O'Connor was specially keen about this ; and Miss Carter and a friend of hers, a Miss Rawlins, were to take the ladies' parts. Green and Morrison were also enlisted, and to me, who had had some little experience of acting at home, fell the thankless task of stage-manager.

The Carters gave up their drawing-room, and for a time things went swimmingly. O'Connor did a deal of flirting with Miss Carter; though I thought I perceived that she paid a great deal more attention to Green, whenever he condescended to make himself agreeable. Three days before the date fixed for the performance, Miss Rawlins fell ill, Mrs. Carter objected to allow her daughter to be the only lady acting, and it seemed likely that the whole thing would fall. through. Suddenly it occurred to the irrepressible O'Connor that I would make a capital lady. I admit I had a good complexion, and no whiskers ; but then I was far too tall, and I possessed a promising moustache which I much cherished. At first, I firmly declined the arrangement ; but the Carters got me to dinner there, and bullied me so unmercifully about my selfishness that I gave way, and consented to take the part of Annie in " Little Toddlekins."

The theatricals finally came off, with the result that is usual in such cases. All the actors thought they had gone off splendidly ; and the audience were good enough to applaud, and say they thought so too. The absence of ladies made them much less interesting ; this we all admitted afterwards in the quiet of our own house ; and then O'Connor, who seemed to long for further excitement, and was also anxious to follow up the impression he supposed that he had made on the Carters, propounded the audacious suggestion that we should have a ladies' party, *i.e.,* a dinner party, at which some of the guests should be ladies.

This idea I received with the scorn I supposed that it merited ; but to my surprise Green accepted the proposition very favourably, and Morrison didn't care a fig which way the matter was decided. So finally invitations were issued to the Carters, parents and daughter, to Miss Rawlins and her father, Colonel Rawlins, and accepted.

The interval between this and the date of the entertainment was a time of some anxiety to me ; for though our house was a good one, and we had all the necessary means at command, yet I felt that our servants were not quite reliable, as indeed young bachelors' servants seldom are, and I had a presentiment that some contretemps would occur. O'Connor devoted himself to the supply of bouquets, something very suggestive being procured for Miss Carter. For my part, I acceded to all the demands of the khansamar, the chief of which were, two fowls per head for each person dining, for the stock of the soup, plus two for the pot; a "ticca" (hired) cook, a "ticca" "mesalchi," or plate-washer, to assist our own men, and various articles in tins and bottles.

It was now well on in the rainy season, when no vegetables or fruits are procurable, and it was necessary to eke out the limited supplies of the country with articles obtained from Europe in hermetically sealed tins or bottles. Every conceivable thing is so procurable, and the native servants hold them in high estimation. There is a story of a man who had recently returned from furlough telling a very worthy half-caste lady who had never seen England, that he had had the honour of dining with the Queen during his absence; on which she remarked, "Ah! everything in tin, I presume." Her ideas evidently coincided with those of her servants.

My experience of Calcutta dinners at that time was, that they very much resembled each other. They were served *à la Russe.* The centre piece of the table was invariably a large citron melon (called by the natives, "batavee nimbo") with its thick rind cut into ornamental shapes; and the fish almost always tinned salmon. The table was prettily adorned with flowers, for the natives have a wonderful natural taste for combinations of colour; and a curious fact about Calcutta was, that though very few people had gardens, everybody had a gardener. Whence the flowers are procured is to this day a mystery.

On looking into the dining-room before the arrival of our guests, I thought the table looked very much like other people's, whereat I felt contented.

At length the critical moment arrived when we were all seated at table, at one end myself, flanked by Mrs. Carter, and Colonel Rawlins, at the other Green, with Miss Carter on his right and her father on his left. He had somehow successfully asserted his right to take her down; but O'Connor was consoled by having a seat next her. I was a prey to the hundred and one anxieties that fill the minds of young married women on such occasions; and these were not alleviated by observing that Mrs. Carter appeared not to swallow her soup, but to make a show of doing so; while Rawlins, after tasting a spoonful, growled to his servant, who was standing behind him, " Isko lejao, jaldi " (Take this away quickly). On my own turn arriving, I found to my indescribable horror that there was a marked flavour of castor oil in the concoction; and on looking round the table it was clear that every one else had discovered it also.

The khansamar was standing by the sideboard with a self-satisfied look, totally unconscious that anything was wrong; and Green had to tell him a second time very peremptorily to take everybody's soup away, before he appeared to conceive the possibility that there was some reason for its not being drunk. The horrible mystery was afterwards explained. It is the custom in all Indian kitchens to strain the soup through a duster, and every day the bearer used to give out a clean duster for the purpose. It was also the custom in our house to burn castor oil in the lamps. It appeared that the duty of straining the soup had been delegated to the wretched " ticca " cook, who had taken for the purpose a duster that had been already used for cleaning the lamps, and hence the communicated flavour. This was rather trying; but everybody was anxious to make the best of matters, and the rest of the dinner proceeded smoothly enough until the sweets were served. Among other dishes was one of preserved green-gages, with a lot of fluffy white cream at the top, of which I felt a little proud, and was somewhat disconcerted that Mrs. Carter refused it when offered to her. It was next handed to old Rawlins, who helped himself pretty liber-ally; but no sooner had he tasted it than he flung himself back in his chair with the exclamation, " Olives, by God." Alas! it was too true. A bottle of preserved greengages and another of remarkably fine Spanish olives had been given out for the occasion; and now for the first time I noticed the greengages lying innocently in a cut-glass dish among the dessert.

This was too much for Carter's power of self-restraint, and he burst into a loud laugh, in which finally all assembled joined. It was the best way of getting over it, though I saw in prospect some very pretty stories about the Wallahs' dinner-party; and for three weeks or a month afterwards I was frequently consulted as to the merits of " olive tarts."

The evening passed off pretty well. O'Connor and

Green were both musical, and the latter sang one or two duets with Miss Carter, and made very decided running. O'Connor *en revanche* sang, accompanying himself,—

" If she be not fair to me,
What care I how fair she be ? "

and was finally allowed to take Miss Carter down to her carriage.

Certainly after this our chummery was not so united as it had been. O'Connor confided to me that he thought Green intensely conceited ; while Green intimated his opinion that O'Connor was exceedingly common in manner, and could not have mixed much in society before coming to Calcutta.

This was about the first week in August ; and two or three days after O'Connor received his certificate from the Board of Examiners of passing in his second language, which would necessitate his proceeding to his station in the interior very ·shortly. About the same time we received information that our landlord was about to return from the hills, and so we were driven to seek quarters elsewhere.

Green and I had been elected members of the United Service Club,—a very excellent institution, where, considering the comforts available, a bachelor can live more enomomically than anywhere else in Calcutta. It was formerly exclusively for military men ; but they got into difficulties, and a lot of civilians joined it, thus preventing its dissolution, while the amalgamation proved very pleasant socially. The Club consists of a number of fine houses, in one of which are the public rooms, while the others are set apart for chambers for members residing permanently in Calcutta, and sleeping apartments for those only making a short stay. Stabling is also available. The rent of these is moderate ; and I found that my Club bill, including eating and drinking, seldom exceeded 200 rupees monthly. This was much more economical than the chummery.

Morrison and O'Connor had found a resting-place elsewhere. The latter came to dine with me one evening, and over a cigar afterwards began to express regret at leaving Calcutta, and some fears as to the dulness of life alone in the Mofussil. I was somewhat interested as I understood his drift, and further amused when he proceeded to show a curiosity about the price of table-cloths, plated ware, and other articles of domestic economy.

Alas that all this provident foresight should be needless ! Two days afterwards, all Calcutta knew he was a rejected suitor of Miss Carter's. He was so crestfallen that I really felt sincere sympathy with him, though this was somewhat abated when I discovered that he attributed his failure, at any rate in part, to the castor-oil soup and the olive tart.

Early in September he left for the Mofussil, and I saw no more of him for a long time. But some three years after I had a letter from Green, who was then at Delhi, and the father of two children, Miss Carter having consented to become Mrs. Green before the Christmas following the above narrated events. He told me that O'Connor had gone up to Delhi on a month's " privilege " leave, and had called at his house during his absence at office. His wife

had received him cordially, and, with natural matronly
pride, sent for her two children to show him. "Ah," said
O'Connor, with a deep sigh, on seeing them, "they ought
to have been mine."

The last three months of my stay in Calcutta passed
very pleasantly. I became a member also of the Bengal
Club, conducted on principles similar to those of the
United Service, but open to men not in the services. This
was frequented by the leading members of the mercan-
tile community and the learned professions, with a good
sprinkling of civilians. It was interesting, though not
always satisfactory, to know what non-officials thought of
official proceedings; and opinions were expressed here with
very considerable freedom. Being up to this time in no
way connected with any acts brought under criticism, I
was able to listen with perfect impartiality; and the
impression I received was, that, speaking generally, all
official proceedings were wrong, at least from the point of
view of non-officials.

On the whole, at this club there was more luxury, everything was more expensive, the whist points were higher,
and there was generally a more free expenditure of money
than at the other; and I think it was more lively. On
coming back to Calcutta a dozen years afterwards, I found
this still to be the case.

Towards the end of September the snipe begin to come
in in the neighbourhood of Calcutta, and this makes a
very great difference in the daily life of the man of leisure,
such as I was. I speedily became acquainted with a good
"shikarree," who knew every inch of ground within a

radius of twenty miles round, and seldom took me out without affording me a chance of making a full bag. Snipe are very particular, and sometimes very capricious, in their choice of ground ; and occasionally one may walk for hours without seeing a bird, and at another time bag sixteen or twenty brace without moving 200 yards. The shikarrees are exceedingly clever in discovering their favourite haunts, and thus save one much weary wading through slush above one's knees, an hour of which, with a hot October sun overhead, is a very serious matter. They generally have one or two boys with them who are better than any retrievers at picking up the dead game. I suppose the snipe-shooting round Calcutta is as good as any in the world ; and I have known four guns bring back, after five hours' shooting, 150 brace of snipe. They lie best between 11.30 and 2.30, the very hottest part of the day ; and the glare of the sun on the water in the rice fields is very trying both to the eyes and the skin of the face. Many a man's eyesight has suffered from his devotion to this fascinating sport ; and I felt very painfully the sacrifice of my moustache for the sake of those confounded theatricals, as I lost the whole of the skin from both my lips, and they were in a very bad state for some time. On the whole, I should say that before November the game is scarcely worth the candle, for till then the sun is intensely hot, and the birds are not very numerous ; but after that there is, I think, compensation for all risk.

About this time, too, military men who had taken leave to Cashmir and other parts beyond the hills on " urgent private affairs," began to return with wonderful accounts of the "ibex" and other rare animals they had slaughtered, stirring up a keen desire of sport in the breasts of the less fortunate listeners.

There was a freshness in the mornings and evenings which seemed to dispel, both in man and beast—that is to say, European man—the languor induced by the hot weather and the rainy season; and life became altogether more animated. At length, in December, the certificate reached me from the examiners, announcing that I had passed in my second language, Bengali, and was therefore fitted for service in the interior.

In those days, when the miles of railway opened in the country were "easily counted" (εὐαρίθμοι), the old rules relating to the time allowed for joining stations were still in force; and these gave me one week for preparation and some thirty-five days or more for the journey, the district to which I was appointed "Assistant Magistrate and Collector" being between 350 and 400 miles from Calcutta, and the rate of progress demanded only ten miles a day. The railway helped me as far as Bhaugulpore, considerably more than half-way on my road ; and as this portion of my journey would only occupy one day, I was enabled to spend the time thus saved in Calcutta, to play in one or two cricket-matches, assist at Green's wedding, and eat my Christmas dinner in a house where I left a portion of my heart, and where the leave-taking was the most serious thing I went through during this sojourn in the Indian metropolis.

CHAPTER III.

JOURNEY UP COUNTRY.

BHAUGULPORE.—A MOFUSSIL BUNGALOW.—HAPPY-GO-LUCKY PRO-
GRESS TO PATNA.—STAY AT PATNA.

ON the 26th of December, in the early morning, with a
couple of cart-loads of baggage, two horses, and four
servants, I found myself at the Howrah terminus of the
E. B. Railway, and by 8 a.m. was rolling along through
the flat swamps of the Hooghly district, disclosing wide-
spreading and luxuriant rice crops, and many a snipey bit,
which it was irritating not to be able to try.

My destination was Tirhoot, a district lying between the
boundaries of the Nepal kingdom and the Ganges. I had
been persuaded to apply for this by a friend whose acquaintance I had made at the Eton dinner given by Lord
Canning at Government House, on the great Eton anni-
versary, the 4th of June, and where I had the honour of
occupying one end of the table, as junior Etonian present.
My friend, Bertram by name, had been appointed as
Additional Judge of the District, and had taken and
furnished a large house at Mozufferpore, the capital
town, as he expected to remain there some time, and had
proceeded to join his appointment about a month before
I left Calcutta. As far as Bhaugulpore my route was
easy enough; but after that I had to trust to chance

about getting over the remaining 130 or 140 miles of my journey.

The train rolled on through vast alluvial plains till, about 3 or 4 in the afternoon, we came among the jungle-covered hills of Rajmahal. They looked wild and lonely, the jungle growing densely on each side of the rail; and as the shades of evening closed in, I began to feel very solitary and full of regret for the animated though idle life I had left behind me. A retrospect showed me that I had spent ten months in acquiring a mere smattering of the languages, and that I had learned nothing of the manners and customs of the natives among whom my future life was to be spent, and no more of the active duties I had to perform, while I had got through a certain amount of money. I had certainly made many friends; but I was now leaving them all, and the chances were that scarcely any of them would be left in Calcutta when I might next revisit it, such is the migratory character of Anglo-Indian society.

However, these somewhat cheerless reflections were agreeably put an end to by my arrival at Bhaugulpore, where a contemporary fellow-civilian met me, and hurried me off to his bungalow with eager hospitality. He had passed his examinations some three months previously, and had been exercising the powers of an Assistant Magistrate and Collector for that period. He had come out to India married, and seemed to enjoy considerable domestic happiness with very limited accommodation. His habitation was a bungalow with a thatched roof, very high in the centre, and sloping, so as to cover a good-sized area. The interior of this area was occupied by three largish rooms, while a strip some ten or twelve feet in width, running all round the four sides of these, formed a very spacious verandah. This verandah was broken up into various partitions on one side of the house by walls of bamboo matting, which made several convenient small rooms. The servants all lived in outhouses made of "cutcha pucka" masonry; that is, bricks cemented together with mud, and thatched roofs. The kitchen and stables were of similar construction.

For my accommodation a tent borrowed from the Magistrate had been erected, and so I passed my first night under canvas. During and after dinner, my host regaled me with an account of the many and various duties he had to perform; and before the evening was over I became quite cheered with a sense of my own importance, and eager to reach the tract of country where my personal official powers would commence. I was a little surprised the next day to find that his presence was not necessary at Cutcherry, and that he would be able to devote himself to me; but I afterwards discovered that all young civilians, who really have very little official work—and very properly so—for the first six months after joining their stations, are most anxious to impress upon others the importance of their duties. I fell into the same way myself; and I recollect a friend, who had gone up to the North-west Provinces some two months before this, writing to me that the work was "crushing." All the same, I was very glad to have the benefit of his three months' Mofussil experience to assist me in forwarding my traps to Mozufferpore, and in helping me on myself; for in most parts of India it is even more necessary to "speed the parting" than "welcome the coming guest."

After a great deal of jabbering four "bailgarees" (bullock carts) were engaged for some very moderate sum, half of which had to be paid in advance, to take all but the things I wanted for use on my journey, direct to Mozufferpore, which they hoped to reach in ten days; and my horses started with them. They left about mid-day, and we were free to devote the afternoon to seeing the station, by which I mean the civil station of Bhaugulpore, and not the railway terminus.

At the Collector's house we found a lot of people playing quoits before sunset, among them the Resident Railway Engineer, who said he could send me by "trolly" to Jamalpore, some thirty miles along the line (in course of construction) next day, and further, give me a letter to the next engineer. This suited me exactly.

We had a very pleasant evening at the Collector's, who gave us hospitality in the shape of dinner; and the next morning at sunrise I started to walk over a short break in the railway, and before nine was being pushed along by coolies at the rate of six miles an hour. It was a lovely day, and the mode of progression very pleasant; and further, I was surprised at the endurance of our propellers, who appeared able to keep up their efforts at this pace for any distance. I found a young officer, who was making his way north-westward as best he could, had also been accommodated with a seat on the trolly, and he proved a very pleasant companion.

All went smoothly till we reached a place called Sultangunge, where there was a break in the line, and from which point our coolies said they must take back the trolly, as they had orders to do so. On this a certain babel of tongues arose, to which my companion contributed some very vigorous English, when suddenly a European under-official of the line appeared, and told us that an engine was going on to Jamalpore about three in the afternoon, and we could get on that. This settled matters satis-factorily, and shortly after sunset I proceeded to climb the hill through which the Jamalpore tunnel runs, and at the top of which my host for the night resided. My com-panion walked on into the town of Monghyr, only four miles distant, where he had friends.

At the house on the hill I was received as if I had been an intimate friend of the family. My host was married, and all the rooms in his bungalow were occupied, but a portion of the verandah was quickly converted into a room by the erection of some bamboo mats, in which I was enabled to pass the night very comfortably. The next day was Sunday and wet; and as my host had somewhat Sabbatical tendencies my departure was postponed until the Monday morning. The desire of entering upon my official duties was now strong within me, and I found this delay very irksome, to say nothing of the natural dulness of a wet Sunday in a Mofussil bungalow. Early on the Monday I was forwarded by "trolly" to the next engineer's; but though I reached this by the middle of the day, my next host, possibly with the desire of a companion for dinner, let me understand that I could by no means get forward until the following day. He made himself very

agreeable, however, and had a good many stories to tell
of encounters with tigers, which are very numerous in
the jungly hills through which the line runs. They appeared to be very fond of coming on the line itself;
but being very inexperienced in these matters I felt
some of the incredulity of ignorance as to some of his
details.

The next day, the 31st of December, I rode five miles
on a rather vicious pony to a large river, the Joas, over
which I was ferried, the bridge not being completed, and
on the other side found the next engineer, who had come
to look at the works. He had a horse and a palanquin
with him, but made the latter over to me, and sent me
in it to his house at Malpore, some sixteen miles further, and said he would follow on horseback. We arrived
at his house almost simultaneously and found the regular
Mofussil one o'clock breakfast awaiting us, for which I at
any rate had a keen appetite. My host was really the
prince of good fellows; as to going any further that day,
it was, he said, simply out of the question. It was the last
day of the old year; some neighbouring engineers were
coming to dinner, and I must assist in welcoming in
the 1st of January. He had a very fair billiard table, and
the afternoon passed by no means disagreeably.

About six the guests arrived—four engineers and the
doctor of that part of the line. Two of the former and
the latter were Scotchmen, as might have been expected;
indeed such a proportion of that nationality, under the
circumstances, may be considered small. Their appearance
was not what one would call polished, for there were no

European ladies within a pretty good circumference, and
men do not dress for each other. However, they were all
men of education, and had seen professional service in
many parts of the world. The doctor, a very weather-
beaten old fellow, had been everywhere; and his conversation was both instructive and amusing. I wish I could
recollect some of it, but after dinner the talk became somewhat fast and furious.

At midnight we welcomed in the New Year, and after
singing "Auld lang syne," with more vigour than tune,
I turned into a palanquin belonging to my host, which
was to convey me some nine miles to the house of one
of the guests, where his palki and bearers would be at
my service. At this place, called Chunar, I arrived
between two and three in the morning; and the bearers,
with the usual *insouciance* of natives, set the palki down
on the left edge of the road, which was an embanked one,
with deep ditches on both sides. They there woke me
suddenly by rapping on the outside of the palki, and
intimated that I must get out and change mine for
that of the "Chunar Sahib." I opened by chance the
left-hand sliding doors, got out hastily in the dark, and
rolled at once into the ditch. It was luckily quite dry;
but the shock was rather startling, and I gave one of my
knees a sprain which I felt for months afterwards. This
was, I believe, the only contretemps that befell me on this
happy-go-lucky journey.

I was naturally very angry, and this induced the coolies
to bestir themselves more than they otherwise would, to
get the other palki ready, so that in a very short time I

was again *en route* for Barh, my next halting-place, about seventeen miles distant.

This I reached about 8 a.m., and was deposited at the bungalow of the deputy magistrate, who received me with hospitality similar to that I had experienced all along. He had been in the army, but had come to the conclusion that the peaceful life of a civilian, even though in the "uncovenanted" service, was preferable to the harassments of war; and so some years previously, when examinations had not been thought of, and such transfers were easily made, had succeeded in getting the exchange he desired, and seemed, I thought, contented.

To me Barh appeared the dullest place that it was possible for a civilized being to inhabit. It is a good-sized native town on the right bank of the Ganges, some forty-two miles from Patna. There was one other European official there, a subordinate in the Opium Department, and this was all the society he and his wife had. The social qualifications of natives are, in relation to Europeans "nil," as I shall perhaps be able to show hereafter. Being the 1st of January, it was a holiday, and his office was closed, so he would much have liked to keep me there for the day; but I had become imbued with a sense of the necessity of pressing on to my own work—though there really was no urgent necessity—and would not be persuaded to stop. Anglo-Indians in out-of-the-way places know that they do you a service in sending you on quickly, and feel that their desire to keep you is really more for their own benefit than yours; so, with a spirit of true hospitality, the advent of breakfast was accelerated, his palki was ordered, and by ten o'clock I was once more *en route*, and furnished with provisions for the day.

The speed and endurance of these Behar "palki bearers" is extraordinary. By 4.30 p.m. I' was at the entrance of the Patna bazaar, some nine miles in length, and thirty-three miles from Barh ; thus they had brought me at an average rate of over four miles an hour, including a stoppage of over half an hour for their midday meal. It is true, I was a light weight ; but I once with a friend tried to carry an empty palki, and found it so galling to the shoulder that I could not get beyond a few yards, while these men, who lived on little else than rice, could carry a loaded one over forty miles, at the rate mentioned above. There were sixteen of them, and four at a time carried the palki, the remaining twelve resting themselves, if so it may be called, by running along side it.

Extraordinary as this may appear, people get so accustomed to the fact, that they look upon the palki in the same light as any other conveyance, and show little consideration for their human beasts of burden. Indeed, I have known young officers put a stone or two of ammunition in addition to the other necessary articles they had with them into the conveyance, on the chance of sport by the way side. The skin on the shoulders of these men becomes thick and hard like that of a rhinoceros.

The last portion of my journey through the bazaar was anything but pleasant ; the dust was choking, and the stench of oil and rancid .ghee was overpowering. It being the cold weather too, a great number of wood fires were lighted, the wood being by preference damp, and emitting a most pungent smoke, hostile indeed to mosquitoes, but very trying to the eyes and sense of smell. The latter, I imagine, natives do not possess, or only in some very modified form.

At length, after nine miles of native huts, smells, and noises, without seeing one single European, I reached, about 6.30, the old " Foujdari Cutcherry " (Criminal Court House), in a portion of which my next host had taken up his residence. He was a civilian, Rawlinson by name, like my friend of Bhaugulpore, who had passed his examinations some three months previously, and had been for that period in the exercise of his official duties.

On arrival I found him absent, " at the Commissioner Sahib's," his bearer told me ; and so I had time for a bath, always available in an Anglo-Indian establishment, and by the time of his return was clean and clothed and in the right mind for dinner.

The principal feature in the entertainment seemed to be the multitude of bats of all sizes, which were attracted by the lights in our room, from all parts of the huge old building, and gyrated in orbits of varying dimensions round the table above our heads. One small fellow finally deposited himself in my host's soup, whereat I was somewhat disgusted ; but he, being a bit of a naturalist, was much interested, bade me observe that the creature had only fainted, requested me to watch the details of its recovery, which duly took place in a few minutes, and he then released it to resume its gyrations as before.

After dinner, over a cigar, I was initiated into some of the details of Patna life and society. This place is the metropolis of the province of Behar, and, with the neighbouring military station of Dinapore, separated only by some six miles of good road, contains a larger European population than any other Mofussil station in Bengal proper.

The province of Behar is divided into six districts or counties, containing an aggregate area of 23,732 square miles, and a population, according to the census of 1872, of 13,123,529. All this is presided over by the Commissioner of Patna, in which place he has his head-quarters, though he is expected to devote a certain portion of each year to the personal inspection of the districts and various offices under his charge. As may be supposed, he is a great man; for though he is not a law-giver, he is the administrator of this vast area; and the only official intervening between him and the Governor-General of India, is the Lieutenant-Governor of Bengal. He has also, it is true, to obey the orders of the Revenue Board in revenue matters; but he is not altogether bound by red tape, and is entrusted with a general supervision and control which is conveniently indefinite, and gives him great power. For the performance of his arduous duties, he draws a salary of 3,000 rupees, equal to £300 monthly, plus a consolidated travelling allowance of 250 rupees, or £25 a month for touring expenses.

The present Commissioner, I was informed, was a gentleman of mature age and experience, with, among other qualifications, two marriageable daughters, a matter of some importance in the Mofussil.

The next dignitary in point of rank and emoluments was

the Opium Agent. This functionary exercised control over this great Government monopoly in the provinces of Behar and Bhaugulpore. The interests in his charge were large; but the duties, as far as I could learn, seemed to involve merely probity, and not much work. The appointment appeared to me to be kept for such as desired, and possibly deserved, *otium cum dignitate.* The present man lived a quiet, retired life, and I do not think had much influence on the social life of Patna.

Next in order came the Civil and Sessions Judge, the Collector-Magistrate, the Joint Magistrate, and the Assistant Magistrate (my host), all covenanted civilians. There were also the Doctor, or Civil Surgeon, who had, of course, served some time with a regiment; the Executive Engineer, the local official of the P.W.D. (Public Works Department, irreverently interpreted the Public Waste Department by those who are not members of that branch of the service); two Deputy Collectors, members of the uncovenanted service; three or four subordinate officers of the Opium Department, and several railway officials. To these must be added the Staff officers at Dinapore, with those of the regiments quartered there; and it will be seen that Patna contained, with these and their female dependants, large and varied European social elements. I have not mentioned the native officers, as I did not make their acquaintance on this occasion, and they count for nothing socially.

My host was more of a naturalist than a sportsman, and only kept one quadruped for necessary locomotion; so the next morning we started after our "chota hazri" to walk to the European portion of the station, called Bankipore, situated about half a mile distant. The narrow road of the native portion of the town here widens out into a spacious plain of a circular shape, which formed the race-course. There is scarcely a station in Bengal without this means of providing for our favourite national amusement. Around this are situated the residences of the Europeans, the Church, and some of the Law Courts; and the open green space, with its fine trees, is very refreshing to the eye after the long, dusty, narrow bazaar.

On making our way to the race-course, we found a remarkably stout gentleman pounding round it on a very strong-built Australian horse. He pulled up on seeing us, and saluted my companion; who introduced me to him as the judge. It seemed to me somewhat curious that this very heavy individual should be the only member of the Patna society who cared for equestrian exercise; but I found that in his youth he had been of slender dimensions and a rider of steeple-chases; and as we conversed, it transpired that he had passed a good many years in the district of Tirhoot, to which I was appointed, and he gave me glowing accounts of the fine riding country and the sport and sportsmen I should find there. Our meeting ended with an invitation to dinner that evening, and we went on to pay our respects to the Commissioner, Mr. Coldham.

Him we found hard at work, with bundles of papers tied with red tape before him, in his "dufter khana," or library, the name given by natives to the room kept in the house of every official for writing purposes, and where, thanks to the absence of housemaids, the most comfortable untidiness exists.

I was prepared to treat the great man with reserved respect, for he would be practically my supreme ruler for some time to come, and much depended on his opinion and consequent reports of me. He, however, greeted me right cordially, asked a good many questions about my journey, and appeared amused at the route I had taken, as I might have come by the regular "dâk gârree" (carriage service) from Raneegunge through Gya. All the time he was talking he was taking up bundle after bundle, and after making short notes on some, throwing them into a large basket placed on the ground, while others he reserved for more elaborate orders. This I wondered at at the time, for some of the bundles so unceremoniously treated were at least a foot thick; but I afterwards got into the secret of this method of working, and found that a very big bundle can often be temporarily disposed of by a routine order.

Presently, on a summons, a chuprassie ("badge-wearer," official servant paid by Government) appeared, and carried off the basket, overflowing with the bundles, which would be emptied at the Commissioner's Cutcherry by his head assistant, and the contents distributed to the various clerks, who would elaborate short orders into formal letters, which, when faired, would be returned to Mr. Coldham for signature, and then forwarded to the various officials for whom they were intended.

We now took our leave, Mr. Coldham telling us that his wife and daughters would be delighted to see us to after-

noon tea and croquet; and on our way home Rawlinson
informed me that I might look forward to a very pleasant
afternoon. It was now time to think of bath and breakfast; and we were returning for the purpose, when a dog-
cart caught us up on the main road, the occupant of which
proved to be Alison, the Magistrate and Collector. He
asked us to come and breakfast with him as soon as we
were dressed; and so my first day at Patna was pretty
well filled up with hospitality.

Alison's bungalow was small but comfortable, and
situated on the edge of what, in the rainy season, was the
mighty rushing stream of the Ganges; but at this time
was a vast expanse of undulating sand, with here and
there channels of water half dried up, an alluvial formation
called in this part of the world a "deara," and in Lower
and Eastern Bengal a "chur." It was this Deara, and
the at present comparatively attenuated river, which
separated Patna from my own district, the palm-trees of
which I could see waving on the opposite bank, some six
or seven miles distant.

I found Alison a most pleasant host, full of interest in
his work, and at the same time with a keen capacity for
enjoyment. Afterwards he and I became excellent friends;
but on the present occasion the conversation was principally on the subject of some decision of Rawlinson's
which Alison had reversed. Rawlinson being his assistant
with what was then called "no powers," all appeals from
his decisions lay to him. It seemed that Rawlinson had
convicted one Nazir Baksh of assaulting one Peer Baksh,
and had fined him five rupees, or ten shillings, whereas

Alison was of opinion that no assault had taken place. Rawlinson was rather hot on the subject, and his very keen interest in the matter seemed overstrained.

After breakfast my two companions went off to their respective offices, and I was left to my own resources for a time. Not for long, however, for it was scarcely two hours before Rawlinson returned, and we sat talking over various matters until it was time to go the Commissioner's.

"What have you been doing to-day?" I asked.

"Oh! those everlasting assault cases. They come in shoals, and it would seem as if they were brought simply to give the *chota sahib* (little gentleman) something to do. It's weary, weary work; and I long to pass my examination in March, and get powers to try something of more importance. They are nearly all false. In some of them there is perhaps a substratum of truth; but in many there is none whatever. If a man or woman have a spite against another, their favourite method of gratifying it is by bringing a case in court against them. If of a sufficiently high class to make their own appearance in court disagreeable, they make their servants complain against their enemies themselves, or their servants.

"Here is an instance that occurred only ten days ago. A case was referred to me for trial in which the complaint was to the effect that a respectable mookhtyar (criminal court attorney), by name Nubbee Baksh, had been severely assaulted by two men, Pultoo Singh and Jeebun Mali, at the instigation of a man called Bahadur Ali, that he was lying at death's door, and could not come to Court to give evidence. Alison probably suspected gross exaggeration in the case, or he would not have made it over to me. However, at the request of the mookhtyar in charge of the case, I went purposely down to the bazaar to record his deposition. He was bandaged round the head, and there was a good deal of blood on it, and he seemed in great, pain. The rest of his body was covered with a blanket; and being a young hand, I felt shy about examining him too particularly.

"His story was to the effect that he was coming home from Court the previous day with some valuable documents, and a sum of about twenty-five rupees in his girdle, when Pultoo Singh and Jeebun Mali set upon him with "latties" (bamboo clubs), knocked him down, kicked him, and carried off his turban, his waist-cloth, his money, and his documents. He recognised his assailants as two bad characters who lived in the bazaar. After recording this, I considered it advisable to report the matter to Alison, who merely remarked, 'Has he been examined by the civil surgeon?' 'No,' I said; 'I had not thought of that.'

"'You should very seldom,' he said, 'believe a complainant is really badly hurt until you have medical testimony to that effect.'

"The civil surgeon accordingly, at my request, went down without warning to the complainant's house; but delays were made about his seeing him when he got there, and before he could get into his room he had bolted. After this, I made the best inquiries I could into the matter, and I ascertained what I believe now to be the truth, viz., that Bahadur Ali, the alleged instigator of the assault, is the brother of Hyder Ali, the employer of

Nubbee Baksh ; that the two brothers are quarrelling about a piece of garden land situated between their two houses, and a few days ago their respective gardeners had a quarrel about some flowers they each wished to gather. Hyder Ali, at the advice of Nubbee Baksh, then got up this case, intending to make out that the documents in question were the title-deeds of the land, and thus hoping not only to spite Bahadur Ali by getting his servants Pultoo and Jeebun punished, but also to lay the foundation of a suit in the Civil Court.

"Alison has ordered Nubbee Baksh to be prosecuted for perjury ; but he seems to think that the two brothers will come to terms, and that it will be very difficult to get evidence sufficient for a committal."

"Alison's experience helped you out of that pretty well," I said.; "and yet you seemed very much annoyed at his reversing the decision in the case we were talking about at breakfast."

"Yes ; but that was a different kind of case altogether. He may be right ; but it is not even supposed that there was any cause for the complaint except the actual assault, and it was merely a question of the quality of the evidence. Now I had seen the witnesses, and observed their demeanour, and I felt confident that in this case they were describing what they had actually seen. Alison had only seen the record ; and in such a case, unless there is something really tangible to go on, I think he should hesitate to disregard the opinions of the officer originally trying the case. .

"It is of course right that there should be appeals on

both facts and law from the decisions of us juveniles; but I have little doubt that in India the system is carried much too far, both in civil and criminal matters. You will understand this better when you have seen more of the work. I only hope that at Mozufferpore you will get a greater variety than I do here; but in a big town like this these petty cases are legion, and as all the other officials are useful in other ways, as having higher powers, it is very natural they should all be made over to me.

"But it is time to go to the Commissioner's. There is the station bath in his grounds, and being an Eton man—you must swim. We will send our clothes, and dress there after croquet, and go straight to the Judge Sahib's, which is close by."

At the Commissioner's we found several people assembled, with, "*mirabile dictu,*" an almost equal number of both sexes. We were soon set to work at croquet under the directions of the Commissioner's daughters, two bright-eyed young ladies, whose rosy complexions showed they were not long from England; and Mrs. Coldham was dispensing tea at a table set out on the lawn,—if the term lawn may be applied to the miserable grass that grows in Indian "compounds" in the plains,—when suddenly an ayah appeared on the verandah of the bungalow, which covered a good large area, there being no upper story, and screamed out something which I did not catch, but which caused everybody to rush to the house, myself with the rest.

We reached a room which turned out to be Mrs. Coldham's bedroom, and on looking in I saw, comfortably lying on the bed, a cow, who had settled herself there, quite regardless of the ayah's distress, and appeared to enjoy the elásticity of her resting-place—a new spring couch just imported from England. The room extended the whole breadth of the house, and at the other side opened on another grass plat, where Coldham's cows were kept. The animal had got in from there, and was speedily though cautiously ejected. Hindoo cattle, though so meek-looking with their large, gentle eyes, are exceedingly impertinent and obtrusive. They are left to cater mostly for themselves, and their powers of making their way into the most carefully-guarded enclosures is almost unlimited. This animal was no exception to the general rule.

There was a good deal of laughter over the incident, and then Coldham walked me up and down and gave me some good advice in a very kind manner.

"From one or two things you let fall this morning," he said, "I am afraid you will be liable to a feeling of disillusion and disappointment when you first commence work. Your duties at the outset will not be of very great public importance; and, as you yourself will understand, it is quite right they should not be so. But they will give you plenty of opportunities of learning the language and gaining experience; and if you use these properly, by the time you have passed both your examinations you will be a really valuable Government servant. And you should make up your mind to pass your examinations as speedily as possible. It is dry work, grinding up Acts and Codes, but it must be done; and it is far less weary work to use energy and pass your exams. on the first possible occasion, than to fail and have to go over old ground, and be kept to the same petty work for another six months. You should recollect also, that after passing your first exam. you get an extra 50 rs. a month pay, and after the second a further 50 rs., making your salary 500 rs.; and if reported fit in other respects you are invested with 'full powers.' You must read your codes to find out what 'full powers' mean. We shall hope to see you over here in March, when your first chance will arrive, though I shall not expect you to pass then; but you will have to be examined, that we may see whether you have learned anything or nothing."

It was now time to go to the bath, and Rawlinson, reluctantly leaving the society of the Misses Coldham, strolled there with me. This is an institution at most Indian stations; and it is a great luxury to be able to take a plunge and refresh oneself with a swim before making a toilet for dinner. This was a good-sized masonry bath, with a platform for dressing at one end, the whole covered with thatch and protected by mat walls. It was filled from a well in the garden, from which the water was drawn by a small Persian wheel, worked by a couple of bullocks.

A melancholy incident had occurred here the previous hot weather. A young guest of Coldham's had come in after dark, undressed himself with eager haste to plunge into the cool water, and jumped into the bath head foremost, which, through the negligence of the gardener who attended to it, had been left *empty*. Death was apparently instantaneous. It cast quite a gloom over the place at the time; and since then the bath has never been empty after dark.

On this evening the water was too cold to allow of any dawdling; and Rawlinson and myself soon found ourselves at the Judge's, with quite a keen appetite for dinner. We met Alison at the door with a roll of music under his arm, and in the drawing-room, very much to R.'s delight, found the two Miss Coldhams. There were also present a young officer from Dinapore, and a Deputy Magistrate with his wife and daughter, Mr., Mrs., and Miss Pease.

Mrs. Lawson evidently took pride in the management of her house; and the arrangements, I should say, were superior to those in most Mofussil establishments. The details of the dinner were very similar to those in Calcutta, even down to the ornamental batavee nimbo; and this comparison implies high praise. There was of course no ice; but at this season it was cold enough to prevent its absence being seriously felt.

It fell to my lot to sit next Miss Pease, a young lady who had never been out of India, I found, and whose subjects of conversation were therefore somewhat limited. Her father had come out as second officer in a merchant vessel, some twenty-five years previously ; and, finding a friend at court, had obtained an appointment in the uncovenanted service. He had not been able to send his daughter home, and she had been educated at a convent near Calcutta ; and her experience of the world was confined to the country between that place and Patna, her father having been stationed at Bhaugulpore and Monghyr in previous years. He had been in his present appointment for some years, and his daughter's social horizon seemed to be bounded by the neighbouring town of Dinapoor.

I was entirely out of this of course, and it was fortunate that the young officer was her neighbour on the other side. They soon plunged into such personal gossip that I almost fancied myself once more on board ship. I was a little startled to hear him regretting the "good old times," when, if a servant within the limits of cantonments misbehaved himself, his master or mistress merely sent him with a note to the cantonment magistrate, requesting that the bearer might receive twenty lashes; which request was granted as a matter of course. "Now," he said, "you can't get a man punished without a regular case, just as if he were an European."

Miss Pease, whether from courtesy or conviction, appeared quite to agree with her interlocutor.

"But," I interposed, "you surely would not have a man flogged simply on the *ex-parte* statement of his employer."

"Oh!" he replied, "you civilians always stand up for these niggers. Of course they obey you because they know your power; but now they are perfectly well aware that they can get the law of us, and they treat us just as they like. You ask anybody who is not in your service."

"My dear Williams," said Lawson, who had overheard this, "you treat your servants well, and they will do the same by you. You young fellows come out from England and kick these poor submissive creatures about as if they had no feeling, either mental or physical. You would not dare to do it at home; and yet you expect these people to do all sorts of things for you that you would not venture to ask an English servant to do. ' 'It's a way you have in the army,' and I think it fully accounts for the very low character borne by regimental servants."

"You're a Judge Sahib," said Williams, "and all the natives kowtow to you." And it seemed impossible to get beyond this point with him.

After dinner we had some very good music. Mrs. Lawson had married late, and therefore had time to obtain more of the advantages of " Western civilization " than young girls who come out to their parents at seventeen. Alison, too, sang really well. Rawlinson seemed happy with the Miss Coldhams. Alison at length gave us a lift home behind his fast-trotting mare.

"Hard lines," I said, " for poor Miss Pease, never to have been home to England."

" She does not miss pleasure she has never experienced," said Alison ; " and moreover she is going to be married to a member of our service, who is at present in charge of the subdivision of Sasseram. He is all alone there without a white face near him, and her father was sent down to do some settlement work. He took his wife and daughter with him, and I suppose they both appeared as angels to poor Smith in his solitude. They are to be married next month. She doubtless has much the best of the bargain ; and I dare say when he gets into civilized society again he will regret it, and I have almost ventured to hint as much to him, but without effect. I have seen one or two cases of the sort. You and Rawlinson will have to undergo a similar course; and before you plunge I should recommend you to think of your people at home. I have myself felt

the influence of loneliness.   Here we are.   I won't come
in.   Good-night."

In Calcutta I had made the acquaintance of the Joint
Magistrate of Tirhoot, Darville, who had promised to help
me over part of the thirty-five miles of road between
Hajeepore, on the opposite bank of the Ganges, and
Mozufferpore.   I had informed him of my arrival at
Patna, and I now found a note asking me to be at Gooriah
Ghât, half-way on the road, by the following evening.

Rawlinson told me I need not start till midday, and he
would get me a palki and bearers.

CHAPTER IV.

LIFE AS ASSISTANT MAGISTRATE AND COLLECTOR AT MOZUFFERPORE.

JOURNEY ACROSS THE GANGES.—DÂK BUNGALOW.—DRIVE TO MOZUFFERPORE.—FIND MY QUARTERS LONELY.—FIRST VISIT TO CUTCHERRY, AND INVESTMENT IN OFFICE.—FIRST CASE.—CHUPRASSIES.—INTRODUCTION TO MY MAGISTRATE AND COLLECTOR. —SWORN IN AS ASSISTANT COLLECTOR.

βY noon the palki and sixteen bearers were ready for me, and Rawlinson himself prepared to accompany me as far as the ghât, or place of embarcation for crossing the Ganges. Here we said good-bye, and I was once more left alone with my "native beasts of burden." The hospitality of Patna had been extreme ; but I was glad to be on my way again to the scene of my own labours ; and the ferrymen and bearers, knowing that I was a "hakim" (governor), though only in embryo so far, were very deferential. There were a few other passengers in the boat, two or three women among them, who had been chattering away till we appeared, but who on seeing us drew their "chaddars" (female linen garment of great length, wound round the head and body) round their faces and retired to the further end of the boat. The male travellers also got as far away as they could.

It is not satisfactory to experience the constraint which

a white face produces wherever it appears in an assemblage of natives.

The progress of a Ganges ferry-boat is of the slowest. Indeed they are the clumsiest things conceivable, and I have often wondered why improved boats have not been invented ; but the Ganges is a troublesome river to deal with, and vessels suitable for one season do not do for another. At this time of the year the river had divided itself into three channels, and we had to disembark three times, the distance to be traversed on sand in one case being over three miles. My horses would have to cross some fifty or sixty miles lower down, and it was a mystery to me how the animals could get into such boats, the sides of which bulge out into semicircles, and the thwarts of which are so close together that a very small space is left to jump between.

At length, after three hours' rowing, bumping, punting, and walking, we reached the Hajeepoor Ghât on the opposite bank; and when the jabbering inseparable from a fresh start had been got through, I found myself once more swinging along to the monotonous chant of the bearers at a little over four miles an hour.

It grew dark soon after we started ; but I had sufficient time to observe that instead of the dry, cracked, mud plains of the Patna district, capable of growing the heavy rice only, and which in the dry cold season are perfectly bare, we were passing through crops of oats, linseed, and pulse, with frequent plantations of the castor-oil plant, which attains a very considerable height.

I was very glad about 9 p.m. to reach the Gooriah Ghât

dâk bungalow. Dâk bungalows are buildings erected by Government at certain places along the road for the convenience of European travellers, and are absolutely necessary in the absence of inns and innkeepers, of whose extortions we are so apt to complain in the West. They are generally placed under the charge of a khansamar who receives a small salary, and is supposed to make his profit as a "licensed victualler." Government charges one rupee, or two shillings, for the use of the bungalow by each traveller.

That at Gooriah Ghât consisted of three small rooms, covered by a thatched roof, and with a short verandah on two sides. Outside I observed the dog-cart of Darville, the Joint Magistrate, who had come to meet me, and inside I found its owner reading by the light of a candle stuck in a bottle. The number of visitors was not large, and the resources of the place were small.

The khansamar was able to provide me with a skinny fowl, which, by the way, took refuge under my chair before being killed for my meal (Darville had expected me earlier, and dined previously), and some "chupatties" made of "sujee" (flour ground coarse, and water); and off this and some potted meat, which Darville had brought with him, I feasted with a fair appetite. He had been mindful of tea, sugar, and a candle, but had forgotten bread.

He was glad to have some one to talk to, and to hear the Calcutta and Patna news; but the one candle did not admit of a late sitting, and so we turned in by half-past ten.

The bed-furniture struck me as scanty. There was a

mattress and a pillow, and mosquito curtains, but nothing in the shape of sheets, blankets, or pillow cases ; and I was glad that I had brought a couple of railway rugs with me. Sleep, however, came very willingly to this not very luxurious couch ; and I was quite surprised when Darville woke me up at the screech of dawn, saying he wished to make as early a start as possible.

Tea was soon ready, and after paying my bill, amounting to three shillings, including the Government charge, we walked to the ghât of the little river, which is here only some twenty yards wide, and across which the dog-cart, with the horse harnessed to it, was ferried in a sort of raft boat.

The road was of a light sandy soil, overgrown with short grass, which keeps the surface well bound together, and sufficiently hard for the traffic to which it is subjected. We had only seventeen miles to go, but to do this we made use of three horses ; and I found it was the Tirhoot custom not to drive a horse a dâk, or stage, of more than five miles. In comparison with the rest of Bengal, it is a great district for roads, but they are none of them metalled, and get heavy in the very dry season and the height of the rains. Horses, too, can be kept cheaply, and as the planters dotted about the country all keep a large number, and help each other when required, a " dâk," as the expression is, of twenty horses can be laid for one hundred miles without much difficulty. Darville had two of his own horses out, and one belonging to a planter, Colville by name, whose factory was quite close to Mozufferpore.

The country as we drove along was quite flat and uninteresting, though there is no doubt that Tirhoot consists of a series of undulations, but they scarcely strike the eye, as the elevations in most cases are probably not over three or four feet. Such a rise, however, makes all the difference in the nature of the crops that the soil can grow, as water lodges in the depressions, and makes them fit for rice only.

Our conversation turned naturally on the station society, and I found it consisted of the following elements: the Judge, who was just about to retire, and a new man was expected in his place; the Additional Judge, Bertram, with whom I was going to chum; the Collector, Blake, with his wife and some young children; the Doctor, Macpherson, with a very charming wife, and no children; the Clergyman and his wife; the planter, above mentioned, with his wife and family; A Deputy Magistrate and a Deputy Opium Agent, with large families; and the planter's doctor.

Many planters were frequently coming in on business, and had leased a bungalow in the station, which they had formed into a club.

Last, but by no means least, was the manager of the estate of the young Rajah of Durbhungah, which had been taken under the care of Government, and who was supposed to reside at Durbhungah, which may be called the capital of the property, but who passed the greater portion of his time in a palatial mansion at Mozufferpore, called Secundrapore, and was of great importance in assisting the station festivities.

About 9 a.m. we entered the town of Mozufferporé. the

breadth of the road at this its southern side, and an avenue of tall trees, rendering the appearance of the bazaar huts specially insignificant ; and after about a mile of this debouched on to the plain which exists in nearly all Bengal stations, at the further side of which appeared three houses —one Darville's, one the Doctor's, the third being empty. On our left was the dâk bungalow ; on our right, the racket court, the Judge's new Cutcherry (Court House), the Foujdari Cutcherry, in which Darville dispensed criminal justice (and where I should at first be principally occupied), and further on the main bazaar of the town.

Darville rather apologized for the appearance of his house ; and externally it did look a little tumble-down ; but inside the rooms were large and comfortable enough, and at the back was an expanse of water called the "lake," which had formerly been the main bed of the Gunduk ; but the river, with the usual caprice of Bengal streams, had turned off to the north, after passing round a piece of rather high land which formerly formed the race-course, and on which the above-mentioned mansion of Secundrapore was situated, also the Circuit House, or Government building for the use of the Commissioner of Patna and other peripatetic dignitaries when they happened to visit this station.

At one end of the lake was Colville's factory, and at the other a sort of embanked bridge, over which lay the road to the high land above mentioned, and which formed the fashionable evening drive of the European community. The lake water percolated through this embankment, and found its way into the old bed of the stream along the back of the main bazaar, joining the new current just above the Collector's house, which was situated at the other end of the town. The old channel was in the dry season a series of shallow pools and a great producer of mosquitoes.

This much I learned while enjoying a cigar in the verandah with Darville after bath and breakfast. The sun was bright and the sky blue, there was a gentle cool westerly breeze, just sufficient to wrinkle in patches the surface of the lake without raising dust on land, and, looking northwards, a faint glimpse of the snowy Himalayas was obtainable. The general effect, as we sat with our legs supported by the long arms of our cane chairs, and the smoke of our cigars curled lazily upwards, was deliciously soothing.

Three months afterwards how different was the scene! Every window closed, to keep out the dense clouds of dust whirled along by the howling, tearing west wind, everything reduced to a state of tinder by the extreme dryness, the backs of all the books curled up, the ink too thick to flow from the pen, one's hair like tow, and a general sense of grittiness and hot discomfort that must be felt to be understood.

Our tranquillity was interrupted by the sound of wheels, and in a moment the chuprassie informed us that "His Highness the Judge Sahib Bahadur and his Highness the Additional Judge Sahib Bahadur, having put the blessed honour in a dog-cart, had brought it to the door," by which he merely intended to express the fact that the Judge and the Additional Judge (my friend Bertram) had called in a dog-cart.

I was very glad to see Bertram, with whom I was to chum ; but my pleasure was much damped by the announcement that he had to start that very evening for the neighbouring district of Purneah, to which he had been appointed. This initiated me into the very migratory nature of Anglo-Indian society. He carried off my modest amount of traps in the dog-cart, saying he would send me a horse to ride down in the evening. The animal, a beautiful bay Arab, turned up about 4.30, and I found my way across the embankment, past Secundrapore, down a newly-made road that ran between the new and old beds of the Gunduk river, to his house.

We dined early, as he had a long palki journey before him, and at 7 he started, with the usual noise and jabber, and a flaring torch emitting a most disgusting stench, which I observed at the time the torch-bearer carried to windward of the palki, and which I have found that torch-bearers invariably do so carry, notwithstanding all possible persuasion to the contrary. Palanquins are happily not such necessities in many parts of India as they used to be ; but even at this lapse of time the most lasting impression left upon me by that method of travelling is the smell of those disgusting torches.

I turned back into the house and felt lonely. The dining-room was about forty feet long, and the other rooms in proportion. The furniture in England would have been thought very scanty ; but for India it was decidedly above the average, for Bertram was a man who liked to be comfortable. He hoped to return in a month or two ; and in the meantime I was left in charge of his effects, and he was to pay half the rent of the house, the whole being ₹20 rs., or £12, monthly, which included the salaries of two gardeners. This was moderate enough, considering its size, but would have made a considerable hole in my pay of 400 rs., or £40, a month, from which had to be deducted a four per cent. income tax, and another eight per cent., or so, for civil and widows' and orphans' funds, to support my possible widow and orphans.

We young bachelor civilians used to grumble at this; but I am free to confess now that I am very glad that this provision for such contingencies was made compulsory. It is this that makes us all worth £300 a year, dead or alive, and prevents the probability of starvation of invalid sons or unmarried daughters.

I retired to the drawing-room to read till bedtime, and began to wonder whether Darville felt lonely also, and thought he must, for he was a married man and temporarily separated from his wife and two children, whom he had left at the station of his last appointment, having been sent up to Tirhoot to learn Hindustani, in which he had not yet passed his final examination. I also began to think it would be less lonely if he would come and help me to occupy this big house for a time; but my meditations were interrupted by a sound like that of a muffled gong, caused by the rising of such a swarm of mosquitoes as I had not before experienced.

I tied a handkerchief over my head, lighted my biggest cigar, and put my hands in my pockets; but it was all useless, and I was obliged to take refuge in bed under the mosquito curtains. This was a great drawback to this house, which, as I have said above, was situated on the bank of the old channel of the Gunduk, and rendered it almost intolerable to be alone in it after sunset in the cold weather. Mosquitoes, I have observed, are much less troublesome in a room where there is plenty of light and conversation. It may be that one's attention is diverted from their noise, but at any rate they don't bite so much.

The next morning I had a canter on Bertram's horse, and reconnoitred more of the town, which seemed very small for so large a district, Tirhoot comprising an area of 6,343 square miles, and containing a population of 4,389,250, according to the last census. About a quarter of a mile from me was the residence of Blake, who governed all this, and I looked at it with a certain amount of awe. He was away in camp with his wife and family, and not expected to return for a day or two. Opposite his house was the church, of the dimensions of a good-sized room, and next to it the parsonage, very small indeed.

My official labours were to commence to-day, so I returned early to bath and breakfast, and made my way about eleven to the Foujdari Cutcherry. Darville I found had not arrived, though there was already a busy crowd around the building. Nothing could be done by me till he came, as he was to administer to me the customary oath, and make over to me such cases as I might be empowered to try.

I went over to his house, which was just opposite, and found him looking rather worried, with three native clerks seated on the ground, and a mass of papers in the vernacular round them. He was reading, and two were writing. "I'm awfully late," he said, on seeing me; "but Monday is always a bad day, as there are a double lot of reports. Sit down, and it may help you to learn something of what you will have to do some day."

I listened,; but, by a not very sensible arrangement, I had taken up Hindustani first in Calcutta, devoting the last five months of my stay there to Bengali, and consequently I now knew very little Hindustani beyond the amount necessary for giving orders to servants, and I understood very little. I gathered, however, that they were police reports.

The district was divided into so many police jurisdictions, called "thannahs," each of which was presided over by an officer called a "darogah," who had under him "naib," or deputy, "darogahs," and "burkundazes," or constables. From each of these thannahs came in daily reports of everything that had happened, or so much of it as the daroghah chose to tell; and if any serious crime occurred, special reports of such, and of the progress and results of the investigation, were submitted. All these the Joint Magistrate had to listen to,—for the new police, to be treated of hereafter, had not been introduced,—and this threw a very heavy amount of work on his shoulders.

One report might be to the effect that a part of the thatch of the thannah building was out of repair, or that the ferry-boat on the neighbouring river was leaky; while the next might report a serious gang robbery with violence, or even a raid of Nepaulese bad characters from the other side of the frontier.

On all of these, orders had to be passed at once. They

were given verbally, and written down by the two clerks who were not employed in reading the reports; and when the whole were finished, the reports, with the orders written on them, were placed before Darville for signature, and formed a heap about two feet high. The clerks were dismissed, and Darville, after devoting ten minutes to a hasty breakfast, was ready for Cutcherry.

The crowd had increased by the time of our arrival, and the noise also, the whole interesting enough to an initiated observer. There were various groups, of which the centre figure was a respectably-dressed man, with a white turban and tolerably white garments, surrounded by individuals with scanty clothing and of unkempt appearance, who listened intently to all that he said. These were the mookhtyars, or Criminal Court attorneys, teaching the witnesses what to say in their respective cases, and suggesting answers to all possible questions, the whole thing having been previously rehearsed at the mookhtyar's house. In other places were seated the sellers of stamps, by means of which the Government Court fees are collected; in another were some twenty prisoners waiting trial, all squatting on their hams, and kept together by a string passed round them, the whole under the charge of three burkundazes, armed only with swords, which subsequent experience taught me could not be drawn from their scabbards under a quarter of an hour at least. ··

Darville looked at these with a weary eye. "I shall be in till dark to-day," he said; "this New Criminal Procedure Code makes everything so long."

I scarcely understood the force of the remark at the

time; but I knew that the New Penal Code and the Criminal Procedure Code had come into force at the commencement of the current year.

Before this, the custom had been to tell off a clerk to record the evidence tendered in each case, and, when completed, to bring the parties before the presiding magistrate, to whom the depositions were read over, and who then could put questions to each witness by way of cross-examination. If there were more cases than usual, it was only necessary to turn on two or three extra clerks, for there were always plenty of "ummedwars," or "hopefuls," ready to work without pay for any length of time, in the hope of getting an appointment finally; and it might happen that the evidence of five or six cases would be recorded simultaneously in different corners of the Court Room. This, of course, tended to great economy of the time of the presiding magistrate; but the power it placed in the hands of corruptible clerks is obvious, and needs no comment.

The Indian Penal Code Act XLV. of 1860 consolidated the criminal law of India; and every conceivable offence is punishable under one of its 511 sections. The Criminal Procedure Code Act XXV. of 1861 was framed to suit this; and they came into force together. Under this Act, the magistrate has to take the evidence down in English in his own hand, and then read it over to the witness in his own vernacular, and ask him if it is correct. And when the witness has admitted it to be so, the magistrate has to add a memorandum to the evidence, to the effect that this has been done, and to sign the whole. No wonder poor Darville, who had been accustomed to the old easy method, considered the new process a long one. In very petty cases, such as trifling assaults, it is only necessary for the magistrate to make a memorandum of the substance of what the witness says ; but this he must do with his own hand, and sign it.

The Court building struck me with astonishment and disgust. It resembled in construction the bungalow of my host at Bhaugulpore, described in Chapter III., though it was a little larger. It contained really only three rooms of moderate size. In one of these Darville sat ; in one, a deputy native magistrate ; and another was reserved for Blake, who came here once a week to do magisterial business, the rest of his time being engaged in Collectorate (revenue) work, in another office, situated two miles off, at the other end of the town. The rest of the building was broken up by mats and an occasional masonry wall, into a record room, clerk's office, small retiring room for the magistrate, and a hole for unclaimed property. And this was the chief Criminal Court of a district of over 6,000 square miles, containing more than four millions of people. It is true that the plan of a new Cutcherry, which would contain accommodation for all the collectorate and magisterial officials, had been laid out, but, up to date, this was all that Government had considered necessary for this purpose.

Such economy, arising from a laudable desire to avoid increase of taxation, can scarcely be harshly criticized ; but I *was* "riled." when, a few years after, I read an account of the magnificent new India Office in London, and the ball given to the Sultan of Turkey at the opening thereof, at a cost to India of £10,000.

The interior of the Court-house more than equalled the exterior in squalor. In the centre of the room where Darville sat was a raised platform of masonry, some three feet high, on which was placed a long writing-desk, dented and inked all over, with a very old arm-chair for the presiding official. At right angles to this, on a platform about six inches lower, were placed seats for the clerks, and beyond this again a railing was erected on which the mookhtyars and pleaders could lean when addressing the Court, and which served as a barrier between them and the desks. At each end of this railing was a small space of two feet square, railed in on the platform, for the witnesses and defendants ; and in the space left outside these arrangements the crowd of those interested in the cases and other spectators jostled each other, and accommodated themselves as they best could. The room was perhaps twenty feet square. The walls *had* been white, but were now of various hues of black and dirty brown. Ink seemed to have reached everywhere, even to the punkah, which in this, the cold season, hung motionless and dirty over Darville's head. I shuddered to think of the consequence of its being pulled in its present state ; but I afterwards ascertained that a small sum for contingencies was allowed to be entered in the magisterial budget, and that a portion of this was applicable each year to the cleansing of punkahs. '

Darville now took his seat ; and I observed that notwithstanding the squalor of his surroundings, the deference with which he was treated was great. The whole assemblage salaamed in the most profound manner, and all the clerks present rose and remained standing until he had seated himself, and another chair, with a weak leg, had been brought for me.

I may state here, that these remarks about the office accommodation are applicable to at least two-thirds of the districts in Bengal, even to the gaols, which in many cases were not intended in the first instance for the purpose to which they are now applied.

Darville's first proceeding was to distribute the new cases which were ready for trial that day. There were some three or four trivial cases of assault and cattle trespass, two of housebreaking and theft, and one of dacoity, in which most of the prisoners I had seen outside in the string were implicated. The petty cases were made over to the native magistrate sitting in the same building, and the theft cases to another Deputy Magistrate, who was obliged to sit in the Collectorate Court, situated at some two miles distance, as mentioned above, and whither the mookhtyars, witnesses, and others concerned, had to make their way. The dacoity (gang robbery) case Darville kept for himself, as most important.

He then ordered petitions to be collected. This was a process generally gone through at the end of office hours; but he had it done at once on this occasion in order that some fresh case on which I might try my virgin hand might be forthcoming. The petitioners were a little taken by surprise, and there was a rush out to get complaints written out, though many were ready; and in about ten minutes some twenty flimsy bits of paper of various sizes and colours were in the hands of the Sherishtadar, or head ministerial clerk, who proceeded to read their con‐ tents.

Darville selected two, which he told me were complaints of assault ; and one of the clerks, who was said to have a slight knowledge of English, was ordered to accompany me to the Court-room I was to sit in and help me through the case. I was then sworn in as a magistrate, and at length found myself sitting on my own bench, with power to inflict a fine of 50 rs., or a sentence of one month's im- prisonment, with or without hard labour, in all cases which were triable in accordance with the Criminal Procedure Code by a magistrate of my calibre.

It was rather an undignified proceeding. First, the complainant in each case was put on oath ; and though the form is simple enough, it is a matter requiring consider- able patience to make a novice who has not been in court before repeat the words properly. It is necessary to be careful about this ; for though I do not think the oath has any effect on ninety-nine witnesses out of a hundred, the possibility of a prosecution for perjury is always in the mind of the presiding officer, and somebody must be in a position to swear that the oath was properly administered.

In the old days Hindoos used to be sworn over some Ganges water, or holding a cow's tail, or with the hand on the head of their eldest son ; but all these forms have been abolished, and the form of oath is now,—" According to my religion, in the presence of the Almighty, whatever I shall say in this case shall be the truth, and nothing but the truth." For Mohammedans the form is similar, only the word "Imam" is used for religion instead of "dharm," and "Khuda" for the Almighty instead of "Permeshur." A late Lieutenant-Governor of Bengal introduced a bill into the Governor-General's Council for the resuscitation of these old forms ; but it was not successful.

On the present occasion one of the complainants was a woman rejoicing in the name of Lakshmee Telinee. She was a small shopkeeper in a neighbouring village, who sold oil and other things. It is not an unusual idea with complainants in petty cases, that they can take the "Hakim" by storm. Now, I had seen this old lady sitting quietly outside with her mookhtyar ; but when her name was called out by my chuprassie (of whom, by the way, *four* had been allotted to me), she rushed in and threw herself on the ground, exclaiming with great volubility,—"Justice, O lord of generosity ! Justice, O nourisher of the poor ! I am very poor. I am dead altogether. I am a widow. Ram Singh came to my house——"

Clerk (quite unmoved). "Stand up, take the oath."

Complainant (standing up). "What ? "

Clerk. " Say, ' According to my religion.' "

Complainant. "Justice, O lord."

Clerk. " Listen. Say what I say."

Complainant. " Well ? "

Clerk. " According to my religion."

Complainant. " According to my religion."

Clerk. " In the presence of the Almighty."

Complainant. "In the presence of the Almighty" (breaking away again). " Justice, O lord. Ram Singh came to my shop——"

Clerk. "Will you take the oath ? "

Complainant. "Justice, O lord. I don't understand. I am a widow. Ram Singh came to my shop——"

Clerk (getting angry). "Go to, baseborn; will you take the oath?"

Complainant. "Justice, O lord" (rather subdued).

Clerk. "According to my religion, in the presence of the Almighty, whatever I shall say in this case shall be the truth——"

Complainant. "In accordance with," etc., "shall be the truth," etc. (Breaks away again.) "Of course I shall tell the truth. Have I come here to tell lies? It's all true. Justice, O my father and mother (*mabap*)! Ram Singh came to my shop——"

Clerk (utters some abuse, *sotto voce*, against the complainant's female relatives. Addresses the mookhtyar). "Make her understand she must take the oath."

Mookhtyar (wishing to enlist sympathy of young and inexperienced Hakim). "She is a poor woman."

Clerk. "Listen, you Lakshmee; if you won't take the oath, the Hakim cannot listen to you."

At length, after two or three more attempts, the woman was made to repeat the words of the oath properly; and with considerable delay and difficulty I elicited the gist of her story, that Ram Singh, the accused, had come to her shop and purchased some oil, and had not only refused payment for the same when demanded, but had cuffed and kicked her, taking away her "chaddar" (a garment) and leaving her senseless. There were five witnesses of the occurrence. It further appeared that all this had taken place some ten days previously, which made me think the violent emotion of the woman all the more surprising. I issued a summons on the defendant and the complainant's witnesses for that day week, and having gone through the other complaint, closed my Court for the day.

It was capital practice for learning the language; but I was much shocked at my own deficiency. It occurred to me to imagine what would be the feelings of the English public, should a magistrate with a knowledge of the language equal to mine proceed to try a case.

My four chuprassies contended for the honour of carrying my empty Cutcherry box, and so escorted I walked across to the Racket Court.

These chuprassies are attached to each official as personal servants; and though paid by Government the magnificent salary of 4 rs. monthly, can be dismissed at the option of the officer to whom they are attached. Their first duty is, of course, to carry official letters and messages; but they also perform all sorts of domestic work, and are particularly fond, in a married household, of looking after children. Their pay is small; but the post is eagerly sought after, as I am afraid they get a good many small pickings, at any rate in a district so remote from head-quarters as Tirhoot, and they are most anxious to please their masters. The moment a man becomes a court official in India, in however subordinate a position, his status is raised, and he himself proceeds to take advantage of it.

What profit a native may expect to make by bribing a chuprassie I do not know; but it is his nature to do so, and he has the idea, I suppose, that by being generally pleasant to the great man's servants, he is more likely to be agreeable to the great man. It seems impossible for us to make them understand how abhorrent to us is this system of currying favour. Their minds are differently constituted, and they like it, and would rather gain their point in this way than by straightforward conduct.

Government, however, does exercise a sort of moral supervision over the treatment of these men, and this may be shown by the following instance. Years later I was Magistrate of Dacca, and had just returned from office to complete some official correspondence in my private "dufter khana." It was intensely hot, and I called out to the chuprassie in waiting to find the punkah wallah. He said there was none present, so I ordered him to pull the punkah himself, if he could not find one. He came into the room and said respectfully, but very positively, that he had never pulled a punkah and never would, for if he did his "izzat" (social status) would be lowered. I replied that he must either obey my orders or leave the service. To which he answered that he would leave the service; so I told him to go.

The natives of Dacca, I should add, were far more independent in their manner to officials than those of Tirhoot; and I believe the native subordinate officials got far fewer illegitimate gratifications. There was steamer and rail communication with Calcutta, and this brought the district into sufficiently close contact with the metropolis to allow apparently the diffusion of the knowledge that the local official was, in fact, not all-powerful, but subject to the real and substantial control of the Supreme Government.

For some four or five days the chuprassie did not appear to perform his duties, and I appointed another man in his place, a little surprised at his quiet acquiescence ; but at the expiration of this time, on my going to Cutcherry one morning, he came to my buggy, salaamed, and wished to take out my official box. I ordered him off, and thought no more of the matter.

About a fortnight afterwards I received a demi-official note from the Commissioner, inclosing an autograph letter from the senior member of the Board of Revenue in Calcutta, to the effect that this chuprassie had appeared before him and stated that he had been dismissed for refusing to pull my punkah. That he had censured the man for his disobedience, as it was part of his duty, and told him he could do nothing for him. However, he thought that the Commissioner should intimate to me that I should reinstate him after six months' suspension. The Commissioner requested me to act on this suggestion, and said he should personally inquire, after the expiration of six months, whether I had done so.

It seemed that this man, knowing me to be on friendly terms with the Commissioner, had thought it advisable to go all the way to Calcutta to the senior member of the Board of Revenue to make his appeal, spending at least four months' salary in the journey. What he actually said I do not know ; but he was a venerable-looking fellow with a long white beard, and probably made out my conduct to have been much more arbitrary than it had been. I waited till the end of the period, having in the meantime taken the precaution to make all my chuprassies pull the

punkah occasionally, which they did submissively enough
I then asked for news of this man, and of course received
a heartrending account of his wretched state ; so, pretend-
ing to have compassion on him, I had him reinstated, and
thus obtained, though perhaps undeservedly, a reputation
for kindliness of heart while preserving my own " izzat."

This anecdote seems to me worthy of record, as showing
the care that the highest Government officials would take
to prevent even seeming harshness or injustice to the
meanest of their subordinates.

The spirit of economy has been abroad ever since I
entered the service, and the number of these retainers has
been very much reduced, an Assistant Magistrate having
now only one instead of four, and a Magistrate Collector
only four instead of sixteen.

At the Racket Court I found two indigo-planters, who
turned out to be the sons of the Deputy Collector,
Arkwright,—and the Civil Surgeon, Macpherson. They
were in want of a fourth, and so my advent was welcome.
I found they were all beginners, and I had had a good
deal of practice, so I could do what I liked with them ; and
this was some satisfaction to me, as it tended to dispel the
preconceived idea that, as a Wallah, I must be a muff all
round.

Darville came over just in time for one game before dark ;
but his work followed him, for there was a regular stream
of clerks with bundles of papers, warrants, and summonses,
etc., for signature, while two or three batches of newly-ap-
prehended prisoners were brought up, for orders whether
they should be admitted to bail or detained in custody.

Darville stood in flannel shirt and trousers with his arms bare, panting from his recent exertions, and gave his orders verbally, which were reduced to writing in the vernacular and then signed by him. The scene was new to me ; but I very soon got accustomed to this way of doing things. I also observed with curiosity that a native writer does not require a table for his purpose, indeed he rather prefers its absence, and holding his paper upright in his left hand writes sitting or standing with the most wonderful celerity.

At length they were all disposed of, and the conversation turned on the forthcoming races, which were to take place in about ten days' time. The merits of various horses were equally discussed, and all my companions had animals entered for the occasion. Darville was going to ride his own, and the two Arkwrights, whom I found to have considerable notoriety as race-riders, seemed to be engaged in every event. I was a little out of all this, as my racing knowledge was very limited, my personal experience being confined to Bullingdon. The Arkwrights gave me a lift home to the door of my house, and there left me to my loneliness and mosquitoes.

The next morning, very early, I was considering what on earth I should do with myself till Cutcherry time, when in came Macpherson. "I say, Gordon, will you ride my horse Lunatic in the hack race."

"I am quite inexperienced in race-riding," I said ; "but if you care to entrust such important interests to me, I will do the best I can."

"All right, you're a light weight. It is a catch weight

race for gentlemen riders; and if you can manage to keep his head straight I think he must win."

"I am much obliged," I began. .

"I am the obliged party," he said. "I'll send the horse down for you to ride this evening. He is rather troublesome at times; but the syce will tell you all about him. Good morning."

In the afternoon I told Darville of what I had undertaken. "The horse is a brute," he said; "but he has a turn of speed."

On reaching home after office I found the "brute," being led about my compound by two syces; both of whom kept as near as they could to the end of the rope attached to his bridle.

On preparing to mount him, the syce begged me to be careful, as he said "Age piche se bahut lat marta" (He kicks out very much, both before and behind).

And in truth, the moment I approached his head he struck out at me with his fore feet in the most violent way.

"He bites too," said the syce. "Then how on earth am I to mount him?" I asked.

"He must be blinded," he said. And untwisting his puggeree, or turban, he managed to throw it over the animal's head, and so blindfold him.

"Be pleased to be quick," he said—a piece of advice which I scarcely needed. However, he let me mount quietly enough, and once on his back, I proceeded to try a little patting and coaxing, what the natives call "phusalana."

"That is no use," said the syce. "If your highness can

frighten him a little he will go better." And as I went
out of the gate he added, " He shies occasionally."

The fact was, he was a type of animal by no means
uncommon in India, which may be described as actually
ferocious, but generally endowed with courage and endurance in proportion to their ferocity.

Turning out of my gate I met one of the Arkwrights
on his way to the Racket Court. " Mind you don't
tumble off," he said, " or you will be eaten up."

" A great incentive to stick on," I replied ; but I did
not feel comfortable.

A little way from the gate the bazaar road narrowed
somewhat ; and the shopkeepers, with that utter disregard
of public convenience which characterizes all natives, had
appropriated a considerable portion of the thoroughfare
for the display of their wares. The European officials
have to wage constant war against this habit ; for native
magistrates are, of course, of the same way of thinking as
their fellow-countrymen, and the police would never dream
of interfering unless they wished to spite some individual.

I had just piloted Lunatic, who was showing signs of a
desire to indulge in one of his occasional shies, as far as
the shop of a potter, or rather potteress, who had arranged
nearly the whole of her fragile stock-in-trade on the road ;
water-pots, cooking vessels, of all shapes and sizes, were
there. Just then there was a sound of wheels behind, and a
dog-cart with a lady and gentleman and two children in it
passed me at a rapid rate. Lunatic gave a tremendous
bound to the left ; there was an awful crash and clatter
and a good deal of screaming. On collecting my scared

senses, I found that Lunatic had fallen right among the pots and pans; but had recovered himself, and now was standing, still fortunately, but quivering with fright. I had been shot into the shop. The syces, who were following, promptly got hold of the horse. The dog-cart had pulled up, and the gentleman, coming towards me, trusted I was not hurt. Strange to say, with the exception of some cuts in one of my boots and two scratches on Lunatic's quarter, we had suffered no injury at all.

"You are Mr. Gordon, I presume?" said my interlocutor. "My name is Blake; I have just returned from camp."

"I am sorry to make your acquaintance in such an unceremonious fashion," I said; "but these people ought not to block up the road in this way."

"No," said Blake; "and I am going to pitch into the old woman at once." Whereupon he threatened her with the direst penalties of the law; and she protested, as natives always do in these cases, that she was not only ruined but dead.

Having scolded her well, Blake told her that out of compassion I would give her 1r. (2 shillings); explaining to me that her whole stock was probably worth 5rs., and if I paid her on the calculation that I had destroyed a fifth part, I should be treating her very liberally. Apparently she thought so too; for on receipt of the coin her face assumed quite a radiant expression; and I believe she would have been glad of a recurrence of the accident daily.

Here the syce interposed, and suggested I should mount at once, before Lunatic had got over his present submis-

sive state, or otherwise I might find it difficult. " Good
evening," said Blake. " Come to my house to-morrow about
eleven, and I will drive you down to the Collectorate and
swear you in as an Assistant Collector; besides, I have a
little work for you."

On getting out of the bazaar on to the sandy road by
the river, I let Lunatic out a bit, and he went freely, and his
paces were perfect. On the old course he showed me that
he could gallop in very fair form; and we got home finally
better friends than I expected.

On my return I found that my bearer with my baggage
and my own two horses also had arrived. He was
terribly dirty and travel-stained, and one horse had a bad
cut from a heel rope, and the other had a swelling as large
as a small turnip on his off knee. They would be no use
to me during the race week, that was certain. I am bound
to admit, however, that of my goods and chattels nothing
was lost and nothing was broken ; though dust seemed to
have penetrated into everything in an incredible and indescribable manner. I was very glad to see them ; and even
pretended to believe my bearer's account of the unparal-
leled efforts he had made to avoid delays on the road.
It was vexing about the horses ; but it could not be helped.
Besides, I had Lunatic to occupy me for a time at any rate.

The next morning I found my way to Blake's as directed,
and so commenced one of those Indian friendships which in
out-of-the-way places ripen so rapidly into the most mature
intimacy. We drove down to the Collectorate Cutcherry
together, which I found as dilapidated and disreputable-
looking as the Criminal Court. Here I took a second oath

to collect the revenue justly, etc., and not to accept any gratification other than my lawful salary.

"The first thing you have to do," said Blake, "is to draw. up some rules for the cultivation of cotton." "Don't look surprised," he added, seeing probably by my countenance that I felt so. "A civilian must know, or pretend to know, everything; and it is as well that you should understand this at once. Government thinks it right to introduce cotton-planting here if it can. Here are two little pamphlets; you must read these, and draw up some fifteen or twenty rules in the simplest language possible, which will be translated into the vernacular and distributed to the more enlightened 'zemindars,' with little packets of cotton seed. I shall have to use what is called my 'moral influence' to induce them to plant it and look after it, and then I shall have to send a report on the result to Government at the end of the season. Those zemindars who have succeeded in rearing any plants will be mentioned in the report, and metaphorically patted on the head like good schoolboys; and those who have not will probably be accused of 'apathy.'"

"Is the soil of Tirhoot supposed to be specially suited for the growth of cotton?" I asked.

"No," he replied; "but Government has thought fit that it should be introduced into India, and so a circular order has been drawn up in the Secretariat and a sufficient number printed to allow copies for every district, and I have got one like every other district executive. When you become a Collector yourself you will find this system a little troublesome. If an idea strikes any clever Secretary attached to the Government of India, the circular orders for report go to the whole of India; but if it occurs to a member of any of the Local Governments, as a rule, only the officials within the local jurisdiction are worried. A short time ago a clever Secretary in the Home Department of the Government of India evolved the idea that something might be done with the porpoises that roll about in the Ganges. You have probably seen some. Consequently every district executive officer in India was called upon to send up a treatise on the 'Gangetic porpoise' within one month. As you may imagine, a good many of these treatises were similar to that on 'Snakes in Ireland.'"

Here the Sherishtadar appeared with a mass of papers, and informed Blake very deferentially that some urgent work was waiting. Blake asked if there was any room where I could sit and do any work. The Sherishtadar replied in the negative, so it was arranged that I should come to the Collectorate only on the days that Blake went to the Criminal Court, that is, twice a week, and make use of his Court room. "Government," he said, "ought to have sufficient accommodation for its officers ; though I am not prepared to assert that it loses much at present by not having a room in which you can exercise your talents to-day. You have seen that new Courts are in progress, and I hope that in the course of a year or so this rather disreputable state of things will be obviated. In the mean time you can go to the Criminal Court and see if there is any work, and, if not, you can draw up your cotton rules. And here are some examination papers on revenue matters, which you had better look through and see if you can answer. You can take my dog-cart and send it back here when you have done with it."

I went away much chagrined at my utter want of importance, and thought how very unnecessary my eager hurry to get to my station had been. It was a consolation, however, to observe the deference with which all the clerks, mookhtyars, and hangers-on about the Court treated me, and led me to understand that my possible future importance was fully acknowledged.

CHAPTER V.

AT MOZUFFERPORE.

FORMAL CALLS. —FURNITURE.—A CURIOUS OPERATION.— AN AFTER-
NOON'S SPORT.—A REVENUE CASE.—A SUNDAY'S WOLF-HUNT.—
END OF CASE OF LAKSHMEE TELINEE.—MOOKHTYARS AND WIT-
NESSES.—THE RACE-MEETING.—HOT WEATHER.—NATIVE CHRIS-
TIANS.—NATIVE VISITORS.—A SOCIAL CONTRETEMPS.

AT the Criminal Court there happened to be no case
suited to my limited powers, and so I went my way home,
and set myself to draw up my rules for the cultivation
of cotton. The task was much easier than I anticipated,
and I was able to complete and send them over to Blake
by the evening, who complimented me on my expedition when I met him on the Old Course, taking the usual
evening drive, while I was exercising Lunatic. That Old
Course was rather dreary after the Mall of Calcutta, with
at the most four equipages of different kinds, and perhaps three equestrians.

However I met Darville, who informed me that he had
received permission to rejoin his old appointment and his
wife ; but that though he intended to stay in Tirhoot until
after the race meeting, he must send his traps off at once.
Would I put him up until his departure ?

Of course I was only too delighted to have a companion
in my loneliness, and he agreed to come into residence
that very evening at dinner-time.

The next morning Darville suggested, as we were driving
to Cutcherry, that I should take his dog-cart and make
a round of formal calls; for he said, "You've been here
nearly a week now, and it should be done." Accordingly
I went round, and called on the Doctor, Colville the
planter, and two Deputy Collectors. The Judge had left,
and his successor had not arrived. Blake did not require
any further formal call, and Darville was living with me, so
that this social duty was easily performed. The forthcoming races formed an excellent topic of conversation ;
and as every lady seemed to know Lunatic's character,
and a certain· amount of interest was evinced with reference
to my proceedings in connection with him, I returned
home somewhat elated, bringing also an invitation for
Darville to accompany me to dine at the Doctor's that
evening.

One feature that particularly struck me in my visit, was
the incongruous nature of the furniture. Bertram had
brought his from Calcutta, and devoted some little attention to its selection ; but he was quite the exception. In
all the other houses, the articles had been got together
as they could be purchased from persons leaving the station from time to time ; and as these had previously
been obtained in a similar fashion, the general result
can be imagined. The only new pieces of furniture that
ever appeared to make their way to the station, were
the cane chairs used on board ship on the way out
from England, which, with the aid occasionally of a
cushion or an anti-macassar, formed no unimportant
addition to the drawing-room suite. The mahogany,

where existent, was the blackest of the black, from age I suppose, and gave some of the dining-rooms rather a funereal appearance. It had been brought into the district, I imagine, about the time of the Permanent Settlement; but whence, it would be difficult to say. None of the houses, however, could be said to be over-furnished, and there was space enough to move about without knocking things down.

The dinner at the Doctor's was pleasant enough, the hostess pretty, graceful, and clever, and also musical. The Colvilles and Blakes, with one or two others, were there. There had come too, as a guest, an irregular cavalry officer, a cousin of Bertram's, who had intended to spend a portion of his leave with him, not knowing of his transfer elsewhere. With the usual Indian hospitality, he had been asked to stay at the Doctor's as long as he liked. He seemed likely to prove a useful acquisition during the race week, for he was not only great at riding, but good at theatricals, and moreover fond of getting them up. It was settled before the ladies left the room, that we should have some "tableaux vivants," and that he should draw up a programme in the next two days.

Over our wine, the Doctor told us of a curious operation he had performed that day, viz., the amputation of the leg of a Hindu lady of rank, without seeing any portion of her person except that operated upon. The limb had been pushed through a hole in a curtain, and a high-caste Brahmin who knew something of medicine had assisted in the administration of chloroform, etc.

I learned from the conversation that ensued, that native

ladies look upon their confinement behind the purdah as a badge of rank, and also as a sign of chastity, and are exceedingly proud of it. In fact, they consider that being seen by any man outside the prescribed number of relatives is equivalent to the very extreme of dishonour, and would prefer death as an alternative. The husbands, too, are of the same way of thinking, which is perhaps more easily to be understood.

" After dinner, we had some good music. Bertram sang well; Mrs. Macpherson was an accomplished musician; and, as it was the cold season, the piano was in tune. While listening and enjoying myself, I wondered why it was that so many writers about Indian society should think it necessary to describe it only in caricature. Here was a party of people of cultivated tastes, and quite as free from eccentricities as any other similar number one might find in a drawing-room at home; and this I found to be the case oftener than not. The conversation, possibly, might not be on exactly the same topics; but I could venture to state that it would not be more frivolous than that of an English drawing-room. Our relatives in England have, at best, a very incorrect idea of our mode of living in India. It need not be rendered still more so by portraying every individual as foolish or vulgar.

Just as we were saying Good-night, Colville said, "I have got excellent 'khabar' (news) of quail about five miles out; will you come and shoot some to-morrow?"

I began to demur, like all young civilians, on the score of pressure of work, and finally said, I must see if Darville could spare me. I saw an almost imperceptible smile curl his lip, for he had seen a good many young civilians, as he replied, "Darville is coming too; he can get away early to-morrow, and if you will send your clothes up to the factory, and give us the pleasure of your company at dinner, we shall be very glad."

Of course I was very glad; and the next afternoon, at three, we found ourselves in Darville's dog-cart, having picked up Colville on the way to the scene of action. After driving some six miles, we came upon about a hundred men, seated in two rows on the roadside, all with latties (long sticks of bamboo) in their hands. They were presided over by two men with red turbans, and proved to be a lot of Colville's coolies—men who worked in the indigo vats during the manufacturing season, and who were always at hand when required to make themselves useful. They lived in the neighbouring villages, and on this occasion had been summoned to "sweep the jungle," as the native expression is, for the purposes of our sport. As we dismounted from the vehicle, they all stood up and salaamed; and at an order from Colville moved off in the direction of a piece of grass of some two or three acres in extent. This was bordered by crops of oats, and "urhur," a species of pea (*Revalenta Arabica*), which afforded good feeding-ground for the game in the mornings and evenings, while in the middle of the day they took shelter in the friendly grass. The country is covered in this way with grasses and cold-weather crops, with occasional patches of fallow land, and we only had to walk from one grass patch to another.

The beaters formed in lines, and commenced making a

noise that to me was at first quite bewildering, as we moved through the grass. They seemed to understand that it was necessary to keep line ; and every individual seemed to think it proper to admonish the rest on this point, by shouting "nine karo," "nine rakho," "barabar," "make line, 'keep· line,"—"evenly." The natives always putting n for l, and l for n, in pronouncing English words commencing with these letters. If a bird was flushed, they all said, "urgaya,"—"it has flown," which certainly did seem unnecessary. And yet all this noise was really requisite, for the quail lay like stones, and continually got up behind us, after we must all but have trodden upon them.

However, out of the first piece of grass we bagged three-and-a-half brace, and ought to have got more ; but I missed four out of five shots, bewildered with the noise, and puzzled with the flight of the bird, which I had never shot at before. It goes as if hurled from a catapult for the first twenty yards, and then flies slowly, and is easy to hit, though small. In the next piece of grass a hare got up, and then the self-restraint of the beaters gave way ; every man started in pursuit, notwithstanding the objurgations of their red-turbaned "mates," or overseers ; and the latties were used with considerable skill, with skill indeed very humiliating to me, for the animal passing near me, I managed to miss it, when a beater near me flung his latti at it, and killed it. It was a relief to me to hear Colville's voice rising loud in abuse of this man, and of all his female relatives, for daring to wipe my eye, so to speak ; and all the beaters were admonished that there would be no hope of any "baksheesh" at the end of the day, should such conduct recur. However it did recur the very next time, and every time that a hare was started; and I always found that nothing could keep these beaters in order on such occasions.

In about two hours, or a little more, we had bagged twenty-seven brace of quail and hares, a leash of black partridges, three plover and five snipe, a very satisfactory bag, in my opinion; though Colville seemed to think we ought to have got more quail, as it was such a good season; and he told us of four guns in another part of the district, some day or two previously, having bagged 110 brace in the same time.

In the course of our shooting I observed that some fifteen or twenty men with blue puggrees had joined the beaters, and worked very zealously for us. These proved to be the chowkeydars, or village policemen, who had come to give their assistance on hearing that the "Hakims" were of the shooting party. The village chowkeydar is a somewhat curious functionary; but more will be said about him hereafter. It was a matter of some surprise to me, however, that this should be looked upon as part of their duty.

Notwithstanding all his threats, Colville gave orders that a few pice should be distributed to the beaters, and we left them all jabbering in an excited way round the red-turbaned mates, as we mounted three of Colville's horses that had been sent out for us and started for a delightful canter home, across country. The large area of good riding ground in Tirhoot makes it one of the pleasantest districts under the administration of the Lieut.-Governor of Bengal ; and as I drove home in the moonlight with Darville after dinner, I thought that frequent afternoons of such perfectly free sport, with no keepers and no game laws, and such pleasant rides back in the cool of the evening, would make life anything but disagreeable.

The next day, as Blake had to go to the Foujdarree Cutcherry, I took my seat in his room at the Collectorate, and a perfectly new vista of work opened before me. In the first place I signed a prodigious quantity of papers, most of them being copies of orders given by Blake or of original documents. I must have been at least an hour thus engaged, signing as quickly as ever I could. The ministerial officers generally bring all such papers to the Assistant Sahib (officers in my position), as it is one of the few ways in which they can be useful. Nowadays, however, the Sherishtadar's signature is allowed to authenticate copies of documents, and the Assistant is thus spared so much drudgery.

This over, the Sherishtadar informed me that some 100 Dakhil Kharij cases had been placed on my file. This sounded somewhat important, and it is necessary to explain the nature of these cases. In 1793, Lord Cornwallis enacted the Regulation I. of 1793, which declared the Government revenue assessed on all estates included in the decennial settlement just expired to be unalterable and fixed for ever. But as these estates might be sold or divided, it was considered necessary that the Government should be furnished with information on such points, in order to enable its officers to assess the revenue in accordance with the rules laid down in the above-mentioned Regulation ; and it was accordingly enacted in Regulation XLVIII. of the same year, that all changes in the ownership, either in part or whole, should be, under pain of fine, notified to the Collector and entered in a Register prepared for the purpose.

Dakhil Kharij merely means entry and erasure, *i.e.*, the entry of the new proprietor's name and erasure of the old. This was useful to enable district officers to know who were the actual owners of property in their districts ; but for the purposes of the collection of the revenue it did not much matter, as by the present laws the owners are compelled to pay into the treasury the revenue assesssed on their estates, before sunset on the days fixed in each year by the Board of Revenue. If the amount due is not paid, the estate in default is put up to auction and sold to the highest bidder. The amount due, with costs, is deducted from the sum realized, and the remainder handed over to the owner on his application. This being the case, this useful Regulation had been allowed to fall into abeyance, and was used chiefly by owners or would-be owners, in order that the entries in the Government Register might be cited as proof of possession in the civil courts in cases of disputed succession or purchase.

The procedure is, that on an application for registration and mutation of names, a copy of the same is posted at the Government Courts in the district in which the estate is situated, and also at some conspicuous place on the estate itself ; and any person objecting to the same is warned to come forward and state such objection in the Collector's

Court before the expiration of one month from the date of publication of the notice. In cases where no such objection is filed, mere formal orders for registration of the new and erasure of the old owner's name are passed. Many of these cases now on my file were without objection so that it was possible to dispose of twenty or thirty in an hour.

In cases where objections were filed, the only point I had to look to was that of "possession." It might be thought that this was not such a very difficult thing to decide ; but in fact it proved to be much more difficult to arrive at than the question of real title, into which I was not allowed to go. Occasionally it was impossible to come to a conclusion either way ; and this was not altogether unnatural, as it sometimes turned out that neither of the applicants was in possession, both of them being merely "pretendants." Government suffered nothing by the absence of a decision, for no mutation of names then took place ; and if the Government revenue was not paid by somebody, it did not matter by whom, the estate was put up to auction, as mentioned above.

The question then suggests itself, Why take any trouble at all in disputed cases ? Why not refer the disputants at once to the Civil Courts which had power to dispose of the whole matter ? The answer always given is, that being a paternal Government, we wish to check improper litigation and assist the parties in the right as much as possible. The chances were, that if we could come to a correct decision as to the party in possession, we caused the *onus probandi*, in the Civil Court, supposing litigation should be carried thither, to fall on the wrongful claimant. But until I had

gained some experience, these cases used to bother me
horribly, and I did not at first understand that the coming
to a decision was not a matter of vital importance, or that
in fact my orders were not decisions, but merely recommen-
dations for the approval of the Collector, for that I had no
actual powers in the matter.

But though this was so, the litigants fought the matter
as obstinately before me as though I were the final tri-
bunal, and doubtless with reason; for as I gained experience my orders would have considerable weight. I
recollect that in the first disputed case brought before me
there were fifty-seven witnesses on one side, and forty-
three on the other: both parties had paid in the last in-
stalment of Government revenue, and both parties had
paid income tax, and receipts were filed by both in proof
of possession. All the witnesses on one side swore that
they paid rent to one party, and all on the other side swore
that they paid rent to the other party. Each party had
on more than one occasion prosecuted the other side for
criminal trespass on some of the lands comprised in the
estate; and each had been criminally convicted and fined,
the decisions in the cases being also filed. This was
enough to puzzle Solomon; for I don't think an offer to
divide the land would have settled the question, and it fairly
beat me.

I turned, in despair, to the head native clerk who was
sitting beside me, and who had been assisting to interpret
difficult terms, and otherwise helping me to wade through
the case, and said, " What can I do ? "

He, I feel sure, from the light of subsequent experience

must have taken a bribe from one of the parties (possibly
the right one), for he said : " The decision is in the hands
of your Highness; but something must be decided, or what
will become of the Government revenue ? " knowing full
well that the Government revenue was safe enough.

I finally decided that the party who had brought the
fifty-seven witnesses should be entered in the Register—
rather an unsafe point on which to found a decision ; but it
seemed to me the only salient-point of difference on which
I could seize to give any reason at all for my order. The
whole case was fought over again before the Collector, who
thought my order wrong ; it was then taken on appeal
before the Commissioner at Patna, who confirmed the Collector's decision, and read the other party a little paternal
lecture (I saw his decision) on attempting to use this regulation for wrong purposes ; but curiously enough, when the
thing was taken on appeal before the Board of Revenue in
Calcutta, they reversed the Commissioner's order, and confirmed that originally recommended by me. I am sure I
don't know who was right; but I am inclined to think that
the Collector probably knew more about the actual facts
than anybody else. But after all, this was only the commencement of real litigation, for no right or title was decided by all that had gone before.

My own impression is, that it is a mistake to encourage
the people to fight these matters in courts that have no
power to dispose of them finally, and that the only benefit
arising from the system is to give more work to Assistant
Collectors.

This was the first hard day's work I had had in office,

and I was positively tired out at the end of it; but a good gallop on Lunatic, who was really becoming very amenable, soon drove away the heaviness of " Cutcherry."

The next day being Sunday, I had the opportunity of seeing all our society assembled in our little church, about as large as a good-sized drawing-room. The congregation was swelled in numbers by some visitors who had already arrived for the approaching races, to commence on the Tuesday; most of them planters in the interior of the Tirhoot District, and some from the neighbouring Chupra and Chumparun. Altogether, I should think there were fifty Christians present, of whom over forty were white. With the exception of a very few, the native Christians in the town were either Catholics or attendants at the church of the Lutheran Mission established here. Blake presided at the harmonium, and Darville assisted the clergyman by reading the lessons.

The service over, a very curious assemblage of vehicles appeared to convey the members of the congregation to their respective homes, varying from the Doctor's neatly-appointed Calcutta-built barouche and pair (Blake's house was just across the road, and he and his family walked home) to the lop-sided, forward-tilted, creaking dog-cart built by the young assistant indigo-planter at his own out-factory, with his own materials, and after his own design. This conveyance was as a rule drawn by a ferocious-looking and screeching animal, which was usually intensely anxious to start until its owner had taken his seat, and would then obstinately refuse to move. I have known more than an hour passed in fruitless efforts to make such an animal go on; and finally the brute has jumped forward with such a bound as to break all the harness (probably not very new or strong) and gallop off perfectly free, leaving its disconsolate owner hanging over the splashboard with a couple of broken shafts for contemplation. However, on this occasion nothing extraordinary happened, and all got home safely, to wish, like myself, I suppose, that Sunday was over.

Wherever the Anglo-Saxon congregates, there is a terrible dulness about Sunday. As a Parisian lady once said to me, " You English on Sundays appear to be rather Pharisaical Jews than Protestants;" and this sort of behaviour we carry with us, for the most part, even to India. In Calcutta it is thought wicked, or at any rate it is not etiquette, to ride on Sundays, any more than it is in London, though it is quite the correct thing, morally and socially, to drive on the Mall. In the Mofussil we were not quite so strict; or at any rate the distinction between riding and driving was not so sharply drawn, and so the Old Course on this particular evening might almost be called lively. There were at least fifteen vehicles of all sorts, and about as many equestrians. One of my Arabs had so far got over the bad effects of his journey that I had ventured to take him out for a Sunday's ride. I was walking quietly along by the side of Colville's dog-cart in which he was driving his wife and little girl, when all of a sudden he started up with a loud "tally-ho," and as I looked in the direction in which he was pointing with his whip I saw an animal about the size of a mastiff going at a lumbering canter over the centre of the plain round which we were circling.

It at once occurred to me it was a wolf. These animals are a great scourge in Tirhoot in the cold season. Everybody else seemed to see it too, and simultaneously vehicles and equestrians started off in hot pursuit of the animal. This Old Course (as mentioned above) was bounded on one side by the lake, and another by the new stream of the river; and between the river and the lake was an embankment which formed a road to Colville's factory. On the lake side of this embankment, where the lake grew shallow, was a large patch of reed and grass jungle, and for this the wolf was making. Some of us tried to cut him off from this, and in fact we made a sort of effort to surround him. Sunday was forgotten, and Colville drove off at a gallop to get spear and rifle; and two deerhounds which happened to be following their master, another planter, in his evening ride, were also in full chase. The wolf, however, though he seemed to be going very slowly and without exertion, kept his distance from all of us, except the deerhounds; but though they came up with him, they were afraid to tackle him, and to our great regret we saw him finally gallop into the jungle and disappear. It was just dusk and the jungle was very thick and swampy, so that nothing more could be done, and we had to return baffled' to our homes. My Arab was dead lame again, as I had forgotten all caution, and he himself had been very excited in the chase.

Two planters came in to dinner with us; and the conversation naturally turned on wolves, and their speed and powers of endurance. One of these told us he had succeeded in riding down and spearing a wolf; but he said he had no European witnesses of the feat, and he found his story generally doubted. But he assured us it was true; that he had started the wolf one morning while riding over his indigo cultivation, and that it had taken the line for his factory, that his servants had seen it and seen him coming, and got a second horse ready saddled, and that by this means he had been enabled to overtake it. I myself had subsequently experience of the difficulty of such a feat, for I frequently had the chance of riding after wolves, but never came up with one. They keep up the same sort of lumbering canter; and if their pursuer by an effort increases his pace, they increase theirs too, but apparently without effort, and go on until the horse is absolutely tired out.

In the cold weather in Tirhoot they pack, and attack people at night, if alone, or in twos, or even threes. About eighteen months after this, when I had charge of the Durbhungah subdivision, it was stated in one of my police reports that a man and his wife and child had been attacked by seven wolves after dusk, within half a mile of their village, and the two latter carried off. I sent for the man to interrogate him personally, and he told me that he and his wife with their little child were returning from a neighbouring village to their homes, shortly after sunset. He was in front, and the wife carrying the child behind, when he suddenly heard a scream, and turning round saw two wolves had seized his wife and thrown her down. He had a " latti " (bamboo stick) in his hand, and ran to drive them off, when five others came up and he was afraid, and ran to a mango-tree close by and climbed up it. There he was forced to be a spectator of the horrible sight of his wife and child being torn to pieces. He described it as being very quickly over ; but it was a very long time before he could summon up courage to come down from his tree and make his way to his house.

It was a horrible story ; but I really believe that I felt the actual horror of it more keenly than the narrator did. It seemed to me that his conduct deserved to be censured as cowardly ; but from the countenances of those around me (the story was told in open Court), I don't think anybody else sympathized with me in this feeling. A woman's life was of very little consequence, the infant was a girl, and probably his fellow villagers thought he was quite right to act as he did. Tirhoot is a highly cultivated district, and is frequently called the " garden of India ;" but there are large patches of grass jungle used for thatching purposes, and these afford shelter to the wolves, which come down in the cold weather from the neighbouring kingdom of Nepaul.

The next morning I was in good time in office to take up the adjourned case of Lakshmee Telinee. The accused, a fine strapping-looking fellow, denied that he had been anywhere near the village on the day in question, and stated that he had witnesses to prove that he had been present at a marriage ceremony, that had been celebrated in a village some fifteen miles distant. On behalf of the plaintiff, Lakshmee Telinee, four witnesses were present, who all swore, in almost the same words, to the facts as stated by her. They were subjected to lengthy cross-examination by the mookhtyars for the accused, two being retained by him ; and they stood this test remarkably well, considering the curious nature of the questions put ; though my surprise at their readiness gave way when I found that almost the same questions were asked in all cases of this nature, and that the witnesses had all been prepared to expect them, and furnished with answers accordingly.

The first question was usually, "Are you any relation to the plaintiff?" Answered always in the negative, whatever the fact might be.

2nd. "Who came up first? — you or the other witnesses?"

The first witness had usually appeared on the scene first.

3rd Question. "When the assault took place, were you standing on the north, south, east, or west of the parties?"

There was always a prompt answer to this question, and to those that followed as to the relative geographical positions of the other witnesses. In this part of the country the natives always talked of east and west, and not of right or left. On one occasion, when out shooting, my chuprassie brought me a piece of lighted dried cow-dung (the ordinary fuel) to light my cigar. I had applied the end of my cigar to a corner not so well lighted as the other. So he said, "Will your Highness be pleased to put your cigar a little to the west?"

Of course, as I gained experience, I disallowed this class of question ; but at first I felt bound to go through it all, and spent a long time over each of these wretched petty cases.

Another set of stock questions was about the dates. The lower class of villagers know very little of dates; and though they could generally state glibly enough the date on which they witnessed the alleged occurrence, and the date on which they were giving evidence, they were easily puzzled by asking them the date next Thursday or last Saturday; this, of course, being a point on which it was not possible to furnish them with answers beforehand.

Another curious point on which questions were always framed was, the length of time during which the complainant remained senseless, "behosh," for the assault always rendered him senseless, and it was generally alleged that this state lasted an hour or two. In the present case, there were one or two slips: and the mookhtyars for the defence then addressed me, pointing out that one of the witnesses had said that he stood to the east of the parties, whereas the others had stated that he stood on the north; that another had averred the complainant had remained senseless for one hour, whereas she had declared she had been so for two.

I recollect, even as a novice, wanting to explain that these were not material points: but my Hindustani was not yet good enough, and I had to let them run on. However, it seemed that there was a *primâ facie* case made out, so I issued summonses for the witnesses for the accused. These were not returnable for a week; but I may as well state here, that they duly appeared, and all swore to the *alibi.* They said they had met the accused on the date of the alleged assault many miles from the scene of the occurrence, and asked him where he was going, and he had replied, to a marriage ceremony. There was a lengthy cross-examination of these also, and a final address on the part of the mookhtyars, who seemed as hot about the matter as their clients, and whom I had continually to call to order for interrupting each other.

Indeed, I fear, as a general rule, that the Court of a young Assistant Magistrate is seldom that scene of perfect decorum that it should be. In those days anybody might be a mookhtyar. There were no rules of admission, and any person passing by the Court might turn in and attempt to make an honest penny by pleading, if he could secure a client and present a power to appear written on a stamped paper of the value of one shilling.

However, shortly afterwards, an Act was passed which excluded from practice as pleaders and attorneys all persons who had not passed an examination and complied with certain rules. A tremendous outcry was raised against this; and the Government, with its usual leniency, gave orders that all those previously practising should be allowed to continue to do so, unless there was something special against them, and the Act should only apply to new comers. The result was, that for many years little real good was apparent, and the Criminal Courts swarmed with these uneducated pettifoggers, who eagerly competed for the custom of any one who had any sort of grudge against his neighbour, and used all efforts to foment quarrels on all possible grounds.

In this case I was preparing to write my judgment, for we were bound to record reasons for our decision when both parties, who had retired for a few minutes, burst into court again, saying· "Razeenama khudawind,"—" Compromise, my lord," and it appeared they· had settled the matter among themselves. It is legal in petty cases to allow a complaint to be withdrawn ; and I was delighted to allow it in this case, for I really did not know what was the truth, though my subsequent experience tells me that probably the whole affair was a verbal dispute about the rate at which the oil was sold, and that all the details of the assault and the defence about the marriage ceremony were false.

I believe that even in true cases of this sort the witnesses have very seldom seen the facts to which they depose. I do not think it occurs to 'a native complainant to select as his witnesses those who have actual knowledge of the occurrence ; but he seeks out those of his friends whom he can trust, and can induce for a very moderate consideration, to undergo the trouble of learning their story and appearing in Court. These men, again, seldom discriminate between what they have seen and what they have heard, so that they consider it no harm to state in Court that they have seen what their friend, the complainant, aided by his mookhtyar, had described to them.

. In fact, it is more difficult to arrive at the truth in these petty matters than in those of far greater importance, and yet these fall to the lot of the most inexperienced magistrates to try ; for, after all, wrong decisions are of less consequence here than elsewhere, and until they have passed their examinations there are· few cases of other descriptions with which they can be entrusted.

And yèt these are so numerous that their good or bad management exercises a serious, influence on the criminal "returns" of the district (to be spoken of hereafter), and on the happiness of a large number of the people.

On strolling over to the Racket Court in the afternoon, I found quite a crowd of people assembled, chiefly planters from the interior of the district; for the races were to commence on the following morning, and the first race ordinary was to be held at the Station Billiard Room that evening. There were to be five days' racing, on alternate days ; and it was also intended there should be five dances, dignified with the name of balls, on the evening of each race day.

Nearly all the betting in India is done by means of lotteries ; and I was initiated into the process that evening. There were separate lotteries for each race to be run on the following day. On this occasion these generally consisted of fifty tickets of 8 rs. (equal to 16 shillings) each. When filled, the names of the ticket-holders were drawn from one hat, and those of the horses starting from another. Each horse was then put up to auction, and the drawer could either buy it in or allow it to be sold. If the former, he had to pay the price bid to the lottery ; if the latter, he received the price bid, but the purchaser had to pay a similar amount to the lottery. Further, it was the custom frequently to throw dice for tickets, the loser paying, and the winner and loser both sharing the ticket, so that a good deal of gambling could be had for a small sum of money.

The hack race, in which Lunatic was to run, was fixed

for the following day ; and as there were six starters, the lottery on the race was worth winning. The number of tickets taken made it worth 25 gold mohurs, or £40, and the various horses sold in the aggregate for another £20. Lunatic, after a long pause without a bid, was knocked down to Macpherson himself for one gold mohur, showing that he even had little confidence in horse or rider ; and from the remarks around me I could understand that Lunatic was considered altogether out of the betting.

The next morning Darville drove me down to the Course, as all racing in India is done before the sun gets high and hot. The race-stand was of very simple construction, consisting of eight masonry pillars, on the top of which a wooden flooring was laid, with a mat wall at the back and wooden railing in front, the whole surmounted by a thatched roof. The spaces between the masonry pillars below were filled in with bamboo matting, and formed a room where coffee was served. The appointments of the weighing enclosure were equally simple, and a longish range of bamboo mat erections at the rear of the stand served as temporary stables for horses in training.

There were four events on the card for the day ; the said card having been printed by the local shopkeepers, Messrs. Jones & Co., to whom nothing came amiss in the way of business, from selling tinned provisions and arm chairs to building a dog-cart or furnishing a funeral. Indeed, I don't know what our little society would have done without them ; and, considering the monopoly they enjoyed and the risk of loss they incurred from deterioration of goods not quickly sold, I think their articles were good and their prices cheap, and I trust they have by this time made their fortunes.

The hack race was the last of the day, so I had time to go into the stand, where I was able to count seventeen ladies, which fact enabled me to look forward to that evening's ball with cheerful anticipation. One lady had ridden in with her husband fifty miles the day before, and told me she was quite disappointed when she found Colville's dog-cart waiting for them ten miles out on the road, as she would like to have done the whole distance on horseback. She was certainly none the worse for the journey, for I danced with her that evening, and a lighter partner I could not hope to find. There were two or three ladies from Dinapoor, two from Patna, and the remaining twelve were furnished by our own district.

One great feature of the occasion was the arrival of Colonel Barlow, who commanded an irregular cavalry regiment at Soogowlie, some eighty miles distant, and had brought in, not only several horses, but a pack of fox-hounds. He was an eccentric man ; a woman hater, at any rate a hater of European ladies ; and his two officers, who had also come in, were also bachelors.

After the second race had been run, Macpherson came to me and said, "You had better get weighed, and mount quietly, and get Lunatic away from the crowd and noise. You can walk him about, and when the others are about ready I will come down and tell you. He knows my pony, and won't think that anything unusual is going on."

I took his advice. The distance was only three-quarters of a mile, and so the starting-post was well away from the stand. It seemed a long time before Macpherson's burly form appeared cantering down towards me. "Come quietly," he said ; "I don't know what instructions to give, except to get the brute to start and keep him straight, and then you may win."

As we came to the post we found the other horses just coming up. Arkwright was on a mare called Juanita ; his brother on a horse called Jericho ; Colville, who had ridden in every race of the morning, was on something of his own ; and the other two horses were ridden also by their owners, indigo planters. As it happened, I drew No. 4 place, which put three horses on one side of me and two on the other. Lunatic saw something new was up, and began to make a brute of himself, neighing, kicking, yelling, and rearing, in a way that made me a terror to the rest. Jericho was somewhat of a similar nature, and diverted some of the indignation from my animal to himself. But after several attempts at a pitched battle between the two, we got the animals in line, and the word to start was given. Juanita was on my near side ; and as the forward movement was made, Lunatic made a rush at her open-mouthed ; but Arkwright, who was as cool as a cucumber, gave him a tremendous crack over the head with his whip, which made him swerve to the off, where he was brought up by Colville's knee, who merely ejaculated, "D—d brute !" and shot ahead. However, the two shocks combined had a good effect, for he simply took the bit between his teeth and ran away with me to the end of the race ; and, being really much the fastest horse, came in an easy winner. I believe he would have got off the course opposite the stand, but the railings kept him in ; and after going about half a mile past the post, I was enabled to pull him up, much blown and quite subdued. The by-standers gave him a wide berth coming into the enclosure ; but I don't think he had any vicious intention left in him. My weight was all right ; and while receiving the congratu-lations of Macpherson and others, I felt as proud as if I had won the Derby.

" I believe that crack on the head from, me made you win," said Arkwright, who, I now discovered, had been second in the race ; and I really think it had a good deal to do with it.

There was now a movement homewards, for bath and breakfast, after which Darville hurried off to office, telling me he didn't expect any work from me during the meeting ; and I hastened to the Doctor's for the rehearsal of our *tableaux vivants*, which were to come off on the Friday evening. I am afraid we did more laughter than anything else ; and poor Bertram's temper as manager must have been sorely tried ; but his apparent equanimity was beyond all praise.

The ball in the evening was to take place in Dar-ville's empty house. It was to be what is called "camp fashion." Every resident in the station had contributed something in the way of furniture, and each person brought his own eating and drinking implements. The eatables and drinkables were supplied from the race fund. The resulting appearance was motley, but picturesque. Every one of the seventeen ladies danced ; and though, of course, the preponderance of males was great, that of dancing men was just sufficient to make the ladies feel that they were each and all sought after, and so make them thoroughly enjoy themselves. Many of the assistant indigo planters were exceedingly bucolic, both in appearance and behaviour, and hung in clusters round the doorways, like the characters described in the entertainment at the farmhouse in "Sylvia's Lovers," by Mrs. Gaskell. Supper was announced about 1 a.m., and some confusion was caused by the desire of each ‚kitmutgar to get his own employer furnished with plates, etc., and served with eatables before any one else. The shy politeness with which young men, who had certainly derived no enjoyment from ladies' society all the evening, proffered their knives and forks to damsels who had neglected to bring any of their own, savoured of chivalry.

. It was amusing to see three pretty girls, daughters of an indigo planter of a remote part of the district, drinking champagne out of three pint pewters, which they had brought with them as safer than glass. They were clearly accustomed to "camp fashion." Nevertheless, the supper was probably more enjoyed than if it had been supplied in the best style by Gunter. Dancing was recommenced with extra vigour; and I, with most of the others, did not get home till 4 a.m.

Colonel Barlow's hounds were to meet at the Planters' Club at 5.30, as all hunting has to be done, as soon before and after sunrise as possible, as the scent soon ceases to lie. The Colonel made no allowances for men who were idiots enough to sit up to dance; and as we could expect no consideration for our late hours, it was not worth while going to bed. Colville had offered me a mount; and after getting into boots and breeches, Darville and I drove down to the Club, where we found coffee and cheroots, and a large number of horses being led about, of all sorts and sizes, from the high-caste Arab and well-bred Australian to the screaming country-bred pony of the youngest assistant planter. At 5.30 punctually we moved off, though it was not quite light; but we had a mile to go down the road before reaching any practicable cover, and no minute of the early dawn could be spared.

We found, in the very first grass we drew, a good straight-going jackal; but the hounds were almost too quick, and he was pulled down in ten minutes. It was a very pleasant gallop, with some small ditches and banks and one or two mud walls. But it was always possible to get round the obstacles; and I believe that the whole field really enjoyed the run. The master was delighted with our morning's sport, for by ten o'clock we had killed four jackals and were on our way home. The pack had only arrived from England some six weeks previously, and had probably cost him not less than £1000, all expenses of journey, etc., included. I subsequently had some experience in getting out packs of hounds; and, what with dishonest dealings in England, and losses on the voyage, the result generally was not so satisfactory as in this case. Colonel Barlow was, what is very exceptional in India, a man of independent fortune, who preferred being a despot in a small way in India at the head of his regiment, to leading a conventional life at home.

This sort of life lasted for ten days, and nobody seemed

to feel the want of sleep or rest, though the hours devoted to the former, out of these 240, were very few indeed. On Friday night our *tableaux vivants* took place, and were pronounced a success ; but I am not sure that the audience, or at least the whole of it, could be called critical. I appeared in two pictures ; in one as Rizzio, singing to Mary (Mrs. Macpherson—who looked charming) ; and in the other as murdered, the two assassins (Colville and Blake) standing over me. Blake was behind Colville, and in the spirit of mischief must needs give him a pinch just as the curtain drew up. His struggles to avoid laughing set me off, and I shook all over with restrained merriment. Bertram, always prompt, had the curtain quickly lowered ; and afterwards one of the more rustic members of our audience congratulated me on my share of the performance, saying, "You did the death quiver splendidly."

On the following Thursday, the last racing day, there were to be two steeple-chases. The course consisted of artificial jumps, in which the changes were rung on banks with ditches on the taking-off side, and ditto with ditto on the landing side, and ditto with ditto on both sides. There was one trench, about twelve feet wide, filled with water, dignified with the name of "the brook." In addition to the ordinary stakes, there was a prize for the winner of the first race of a bracelet, subscribed for by all the bachelors present, and which he was to present to the lady he might consider the belle of the meeting. It was a case of owners up, and the ladies looked forward to the result with considerable interest. An exception was made in favour of Colonel Barlow, who declined to ride in person, but was anxious to enter a horse; and in consideration of all he had done for the public amusement, was allowed to do so, and put up one of his subalterns. Perversely enough, he was the winner; and the rider had to give him the bracelet to present, which he at first flatly refused to do. However, he was at length persuaded to go up into the race-stand, where all the ladies were seated in a state of great expectation, and walking up to a young lady from Dinapore, thrust the prize into her hand, saying, "Take this; I knew your father," and walked off without another word.

The general disappointment was mitigated by the anticipation of the next race, in which there were no less than ten starters. I had persuaded Macpherson, against his will, to enter Lunatic, as I had tried him over most of the jumps, and found that he was perfectly able to negotiate them. Macpherson pointed out to me, that it was very different doing this leisurely, and with a good deal of coaxing, to going round the course at racing speed.

However, my previous success had made me very sanguine, and the consequence was that I found myself at the post with nine others, and we got off in rather a straggling way; but I suppose the starter despaired of doing any better. Lunatic put his head down, and seemed determined to make a bolt of it. But he cleared the first jump, —a bank with a ditch on the take-off side,—without an attempt at a swerve; and this seemed to put him in a good humour, for he cleared the next five or six in the same way. The "brook" was the last jump but one; and by way of assistance to keep us straight, a small hedge of hurdles, with boughs of trees stuck in them, had been made up on each side, to a length of some twenty or thirty yards. Lunatic did not like entering this avenue; and when he got to the edge of the brook, turned round, and tried to jump the hedge. I don't recollect anything more until I found Macpherson and one or two others standing over me. But it seems that another rider had come crash against me, and knocked both myself and horse over. He had escaped unhurt, and so had Lunatic; but the ground was as hard as pavement, and I had fallen outside the hedge and, as it turned out, broken my collar-bone. Nothing very serious, but very annoying.

The next morning it was a case of "I told you so" from Macpherson, who nevertheless sold Lunatic at a good profit. ', ,

So ended my first race-meeting in India, which, up to the time of my accident, I had thoroughly enjoyed. But now came a dull time. I did not get well very quickly; and as all outsiders had left the station, and those who remained were well occupied, the days of lying down and keeping still, with nobody but native servants to speak to, were long and dreary. In the meantime, there was a "pig-sticking" meet in the neighbouring district of Chuprah, from which came back reports of fierce boars and thrilling incidents. After this, Blake, the Arkwrights and Colville went on a shooting expedition to the Terai in Nepaul, which is on the northern boundary of Tirhoot—a flat strip of country covered with grass, jungle, and forest, at the foot of the line of hills which are the commencement of the Himalayan range. They brought back a tiger, a bear, and a boa-constrictor.

'I, in the meantime, attempted to solace myself by reading for my law examination, which was to come off in March, at Patna ; but to which I was not able to go, and consequently, could not present myself until the following October.

Darville had gone, and his successor only stayed a month, being promoted to be Magistrate of another neighbouring district, Chumparun ; and his successor, Melville by name, had arrived—a contemporary of mine at Eton, though some two years my senior, now a married man with a large family. Our meeting in this way was a curious coincidence, and a great pleasure to both of us.

The new judge, Percival, was a grass widower, and asked me to chum with him in his house on the lake. Bertram was not to return to Mozufferpore, having been appointed a sort of roving Judge to do work in districts that had fallen into arrear, and had sent instructions for the sale of his goods and chattels ; so that this offer was most acceptable, the more so as Percival was also an Etonian, and an exceedingly pleasant, refined man, and musical. My own belongings were very soon moved ; and after the disposal of Bertram's effects, which gave me occupation for a month or so, I regularly settled down for the dreary dulness of the hot weather.

My work was not sufficient to occupy me for the long days. Indeed, on an average, I did not get more than an houi and a half daily ; and as, until I should pass my examination, the importance and the very nature of the cases I could try was very limited, the endless " assaults," varied only by the still more numerous " dakhil kharij " cases on the Collectorate side, made me feel nauseated at the sight of a mookhtyar or a suitor.

In India it is impossible to lie in bed late; and I was always up before 6 a.m.; and on the mornings when the "bobberee" pack went out, of which Macpherson was "master," and I "whip," we used to be up by 4 a.m. How well I remember the feeling of stifling heat, even at that hour, and the misery of putting on breeches that were a little shrunk with frequent washing. However, these very hot mornings did not come till the middle of April, and up to that time it was a very pleasant way of passing the hours up till nine or ten, until bath and breakfast were due. Knowing that work would come some time or other, I always made it a principle to be at office about eleven, and to do all that I had to perform without dawdling; and the consequence was, that I was generally free for the day about 12.30. I then had to come home to a lonely house and wish for evening.

It is true that I had my examination to read for; but that did not come off till October, and I felt certain of accomplishing that with very little labour. It would only be in the laws and one language—Hindustani, that of the district in which I was serving; and I was prohibited from taking up Bengali until I had passed in this. The fact of having nothing to do that was compulsory, coupled with the enervating heat, made me feel it distasteful to do anything; so I used to watch the shadows as they lengthened, and wish,—not as Hezekiah,—that they would go forward, and not back. About sunset Percival and the others would come from their respective offices; and then we had rackets or a canter on the Course, and so passed the time till dinner. But I shall never forget the dreariness of those long hot afternoons. Occasionally I used to send a note in to Melville, who, as Joint Magistrate, made over criminal work to me, and beg him to give me something to do. His reply was generally,—" Nothing within your powers. Don't be discontented with your leisure, but make the most of it while you have it." And his advice was, no doubt, correct.

One day, however, he sent me a case, wishing me joy of it at the time, in which some seven or eight native Christians and one Christian woman, were accused of assaulting certain Mohammedans and making a row in the bazaar. It certainly involved the hearing of a number of witnesses that, would appal a stipendiary magistrate at home ; for each of the eight defendants had separate witnesses of his own to prove his innocence and absence from the scene of the alleged occurrence. Finally I convicted all the defendants, and sentenced them to a small fine each, with the exception of the woman, who was young and exceedingly pretty, and who I did not believe could have done much in the row. The next day, while wearying through the afternoon, the Chota Padre Sahib, or little clergyman, was announced, and the head of the German Lutheran mission in Mozufferpore came in. He was a really good old man, and much respected by all who knew him.

"Oh, Mr. Gordon," he said, "I cannot talk about any ordinary subjects ; I want to speak to you about having fined my Christians. It is cruel, and they are all innocent; and it is the other side that ought to have been fined."

"Mr. Blumenthal," I replied with some dignity, "I decided the case to the best of my ability on the evidence adduced. If you are dissatisfied, you can appeal to my superior, the Magistrate of the district, Mr. Blake; and if he think fit, he can reverse my decision."

"Oh, I should not like to hurt your feelings by doing that."

"Officials have no feelings on such matters," said I, sententiously, but not truly.

"But if you only knew all that I know," he said; "these men whom you have fined are subjected to persecution for having turned Christians; and those who were the plaintiffs began the quarrel by calling my men 'eaters of pig' and 'drunkards.'"

"Then you admit there was a quarrel. Why did your Christians all assert that they were not there? And why did they all bring Christian witnesses to swear that they were not?"

This was rather a stumper for the Padre.

"Well," he said, "the others, the complainants, whom you didn't fine, were quite as bad; and the woman you let off was the worst of all."

"My dear sir," I said, having now got the best of it, "I decided the case on the evidence, and you have only heard one side. The evidence, very likely, was a good deal of it false. That of your Christians certainly was; and all you have said to-day only confirms me in my opinion that I decided rightly. You cannot be so blind as to really think that a native convert is immaculate because he is a Christian."

Here the poor old gentleman absolutely began to cry. So I stopped, and he thanked me for letting him speak so freely on the subject, and went away.

I don't think he really believed his Christians to be innocent; but he was doubtless much concerned at the triumph of his Mohammedan adversaries.

I cannot say that I found conversion to Christianity improve those converts with whom I happened to come in contact. On the contrary, it appeared to me that they became, both socially and morally, degraded by it; but then it must be admitted that all the converts I knew belonged to the very lowest classes. As far as my experience goes, Christianity is certainly not making progress in India, notwithstanding anything missionaries in Bengal may say to the contrary. Indeed, I have little belief in genuine conversions.

It may be better in Madras, though the Madras Christians that I have known have not borne a high character. The usual run of missionaries are not of a very high order of intellect, and by no means fit to argue with the subtle Hindoo, who is scarcely convinced of the necessity of self-denial, etc., etc., when he sees the preachers of the doctrine so fond of comfortable bungalows and married life, and as exacting with their servants and as careful of their rupees, annas, and pice as the rest of the world. It requires men like Xavier to make an impression on the Oriental mind, and missionaries of the present day do not resemble him.

My afternoons were also occasionally enlivened by the

visits of native officials and gentlemen of the neighbour-, hood, who thought it right and proper to call on the young Hakim. These were a great nuisance, both to the visitor and the visited.

If the visitor were an official, he would probably be a native Judge; and after the usual questions about my health, I would generally ask if he had a great deal to do, and he always had; but, by dint of extremely hard work, just managed to get through it.

If it were a native gentleman, I used to ask about his crops, and if there was any difficulty about the rents ; and as a general rule, the answer was,—

" In consequence of the prosperity of your Highness's boots, the crops are good. (Huzoor ke juti ke ekbal se.) There is a little want of rain ; but we hope that, by your Highness's favour, the rains will soon set in."

To ask after wife or daughters would have been an offence, and set down either to ignorance of the proper way to behave, or to sheer rudeness. We in India are often accused of a want of desire to amalgamate with the natives, and cultivate their society. But how can we under these circumstances ? How can you be on friendly terms with a man who believes that your very touch defiles him, and who would not eat his food if, in passing, your shadow had happened to fall on it ?

The Maharajah of Durbhungah (who had died a short time before), who was thrown into tolerably constant con- tact with English officials, used, it was discovered, to change his clothes immediately on his return home after an inter- view with them, and not wear them again until they had been thoroughly purified, and also go through a personal purification himself. His property was now under the protection and control of the Court of Wards mentioned above ; and the manager, who had much improved and beautified the palace grounds at Durbhungah, and made some ornamental gardens, used to send the widow Ranee a choice nosegay every morning, until he found that she never admitted it to her presence, for fear he should have touched it, as he had done once or twice.

It is true that some few members of the Brahmo Somaj —that is, the new Deist religion—have thrown off the trammels of caste openly, and are glad to frequent European society ; but even these could in very few cases bring the females of their family with them; and many of them, unfortunately, in consequence of the removal of caste restraint, have become dissolute and drunken, and their society is not desirable. It is impossible at present that there can be any intimate friendship between natives of India and Europeans. Before this can be altered there must be a complete change of habits on one side or the other. What we think clean, they think dirty, and *vice versâ.* For instance, a well-bred Hindoo gentleman thinks it dirty to eat with a knife and fork, or with any clothing on but a waistcloth ; but I fancy it will be a very long time before we come round to those views, and it will certainly be equally long before they adopt ours. If newspaper reporters could see what really went on in the domestic privacy of the native potentates presented to the Prince of Wales, after their interviews, I fear their accounts, if true, would not have been quite so flattering and satisfactory.

To show how far this fear of defilement may be carried, I may relate, that when Assistant Magistrate in charge of Durbhungah, I was riding through an out-of-the-way village one hot morning, and met a number of the headmen who expected my coming. They were perfect rustics, but very courteous. I asked them for some water, and some was fetched in a perfectly new earthenware vessel and presented to me on my bridle hand as I sat on horseback; and they begged me, when I had drunk as much as I wanted, to throw the vessel with the contents remaining on the opposite side of the animal, so that the vessel might not be used again in the village, and no sprinkle of the water come near them. All this was done without the faintest suspicion that my feelings could be hurt by it, and I complied as a matter of course.

From the above it can be easily understood that our social intercourse in India is confined to Europeans only; and as their number in small out-of-the-way stations in Bengal is very limited, it is well to be at peace with all, if possible.

One hot morning, just as I was coming out of my bath, Percival sent me in a note that a chuprassie of Blake's had just brought up. It was from Mrs. Blake:—"Dear Mr. Percival,—Will you and Mr. Gordon give us the pleasure of your company at dinner this evening, at eight o'clock?" On this he had written in pencil, "Must we go?" and underneath it I replied, "I suppose we must," and told the man to give it back to the Sahib. Percival, I knew, very particularly wanted to stay at home that evening, as his piano had arrived some half an hour previously from

Calcutta, and he wanted to devote his leisure to unpacking, putting it up, and having a first performance on it; so on meeting him at breakfast I asked him,

"What did you say in answer to Mrs. Blake?"

. "Why, I sent the note in to you, and asked if you thought we must go."

"And I sent it back to you, saying that I thought we must."

"Good heavens! the idiot must have taken it back to Mrs. Blake. What shall we do?"

It was rather trying; but I was not in such a mess as Percival, as the note had been addressed to him, and it was for him to answer it, and he had asked the question, "Must we go?" He was an exceedingly punctilious man, and was evidently in considerable consternation. At last I suggested he should say that he hoped Mrs. Blake would not be offended at an accident that had occurred through the stupidity of a chuprassie; that it always gave him great pleasure to come to her house, though on this par-.ticular occasion he had special reasons for staying at home; however, that if she would receive us this evening, we should both be delighted to come.

This answer was accordingly despatched, and we both went to office; and in about an hour I got a note from Percival saying that Mrs. Blake had merely sent a "salaam," which was equivalent to "no answer." This looked ugly. In the evening I met Blake at the Racket Court; and he said, with a good-humoured twinkle in his eye, "I shall have the pleasure of seeing you to-night." I saw that he was all right, and on going home to dress I found that

Percival had had a formal note from Mrs. Blake, saying that she should be glad to see us at the hour named. It was an awful ordeal, entering the drawing-room ; but Blake was so genial, and evidently so delighted at the whole thing, that we were soon at our ease. I found afterwards that Mrs. Blake had sent our wretched pencilled remarks to him at office, asking his advice, and he had told her to treat the whole thing as a joke. She had scarcely felt equal to this ; but his good humour and good sense had pulled us through, and so a possible big disagreeable had been reduced to a minimum.

About this time a small windfall came to me, though from a melancholy cause. Poor Mrs. Macpherson fell seriously ill, and was obliged to go to Calcutta, and her husband found it necessary to accompany her. In addition to his duties as Civil Surgeon, he held the office of District Registrar, for which he was remunerated by fees paid on the registration of each deed. In those days registration was very loosely conducted, and no doubt a very large number of false deeds were registered. There was nothing to prevent false personation, except the identification by two witnesses, who could be picked up for 6*d.* each ; and unless other parties interested got information that it was sought to register a deed,—and it was more than probable they did not,—there would be no objections offered. All this has since been altered. But, as it then was, the registration of a deed was positively of no value. Notwithstanding this, the number of deeds registered in Tirhoot was very large, and used to bring the Civil Surgeon a profit of about £70 a month, after paying the salaries of three clerks. In his absence the Registrar was allowed to appoint his own substitute, and Macpherson made it over to me, offering half the proceeds as remuneration, which I was only too glad to accept, and which I received for about two months—a very welcome addition to my own pay.

We were all very sorry for him when he came back alone, and the return to his solitary house must have been hard indeed.

CHAPTER VI.

AT MOZUFFERPORE.

DURING that year the Bengal Government had determined
to put into practice the much-talked-of re-organization of
the police. An Act (V. of 1861) had been passed for the
purpose, and it had been decided that this should come
into force first of all in the Tirhoot District.

The Report of the Madras Commission, issued some time
previously, had shown that the police in that province had
not been properly controlled ; and that various malpractices,
including torture, had been carried on. It was thought,
truly enough, that the Bengal District Magistrate had
so much to do that he had not time to look after the
police ; and a good deal of stress was also laid on the
inexpediency of the thief-catcher being the thief-trier ; so
it was thought advisable that a special European officer
should be appointed to each district, called the District
Superintendent of Police, and that he should be provided
with special European subordinates to take charge of the
sub-divisions of districts. Further, the nomenclature of the
native police officials was to be changed. The old officers
in charge of the "thannahs," henceforward to be called

"police stations," were no longer "Thannardar" or "Daroghah," but Inspector, or Sub-inspector. The subordinate stations were no longer "phanre," but "outpost;" and the old burkundaz became "constable." These new names were pronounced by the natives " poleesh-istashun," "inshpektar," "outposht," and "cunnishshtubble." Uniforms also were ordained; and European military caps and jackets were decided upon for the officers, while a red turban, blue blouse with belt, and staff, were substituted for the rather nondescript get-up of the men, who were also taught military drill and provided with muskets. The Commissioners of Divisions, as far as their police powers were concerned, were succeeded by Deputy Inspectors-general; and a sort of Police Minister was appointed under the title of Inspector-general. In short, the police were to become a separate service under separate officers, and sufficiently drilled to be able to act in large bodies if necessary.

The first result to us was a temporary addition to our small society, in the shape of the new Inspector-general (a civilian of some standing), a Deputy Inspector-general, and three District Superintendents, who were to learn their work. Two of these were military men anxious for staff employ, and the third had been in the uncovenanted civil service.

The new great man was a friend of Percival's, and put up with us; the others were distributed among the other officials in the station. Our guest was an exceedingly pleasant fellow, and of a character calculated to make the new arrangements work smoothly if possible, for he at any rate kept Talleyrand's advice of *"point de zèle"* always in view. This was not the case with all his subordinates, especially the military men, who seemed continually to be on the look-out for offence, and constantly exaggerating little molehills of routine or etiquette into mountains of difficulty and quarrel. Blake, however, was the man of all others to steer clear of avoidable disagreeables, and his even temper and clearheadedness enabled all the intricacies of taking over charge to be got through without any open rupture.

It was naturally distasteful to the Magistrate of the district to give up the direct control of the police. As a matter of fact, it did not save him much routine work; for, as I have mentioned above, the reports, except those of extra importance, were heard by the Joint Magistrate; while it deprived him to a considerable extent of the appearance and of the reality of power. As long as the police understood the Magistrate to be their immediate head, they were anxious to please him in every way, and be as subservient as possible; but now they had another set of officers to look to, and these began certainly by being exceedingly jealous of the Magistrate, and encouraged their subordinates to be independent and disobliging.

One feature in the new procedure was, that the Magistrate should give no orders direct to the subordinate police, but through the District Superintendent only; and one of our new arrivals, the first appointed to be District Superintendent of Tirhoot, had instructed his subordinates to carry this order out in the letter as well as the spirit. It so happened that Blake was obliged to go out into the interior of the district soon after he had made over charge of the police, and had sent his tents on, as usual, under the care of his chuprassies. On arriving at his camp he found nothing ready; and his servants told him that the police of the station had declined to give them any assistance in the way of pitching the tents, or getting supplies of straw and other necessaries. They said the Magistrate was no longer their master, and he must look out for himself. Blake went to the police-station and found the "inshpektar" apparently a little frightened at his own temerity, but firm in refusing assistance, as he had received no orders from the District Superintendent. "Very well," said Blake, with the most perfect good temper, "let me look at your station registers." This also the man declined to do on the same grounds. Now in this he was utterly wrong, though he did not know it. The Magistrate was still the chief officer in the district, and responsible for its tranquillity and proper administration; and it was of course absurd that he should be denied access to the information contained in the police registers.

This supplied Blake with a capital peg on which to hang a report to the Commissioner, which was forwarded to the Government; and the result was a wigging to the District Superintendent, and the dismissal of the "inshpektar," who had gone beyond the letter, though not the spirit, of the orders of his superior.

It was now laid down that the Magistrate of the district,—*e.g.*, the official corresponding to Blake,—could give orders direct to the police which did not affect the internal economy of the "force," as it was now called; and also, that the Deputy Superintendent of police should carry out

all orders of the Magistrate, recording his non-concurrence
by way of protest, if he saw reason to do so, and reporting
to his superior officer, the Deputy Inspector-general, who
would confer with the Commissioner, and then, if necessary,
lay the matter before the Government. Under the circumstances, if a Magistrate did give a wrong order, it
would be a longish time before it was rectified.; but it was
far better to trust an official of his position with absolute
authority for the time, than to allow storms to arise in each
district tea-cup.

It was only to be expected that the Commissioners, as
well as Magistrates, should object to the change, for they
too were still held responsible for the peaceful administration of their provinces, and yet found the Deputy
Inspector-general interposed as buffers between them and
the police, just as the Magistrates found the District Superintendents. As years have gone on, the new system has
been much modified; but at first, there can be no doubt
that the thing did not work well. A mass of appointments
were suddenly created, and, as a necessary consequence, a
still more numerous mass of candidates appeared, a very
large number of them being military men, whose sole
qualification for the posts they sought was a desire to enter
staff employ, and get better pay than they did with their
regiments. They were useful in drilling the new police,
practically the least important part of their work; but, as a
rule, utterly without experience in the management of a
body of men, not to be employed in fighting battles, but in
the prevention and detection of crime in a peaceful country.
Many of them knew little or nothing of the. language, and

were altogether in the hands of their chief native subordinates. They could, however, be credited with a sense
of duty, and a desire to do their best; interfered with only
by a strong feeling of what was due to their dignity, and a
constant suspicion that their rights were being encroached
upon.

The most useful class were those who had been Deputy
Magistrates in the uncovenanted civil service, and who had
been tempted by the hope of promotion and better salary
and status to exchange into the police. These understood
the supervision of local police and the conduct of cases,
and did practically well, though terribly pitched into by
military Deputy Inspectors-general for not being up in
their drill.

Another class were the friends and *protégés* of people in
influential positions, and who of course were useless at
starting, though many of them turned out well enough
after gaining a little experience. Another difficulty was,
that a large number of the old "daroghahs" objected to
the new uniform, as entailing loss of caste, and still more
to serving under military superiors, who were generally
supposed to be quick-tempered and imperious, and to be
devoid of the consideration for native manners and customs
shown by the civilians.

Abuse (in Hindustani, "gali") is looked upon with great
dread in India by native gentlemen. Instead of considering that it defiles the man from whom it proceeds, they
think that the person against whom it is levelled is irre-
parably injured by it, and shrink from it more than they
would from a blow. The stain of dishonour caused by the

receipt of an abusive epithet cannot be effaced. I recollect some time after this a native gentleman calling on me, and telling me that he thought he ought to pay a visit of ceremony to a young Assistant Superintendent of Police who had recently arrived at the station ; " But," he said, " I am afraid. He is young and hasty, and how do I know but that some word may come out of his mouth which will disgrace me, without his meaning anything." Admitting that the offensive word might not be intended, perhaps, even not understood, by the person uttering it, the effect on the person addressed would be the same. This being the case, many of the experienced old native police officers threw up their posts, and a great number of the burkundazes, who would not put up with the drill. Their places were filled by numbers of recruits from the more warlike populations of the West and North-West, who knew nothing of the people or the localities in which they had to act, and could with difficulty be made to understand how to serve a summons. They were, also, generally of better physique and greater animal courage than the Bengalees, and bullied the people proportionately, who hated them in return with a bitter hatred.

In due time, the watchful supervision of Government detected this, and orders were issued on the subject of recruiting, with a view to check the evil. As may easily be imagined, the new police, though more expensive than the old, were at first not very efficient ; but as things settled down, and the new officers got to understand their work, and it was more and more definitely settled' that the District Superintendents were the assistants to and subordinates of the District Magistrates, the new system began to work much better, and doubtless the subordinate native police were more efficiently controlled.

All these disagreeables and difficulties were pretty well got over before I attained the post of District Magistrate; but, in the meantime, great changes were made. The Deputy Inspectors-general were abolished as useless, and the services of many of the Assistant Superintendents of Police, so hastily appointed, had been dispensed with. About this time there had been a desire in Bengal to diminish the power and importance of the District Magistrate, and cut him up, as it were, into a number of smaller functionaries; but this was soon found to be a mistake, and recently the "tendency" has been all the other way. However, I shall have to speak on this matter at greater length further on.

During the settlement of the new arrangements in Tirhoot, it was of course necessary for the Inspector-general to move about a good deal, and this he and his satellites did *con amore*, the more especially as there was plenty of small game to be had, and it was still possible to shoot mornings and evenings. On one occasion he was going to inspect a station called Rowsara, whence also "khabar" (news) of innumerable black partridges had been received. I ventured to bet him 1 gold mohur (32s.) that he and his party would not bag twenty brace in the day they could devote to the sport. After some haggling, he backed the guns for thirteen brace only. On his return, I asked him the result; for I had heard that all the forces of the neighbourhood had been put into requisition, and the resident gentry and police had vied with each other in providing means to " sweep the jungle " as the natives call it ; and 200 coolies (chiefly village chowkeydars) and nineteen elephants had been employed to beat the grasses in which these birds were to be found.

" We shot all we saw," he said, in reply to my questions ; and after some time I elicited the fact that they had only seen one partridge—rather a disproportionate return for all the force employed. These black partridges are migratory birds, in the sense that they move in bodies from one heavy grass to another ; and as these patches are very numerous, it is rather difficult to know where to find them.

But a still more annoying fact was the occurrence of a " dacoity " within a mile of his camp, for they had been in tents for one night. A " dacoity " is a robbery with violence by an organized gang,—according to the Penal Code the number must exceed five,—and is the most serious and troublesome class of crime that the police have to deal with. In this case the house of an opulent villager had been attacked by a band of twenty-five or thirty men ; two of the servants and one of the sons had been severely wounded with spears ; and about 1,000 rs. worth in money and jewels carried off. There were plenty of police promptly on the spot soon after news was received of the occurrence, and a deal of energy displayed, but apparently not much discretion, for though a number of bad characters in the neighbourhood were arrested, and an enormous number of witnesses procured to give evidence against them, they were all finally acquitted by Percival when committed to his Court for trial.

This was naturally a subject for cynical remarks, not only by the magisterial authorities, but the subordinate native officials; but it proved nothing either way, for plenty of dacoities had been previously committed in which no clue to the perpetrators had been discovered. It was very perverse of those particular dacoits, however, to choose this time and place for their exploits. Of course, the police officials said the Judge was all wrong, and they had caught the right men. Perhaps they had. I don't know. Personally, I had no feeling against the new police, for they did not interfere with any exercise of power by me, and I looked upon the new comers as so many more racket-players and additional members of our small society. In due time, however, the Inspector-general went off to arrange another district, and we were left with the new District Superintendent and his Assistant, to the dulness of the rainy season, which began this year punctually on the 15th of June, the date given, in geography books about India, for its commencement.

The weary sodden months of July and August passed slowly away, and in September we began to cheer ourselves with the prospect of the approach of the cold weather, though it was still two months off. On the 18th of this month began the worship of the Goddess Doorga, commonly called the Doorga Poojah, which lasts for a fortnight, and answers in Bengal somewhat to our Christmas holidays in England. The festival had not quite such a hold of the people in Behar as in Bengal proper; but nevertheless the Courts, criminal as well as the others, were closed for ten days, the troublesome pettifogging attorneys ceased to seek for clients, and even "dacoits" refrained from their nefarious pursuits during this sacred interval.

Melville determined to make a rush down to Calcutta to see his sister there, the wife of one of the Government Secretaries, and asked me if I would like to go with him. I was only too glad of the chance of a change, and Blake gave us both leave to go on our own responsibility; that is, he undertook to look after the district and do for Melville anything that might be necessary during his absence, while we should have to take upon ourselves the consequences of the Government finding fault with us for absenting ourselves from our districts without regular leave.

We hoped to reach Calcutta in three days, as the railway had now been opened as far as Monghyr, which lay on the other bank of the Ganges, a little lower down than the south-easternmost corner of the Tirhoot district. We were to drive to an indigo factory situated on the river bank, and then take boat, which we expected would carry us to Monghyr, as it was down stream, easily in the course of one night.

We left Mozufferpore on a Sunday morning, and arrived at the hospitable planter's house in time for a midday meal. He had been written to beforehand, and provided a country boat, and sent some food on board. Unfortunately, he had not himself inspected the boat, and on coming down to the ghât to see us off, expressed some misgiving as to its fitness. It was a very clumsy affair, very wide in proportion to its length, and covered with thatch, the covering coming so far forward as to leave very little room in the bows for rowing purposes. In fact, there was scarcely space for four rowers, and our host had stipulated for six. But the weather was calm and the stream was strong ; so we still thought to reach Monghyr very early in the morning, about 4 a.m. We said good-bye to him in good spirits, and for the first two or three hours seemed to make fair progress.

We determined to dine early, and go to sleep as soon as possible, as we had no candles with us, and it would be rather dreary work sitting in the dark, or with the light only of the stinking oil lamp that could be procured from the boatmen. Our provisions consisted of a very small leg of lamb, a small loaf of bread, about half a tin of sweet biscuits, and a bottle of claret. This was considered ample to last us till 4 a.m. the next morning, so we ate carelessly, not thinking we should care to see any of the remnants of the food again. But towards the small hours I was awoke by the boat rolling in a very uncomfortable way, and putting my head out in front of the thatch, I found that the men had ceased rowing, and that we were wallowing in the trough of a pretty considerable swell, caused by a strong south-easterly wind. I woke Melville, and with a little British energy we set the rowers to work again. But it was soon clear that it was impossible to keep the head of the clumsy vessel to the wind, and that, as far as onward progress was concerned, we were utterly helpless. The wind increased in strength every minute, and very soon rain began to pour down with tropical fury. As daylight broke, we saw the right-hand bank, towards which the wind was driving us, about a mile off; and we hoped to reach this, and take shelter until the wind should drop, or, if that seemed unlikely, retrace our steps. But while considering what was best to be done, we felt a violent bump, the boat heeled over on one side, and then remained stationary.

We had stuck on a sand bank, covered with only about half a foot of water. Oars and poles were at once put in requisition to shove us off; but the wind drove us on, and though Melville and I worked as hard as the rest, all our efforts were of no use, and we became convinced that we must stick where we were until the wind should moderate. My solar topee (pith hat) was whirled away during the struggle, but that was the only result. As the day passed on, about 6 a.m., I began to feel hungry, and would have given a good deal for a hot cup of coffee and a piece of toast. We looked at our leg of lamb, or rather the small remnant. There was no bread left, and we each had a bit of meat and a sweet biscuit, not a nice mixture, our drink being drawn from the holy Ganges, which troublesome river we both cursed from the bottom of our hearts. The day wore wearily on, still the same leaden sky, the same torrents of rain, and the same unceasing plash of the waves driven by the wind against our half-heeled-over boat. The thatch, too, was leaking; and Melville and I sat close together on a space about a yard square, which seemed drier than the rest. There was no danger, and consequently no excitement to keep up our spirits. The roof of the boat was not high enough to allow us to stand upright; we had nothing to read, so all we could do was to squat, and endeavour to talk. In this respect the boatmen were better off than we; for natives have any amount of sleep at command, and they lay huddled up like so many bundles of rags, apparently heedless of everything, but probably happy because able to be lazy.

About midday we felt hungry, and again turned our attention to the remnant of our leg of lamb. To our dismay it had turned green. The damp and muggy heat combined had caused this. With many misgivings we committed it to the stream, to be digested by some river turtle or alligator, and satiated our present pangs with a few sweet biscuits each. Evening came on, but with no change, and we were content to dine off a handful of dry rice, given us by the boatmen; for the wind and rain was such that they could not even attempt to light a fire in our exposed situation. They had, moreover, very little rice with them, as they expected to buy some cheap in the Monghyr bazaar. As the darkness settled down, we tried to compose ourselves miserably to sleep, and partially succeeded, so that the night was less dreary than the day. But the morning dawned dismally, without break in the sky or cessation of the wind and the rain. Added to this, our food supply had nearly collapsed, and we were reduced to two sweet biscuits each.

About ten, a steamer passed us, a long way off, but without taking any notice of our signal of distress, viz., a pair of trousers, belonging to Melville, hauled up the mast. We used these in order to show the steamer people that Europeans were on our country boat. We anathematized this vessel pretty well; but two hours afterwards, another passed us with the same result, and then our indignation knew no bounds. I mentally composed a tremendous letter to the *Englishman* newspaper on the inhuman conduct of river steamer captains, which, as may be supposed, was never committed to writing. Probably we, were not seen, and if we were, I doubt if they could have helped us without considerable risk; for it seemed we had got on a long strip of shallow, to which they were obliged to give a wide berth, and down the side of this a tremendous current was running; and had they stopped near, they would probably have been stranded like ourselves. For all this we were not prepared to make allowances at the time; and to add to our discomfort, the bottom of the boat being now pretty well waterlogged, the rats began to make their appearance in our neighbourhood, and to climb about the thatch roof. We consoled ourselves with the reflection that they would not find much to eat, " Unless it should be our own unhappy persons," I added, with a forced smile; but Melville suggested that it might be the other way, and we should eat them.

But even this gale must have an end, and looking out hopelessly about 5 p.m., I thought I detected a light appearance in the sky to windward; and surely enough, half-an-hour afterwards, a gleam of sun shot through the clouds, and the wind had decidedly moderated, and the rain ceased. We also found, considerably to our surprise, that the river had fallen so much as to leave a small dry bit of sand on one side of our boat, and it was a relief to get out and stand on this. Presently we saw shoot out from the bank, some three-quarters of a mile distant, a very tiny dinghy, and, as it approached, we saw it was navigated by an old greyheaded creature, who seemed afraid to come near us when he found we were Europeans. However we got the boatmen to speak soothingly to him; Melville, too, addressed him as his father and brother, and by every other endearing term he could think of, and I made rupees glisten by holding them in the sun, which was now shining.

At length he was persuaded to come alongside; and, with much caution and difficulty, Melville and I got into his frail craft, for the wind was still very strong, and reached the bank. The appearance of this was not very encouraging, for it looked a mass of black streaming mud, about eight or ten feet high. We divested ourselves of our boots and socks, and even our trousers, and tying them in bundles on our backs, plunged on to, or rather into, this, and reached the top, black above our knees and our elbows. There we found a herd of tame buffaloes, enjoying the slimy nature of things in general, guarded by a small herd-boy, who was riding on the back of one of the huge ugly brutes, some hundred yards off. It is a curious fact that these creatures are so amenable to their keepers, who are generally small children, and so irate at the sight of a white man; and this was most disagreeably illustrated by one of them making a rush at me. I turned to fly, but my naked feet prevented my making any progress in the mud; and so I held up both my arms, stood firm, and shrieked. This stopped the animal long enough to give the small boy time to drive him off, which he did quite easily, and then ran away in as great fear as if he had seen two evil spirits.

However, the village was only a couple of hundred yards off, and going towards it we found a pool where we washed our arms and legs, and made ourselves look a little more respectable, and then went on to where a small group had assembled to stare at us, and of whom Melville demanded in as authoritative a tone as possible where the "jeyt ryot," or headman, was to be found. This individual was soon forthcoming, and we then inquired where the nearest police station was; and this to our sorrow we heard was eight miles away. We also found that we were in the district of Monghyr.

"Then," said Melville, "send a messenger to the thannah, say that two Hakims from Tirhoot have been wrecked here and want two palanquins as soon as possible to go to Barh, which we found was some thirty miles off, and tell the police to send information to the magistrate of Monghyr and the magistrate of Tirhoot."

This was done to make the villagers believe that we were *bonâ fide* Hakims, and not European loafers only; and it had the effect of rendering them willing to oblige us. The "patwarree," or village accountant, placed a room, that is, a mud floor covered with a thatch and surrounded by mud walls, at our disposal; and here we prepared to pass the night, for it was now dark, and there was no chance of our getting the palanquins before the following morning. The village was inhabited by Hindoos, and so no animal food, eggs or fowls, could be procured; but some rice and vegetable curry was prepared for us, and presented to us on plantain leaves. This we ate with our fingers. We were starving; and yet plunging my fingers into the greasy mess had such a nauseating effect on me that I could scarcely swallow any of it. Melville was of stronger stomach, and ate all that I left as well as his own share. We then lay down to pass another miserable night on a "takhtaposh," a sort of low table on which the patwarree used to squat in the day-time with his papers round him, and in which I found the nail heads even harder than the boards. Sleep was not possible, and it was an inexpressible relief when day began to make its appearance.

The wind had by this time quite gone down, and the boatmen had managed to bring our baggage on shore. Soon the two palanquins appeared, accompanied by a policeman; and after taking a draught of milk, and signing two certificates, one for the "jeyt ryot" and one for the "patwarree," both written out by the latter, that they had given us all necessary assistance, we started for the nearest European habitation. These certificates would be carefully preserved by these two men, and brought forward as evidence of their being good characters in case of their getting into trouble by any chance afterwards.

We had happened to come upon a low-lying tract of country, suited only for the cultivation of the heavy rice crop, so that there were no planters' bungalows in the neighbourhood. Had there been, we should have been better off. As it was, we were anxious to see who was the inhabitant of the nearest European habitation, for the natives could only tell us he was a "railway sahib."

In about two hours we approached the bungalow, and saw the sahib sitting in the verandah. My heart fell at the sight of him, for it was clear he was one of the lower class of employés, and I longed for something civilized both to talk to and to eat. He turned out to be a sort of overseer, and was for his position a decent enough fellow ; but his means of hospitality were not great. However he did his best, and supplied us with some fried slices of village pig (a food we would not have looked at on any ordinary occasion), and some gin and water. Being all but starved, we found these good ; and when discussed, our host, who had a trolly at his disposal, said he would give us a lift to Mokameh, where his superior the engineer lived, and whom I had met on my journey up, some nine months previously. The rails had been laid as far as Barh in that interval, though the line was not open for traffic. He was a mild-looking man ; but his conversation on the trolly was most truculent. According to his own account, he had killed several game-keepers in England before coming out to India, and committed other exploits of a similar character. We nevertheless parted on good terms about 3 p.m., and were delighted to find ourselves hospitably received once more in a properly furnished bungalow, with a chance of getting something fit to eat.

Our new host was much interested and amused with the recital of our adventures, at which we could now afford to laugh, and promised to send us on by trolly to Barh the next day, after we were refreshed with a proper dinner and a good night's rest. The next day we reached Barh, in the Patna district ; and I found that my former host had taken advantage of the Doorga holidays to go into head-quarters, to consult Alison the Magistrate ; but at the dâk bungalow we found the new Assistant Superintendent of Police, who had only recently been appointed here. He proved to be an old acquaintance of Melville's and with his assistance we soon procured a decent-looking boat to cross us once more to the Tirhoot side of the river. With some misgivings I trusted myself again to the treacherous stream ; but this time nothing adverse happened, and about sunset we cast anchor close to the hospitable bungalow of the Begum Serai factory. Here again our adventures were the source of considerable amusement, and a running coolie was sent into the station with a letter for Mrs. Melville, to allay any anxiety that she might feel, and also to prepare relays of horses on the road, for we had sixty-five miles to drive, and consequently thirteen horses were necessary.

The following evening saw us safe once more in Mozuf-ferpore ; where our movements had been the subject of much speculation, for Melville's brother-in-law had been telegraphing in all directions to know what had become of him ; and Mrs. Melville had in consequence been seriously alarmed. The only practical result was, that we both got a wigging from Coldham the Commissioner, for absenting ourselves from our district without leave.

In due time the police report was forwarded from Monghyr to Blake, for information, stating that two Europeans calling themselves Tirhoot Hakims had come on shore at Barheeia (the name of the village), and that they, the police, had furnished them with palanquins and everything necessary to go on to Barh. For some time after this we were a good deal pestered with inquiries as to how we had enjoyed Calcutta.

I think the adventure is worth relating, as showing to what straits Europeans may be reduced in a highly cultivated and civilized part of Bengal, if thrown entirely upon native resources.

My next journey took place a month later, when I had again to cross the Ganges to get to Patna for my examination. The river had begun to subside ; but yet it was very different in appearance to the series of streams and sandbanks I had traversed in the previous cold weather ; and by making a tour of the large island, which was now only just above water, a boat could go across at one stretch. There was a favourable breeze blowing, and I quite enjoyed the sail. There was a pleasant party at Alison's hospitable table that evening, for several young civilians had come in from the neighbouring districts, and my starvation trip was a source of considerable merriment.

In these days the examination for the whole province under Coldham's jurisdiction was conducted by the Local Committee at Bankipore, consisting of Coldham, Lawson, Alison, and a native Deputy Magistrate. The papers, however, were issued by a Central Committee in Calcutta. There were four papers in all, one containing twelve questions on Revenue Law, Rent Law, and all work done on the Collectorate side ; another containing a similar number on Criminal Law and all work done on the Magistrate's side of the office ; a piece of prose to be translated into very grammatical Hindustani ; and a second piece to be dictated into Hindustani, to be written down by a native clerk. We also had to hear the record of a case read out, and write a decision upon it, and converse with two classes of natives—an educated man·and a· rustic, and read off some ordinary documents written in shikust, or the running hand in the vernacular.

The Revenue was much the tougher of the two law papers, as it embraced a great variety of subjects—among others, the regulations for the Permanent Settlement of Lord Cornwallis; the law of resumptions by Government of illegal grants; the law for the collection of the revenue; . the Excise, Opium, and Salt laws; the Stamp Acts; the law of Batwarra, or division of estates; the law of the acquisition of land for public purposes; and the great Rent Law Act of 1859, which had only recently come into working; and, though mentioned last, by no means least, the Rules of Practice based upon these laws and framed by the Board of Revenue.

The Criminal Paper embraced the new Penal and Criminal Procedure Codes, the new Police Code, the Cattle Trespass Act, the Ferry Laws, ·the Municipal Act, Railway Act, and the Law of Evidence, then Act II. of 1855. The first two of these Codes I think I knew pretty nearly by heart, as this was the only sure way of being able to answer the questions in this paper, the very words of the Act being required by the Examiners. *E.g.;* "When is a person said to use force to another?" In answer to such a question it was necessary to give the definition in the Penal Code word for word, and a precious long one it is. I insert it here as a specimen.

"Sec. 349.—A person is said to use force to another if· he causes motion, change of motion, or cessation of motion to that other, or if he causes to any substance such motion, change of motion, or cessation of motion as brings that substance into contact with any part of that other's body, or with anything which that other is wearing or carrying, or with anything so situated that such contact affects that other's sense of feeling; provided that the person causing the motion, or change of motion, or cessation of motion causes that motion, change of motion, or cessation of motion in one of the three ways hereinafter described :

"*First.* By his own bodily power.

"*Secondly.* By disposing any substance in such a manner that the motion, or change or cessation of motion, takes place without any further act on his part, or on the part of any other person.

"*Thirdly.* By inducing any animal to move, to change its motion, or cease to move."

We examinees used to chafe a good deal at these questions, saying, "What is the use of asking them, when we always have the books at our side for reference in actual practice?" But no doubt the fact of having to learn our laws like this was of great use in making us familiar with them, and enabled us to know *where* to look when we had the books beside us. The questions, possibly, were not always very intelligently set; but the mere reading for the examination, though distasteful, was beneficial.

In the Vernacular Examination the insistance on grammatical accuracy was carried to an almost absurd pitch. There is a wretched particle "ne" in Hindustani, which spoils all fluency and neatness in long sentences, if used in accordance with the exigences of grammar, and which is disregarded freely by native clerks in writing orders and reports, but neglect of which brought many a glibly talk-ing and writing examinee to grief in the translation paper. The paragraph set for dictation consisted generally of long and involved English sentences, and seemed to me as a rule more difficult than that given for translation ; but as what emanated from the mouth of the young " Hakim " was taken down by a subservient native clerk only too anxious to make the result as good as possible, in many cases this was not so trying a test as it was intended to be. It was amusing to watch how civil all we examinees were to this underling ; and it was very important that those who dictated towards the end of the list should be so, for by that time he had got an inkling of what the English really meant, and could be of powerful assistance.

The examinations are now conducted in a much stricter way ; and the Local Committees give marks only in the subject of conversation, all the papers being looked over by the Central Committee, in Calcutta ; but at this time everything was done in a very friendly way. Lawson superintended my conversation with the Deputy Magis-trate who represented the educated gentleman in my case. He had, as I knew, a small boat ; and I directed the con-versation to this, and asked him if he would lend it to Lawson, or if he were afraid, Lawson being stout, to say the least of it. Lawson here interposed very good humouredly, said I conversed very well, and gave me full marks.

Two days after both law papers were finished, I went over to see Lawson in the early morning, and found him engaged in what he called looking over them. Full marks for each paper were 160; and to pass, it was necessary to get 100. Lawson's plan was, to see who had got 97, or thereabouts, and give them an additional four or five marks each, so as to bring them over the ·100. Alison and the Deputy Magistrate had already marked the papers. carefully and conscientiously no doubt, and it remained for Coldham and Lawson to do the same, when an average would be struck by adding the marks given by all the examiners together, and dividing by four. Lawson's theory was, that it was a waste of labour to make four men look over one paper; and that if a man got 97 marks he must know enough about it to make him fit to pass, and therefore, as far as he was concerned, he passed him. It so happened that I had plenty of marks in both papers, so that I did not want any assistance; but it occurred to me that it would be rather hard for other examinees, if members of other Local Committees did not happen to hold the same views.

The reading documents in the vernacular was also easily got over in these days; but now is the greatest stumbling block to examinees, for instead of having to stammer through two or three lines, as I had, they have to write out the whole thing in the Roman character. The shikust Hindustani writing is exceedingly difficult to learn to read, and it requires long and constant practice to do it fluently. On the whole, my few days of examination were very pleasant, and I felt pretty confident that I had passed; for though all the proceedings of the Locals had to be confirmed by the Centrals in Calcutta, yet this was a mere matter of form, and it was only a question of waiting until they should choose to hold a meeting and order the names of those who had passed to be inserted in the *Calcutta Gazette*.

Rawlinson had passed the First, or Lower Standard at the previous examination, and was now in for the Second, or Higher Standard, in which the papers set were on the same subjects, but supposed to be more difficult, and in which an examination in Bengali was included. He was now empowered to try a larger range of cases, and could inflict a fine of 200 rs., or £20, and sentence to a term of six months' imprisonment ; and he could also adjudicate cases under the rent law. In fact, I felt he was ahead of me ; and as he was also now drawing 50 rs. a month, or £60 a 'year, more than I was, I was sensible already of the importance of the time I had lost in coming round the Cape, instead of by the overland route ; and in dawdling in Calcutta.

Further too, his suit with Miss Coldham appeared to be prospering, and he seemed in a fair way to a very successful start.

I felt rather sad on my return journey to the trial of my everlasting assault cases, and looked eagerly forward to the report of the Central Committee ; but they were lazy, and no mention was made of us in the *Gazette* until January. I was afterwards told that one of the senior members of the Central Committee could not be got to attend the meeting, hence the delay, which was altogether uncalled for and most annoying to all of us examinees.

However, in the meantime the cold weather came on ; there were no more dreary hot afternoons to lounge hopelessly through; and on the 16th of November commenced the great Sonepore fair, with which is combined the pleasantest race meeting in the world. This has been described in detail by the able author of "Letters from a Competition Wallah"; but this year was the last occasion in which it may be said really to have been sacred to the enjoyment of the European inhabitants of the surrounding districts, for in succeeding years the railway was open, and the European society was quadrupled.

I will shortly state that we Europeans took up our quarters in a large grove of trees bordering on an open plain, in which lay the race-course. The whole grove was filled with tents, one wide way being kept clear as a sort of street through the whole. Blake had asked Percival and myself to join his camp, as he had plenty of tents at his disposal; and this was a very agreeable arrangement for us. Sonepore itself lies at the point of confluence of the river Gunduk with the Ganges. The Gunduk separates Tirhoot from the neighbouring district of Chuprah, so that we Tirhoot officials had only this stream,—a broad and rapid one it is true,—between ourselves and our own jurisdiction. The route to it was down the Hajeepore road, by Gooriah Ghât, the place where I had slept on my first journey up to Mozufferpore. Gooriah now presented a very different scene to that occasion, as all the accommodation was taken up, and innumerable vehicles quite filled up the road in front of the bungalow. Blake spent a night there *en famille*, but most of us merely stopped to change horses.

Percival and I left Mozufferpore before daylight, and

reached Gooriah just in time to find Blake installing his family in their barouche. They seemed rather crowded and somewhat fretful, and I felt glad that I was unattached, at any rate for this occasion; and I think Percival for the moment did not regret that his family were some 7,000 or 8,000 miles away. We offered Blake a seat in our dog-cart, which he accepted with some alacrity, telling his wife that he would go on ahead with us and see that the boat was ready at the crossing. This, probably, was not his sole reason; but yet it was really a good one, for the resources of the ferry were completely overtaxed on this occasion; and without a certain display of authority and European energy, hours might elapse before a crossing could be effected.

The ghât presented a scene of indescribable confusion. Elephants were being urged into the water, having been first divested of their loads, in order that they might swim across under the guidance of their mahouts. When an elephant swims, he keeps a very small piece of his back above water, or else sufficiently near the surface to enable the mahout to stand upon it and direct his movements. They are very nervous animals, and easily lose their heads. The day previously one had got frightened, refused to obey its mahout, and swam about without approaching either bank, until it sank and was drowned. Its body had been washed on to a shallow; and we could now see it, with numerous vultures and other birds of prey hovering in the neighbourhood, waiting until the tough hide should be sufficiently decomposed to become penetrable by their beaks.

There were horses, cattle, and sheep in numbers, buggies and native carts, and native goods, and European baggage, tents, and tent furniture, waiting in quantities which it seemed impossible should ever get across. However, on Blake's appearance, a boat which had just returned from the opposite shore was kept clear for him and for us ; and by the time we had got our dog-cart on board, the barouche with the rest of his party appeared. Under the Hakim's eye the ferrymen worked hard; and we were soon on our way to the other side, whereas an unfortunate native passenger with any baggage would probably have had to wait for hours. As we drove up the street of canvas dwellings on the other side, from every tent already occupied friendly faces looked out and friendly voices shouted a welcome. Our servants had gone on the previous day with our baggage, so that we found all comforts ready.

Sonepore fair, of course, originates in a religious ceremony, which consists in bathing at the point of confluence of the Gunduk with the Ganges, at the very moment that the November moon is at the full. Such bathing washes away all previous sins ; but it must be done at the exact moment, and to this end crowds assemble and await the signal given by a Brahmin, who sits on a small sand hillock overlooking the spot. He is supposed to give the signal a few seconds before, in order to give as many bathers as possible time to get into the water ; and the crowd at the moment he gives it is a very extraordinary sight. People of both sexes, of all ages and ranks (Hindus, of course), make a simultaneous rush to the water. Many accidents take place, and occasionally some are drowned; but to be drowned on such an occasion is about equal to being crushed under the wheel of Juggernath's car, and the fate of any one so dying cannot be considered a cause of sorrow.

The Brahmins, on the one hand, like a death or two, as it adds to the fame and sanctity of the ceremony ; but on the other, they are afraid that too many would lead to disagreeable restrictions on the part of the officials of the unsympathetic British Government, who, as it is, place policemen here to keep order and prevent all accidents, as far as may be possible. There are too, I am sorry to say, many impious thieves, who take advantage of the frenzied fervour of those who are anxious to wash away their sins, to ply their calling very successfully.

We Europeans further inland, in our pleasant canvas town under the shade of the grove, took little notice of these things, but devoted ourselves to Anglo-Saxon pleasures with very remarkable energy. The amusements were of a nature similar to those described at the Mozufferpore race meeting ; but as nobody's tent was very far from anybody else's, and as everybody had brought a large amount of good cheer which he wished to share with his friends, the amount of eating and drinking was very great. I never saw so much hospitality pressed into ten days.

One additional thing to do, was a visit to the elephant and horse fairs, the latter being accompanied with some risk, as every other animal seemed to be as dangerous as a man-eating tiger. They were mostly blindfolded, and their fore and hind feet securely tied ; but not unfrequently they managed to break loose, and then the fighting and kicking and biting became a serious matter.

The ball-room was in the race stand, a masonry building of some pretensions; and as it possessed a good polished wood floor, and this season was not overcrowded, the dances were very enjoyable. The supper and the utensils wherewith to eat it were provided from the race fund; and the whole thing was on a much grander and more finished scale than that at Mozufferpore.

The weather was lovely, and the nights bright moonlight; and to me ten more enjoyable days cannot be imagined. I had, of course, no cares of state; but Blake had a mass of correspondence forwarded daily, as had all the other District Collectors here assembled. Poor Melville had to rush back in the middle of the enjoyments to take up a serious dacoity case, which some most disobliging dacoits had chosen to commit on the second day of the meeting; and as he had to leave all his family fully established in the canvas town, with a good deal of his household furniture, his bungalow must have looked very bare, and all his surroundings have been melancholy. He doubtless was better pleased than most of us when we all returned to our respective homes and occupations.

In December, Blake went out bachelor-wise into camp, and took me with him, to learn something of district work, theoretically; practically, for company's sake, and to give me a chance of some shooting. I know that I did little else but shoot large quantities of duck and black partridges, and occasionally found the time rather long when Blake was getting through heavy bundles of correspondence sent out to him by post, and in which I could be of no use.

Tirhoot is a very pleasant district for camping out, with numerous pleasant groves of trees under which to pitch tents; but, as a fact, there is not so much actual work to be done here as in the districts of Eastern Bengal, where the great rivers change the whole face of the country in their neighbourhood, one may say, almost annually, and constant re-settlements of the land are necessary.

At length, in January came the news that I had passed by the Lower Standard, and I was empowered now to try various criminal cases of a nature that I could not take up before; and I could pass sentences of six months' imprisonment, with or without labour, and a fine up to 200 rs. Technically speaking, I was invested with "special powers," and on the Collectorate side, I could try cases under the Rent-law Act X. of 1859. Further, my pay was increased by 50 rs. a month, making it 450 rs. monthly, or £540 a year. I had to undergo a further examination of a more difficult nature in the same subjects, and also in Bengali in April.

All this might have come to me some two months sooner, had it not been for the laziness of the member of the Central Committee above mentioned; and I had very little time to get much Bengali ready by April next, the more so as my work increased with my increased powers. My resolution was to work very hard; but alas! in the middle of January came the Mozufferpore races, all the more enjoyable now that I knew everybody, and in February Blake had a shooting party to the Terai, and asked me to go with him. The races passed off much as those of the previous year; but the jungle trip was my first experience of the kind, and I looked forward to it with the keenest anticipations of enjoyment. We had fifty miles to drive to the Nepaulese frontier, where all roads ended and we had to take to horseback. Our party consisted of Blake and a friend, Colville, Macpherson, and myself; and we started in two batches, Colville and myself in the early morning, and the rest later on in the day, they taking on the various relays of horses as we left them at each place.

I think it may be laid down as a rule, that young men in India who have any horses at all, have vicious ones, and I was no exception to this rule. Two that I had on the road were splendid goers when once started, but the difficulty was to start. The one generally refused to move at first,—I had bought her at Sonepore,—but once off, went very fast, and never tired. It required very careful coaxing and management to get her off. The other was only too anxious to start, and gave no time to get into the vehicle to which she was attached; the only plan was, to creep up behind, without allowing her to suspect any designing person of a desire to enter the dog-cart, and be content with being able to get one foot on the step. The moment she felt the pressure on the shafts, away she would go; and if checked, became very violent,—she was a very big, powerful animal,—and generally upset whatever she might be drawing into the nearest ditch.

I understood them both, and Colville understood all horses,—though he rather chafed at having to give in to

their caprices in this way,—so we got on capitally, and
arrived at our rendezvous,—a hospitable planter's bungalow, at the very edge of the district,—in excellent time.
We expected the others some three hours later, in time
to go on all together to our first camp before dark. But
evening came on, and there were no signs of them. I
began to get a little anxious; and as Colville and I knew
that none of the trio behind were good at the management of horses, we were afraid they might have broken
down altogether. Our host was the only person pleased,
as it gave him the certainty of company for one evening
at any rate. We had half finished our dinner, which had
been keep waiting some time, when the sound of wheels
was heard at the door; and on hastening out we found
our three friends, not in the best of tempers.

"You're a pretty fellow to trust to for dáks!" growled
Macpherson.

"Never mind," said our host; "don't say anything
about your misadventures until you have had some
dinner, and then you can grumble as you please."

So our repast was resumed; and in the genial presence
of bottled beer, accidents that had appeared simply irritating before, now began to assume somewhat of the ludicrous;
and finally we got a good-humoured account of the details.
It appeared that the first-mentioned of the two mares
had shown signs of an unwillingness to start, and Macpherson had in an ill-judged way used the whip. This
decided her not to move, and she had stubbornly resisted
all efforts to do so for a whole hour. At length the syce's
plan was adopted, of leaning with all his weight against

one shaft; when the mare shifted a little, the other syce, belonging to the horse recently taken out, began to lean against the other shaft; and so, as she got no ease standing still, she finally elected to go on, and carried them through the dâk splendidly.

At the next dâk, the syce had warned them of the peculiarities of the big mare; but Macpherson, who was to take the back seat of the dog-cart, was not sufficiently quick in jumping in, and as she plunged forward lost his hold and was left on his back in the middle of the road. Blake, who was driving, had to pull up, whereat the mare became violent, backed them all into the ditch, and turned out him and his friend, and all the guns and things they had with them. She also fell down herself. They promptly sat on her head and undid the harness, and hoped to get her out without any breakage; but just at the last moment, she gave one kick and sent one of the shafts flying. Nobody, however, was hurt, and a specimen of the all-useful bamboo was procured and tied on to serve as a shaft; but then it was found impossible to harness her again, and after many vain attempts, it was decided to re-harness the other mare, and trust that she would consent to start. She was somewhat subdued with her previous work, and now an obedient, instead of a capricious servant, for she went off at once, and did her second stage as well as the first.

"And now," said Blake, "what do you mean, sir, by endangering your superior officer's life in this way?"

"I can lend my superior officer horses," I replied, "but I can't give him understanding how to manage them."

Every man stands up for his own animals; but. my remark was not justified by the facts. Blake was much too good-tempered to be angry, however; and I may here mention the end of these animals. The first I sold soon afterwards at the price I paid for her. The big mare I kept obstinately for some two years. She smashed one dog-cart of mine afterwards; and I finally lent her to a friend, whom she upset, and falling down herself too, tried to kick the shaft away as on this occasion; her leg however came in contact with the step of the dog-cart instead, and she died from the effects of the injury.

The fact is, that with us horses were always driven before they were properly broken; and I mention the above to show the sort of thing that constantly occurred when driving long stages. Sometimes the escapes were marvellous. Soon after this, a friend of mine was driving his sister and her little girl over a bridge where a weak bamboo railing served as a parapet. In crossing, the horse took fright at something, and, refusing to go on, began to back against the railing. He saw the danger and said to his sister, "Get out and take the child." She jumped out; but as he was handing her the child, the railing gave way, and he and the little girl, cart, and horse were precipitated into the water, some fifteen feet below. The sister, in relating the story to me, said she recollected nothing more till she found herself in the water,—which was fortunately only between three and four feet deep,— groping for the child, and saw her brother doing the same. He finally caught her by the hair and handed her to his sister. The final result of all this was, that beyond the bending of one step of the dog-cart, and the ducking and fright, no damage was done. The villagers of the neighbourhood came to their assistance, and they were able actually to re-harness the horse and drive on.

The next day we rode on to our camp, some twenty miles across the frontier. Blake had a pass from the Nepaulese authorities, so we entered that country without hindrance and found our camp in the afternoon on the banks of the Bhagmatty, a river flowing down from the Nepaulese hills, now close by, and with big-tree forests all round us. We had four tents, Colville's being the largest ; but we used that also for feeding purposes. This was my first experience of a jungle expedition, and I was quite astonished at the army of followers that seemed necessary for our comfort and convenience. Of course, everything for eating and drinking purposes had to be brought with us, as nothing except water was procurable on the spot. We had too, forty-eight elephants,—a very large number for a private party,—and these necessitated ninety-six men to look after them, and conveyances for their food also. As it got dark, and the various fires flickering caused fantastic lights and shadows among the tall trees, the scene was picturesque indeed ; and it was too delightful to be lulled to sleep by the sound of the river running over its pebbly bottom—a sound never heard further down in the plains, where a stone is never seen. It was cheery too to be roused in the morning by the shrill crow of the jungle cock (our game fowl), which are very numerous here, and to feel that a long day's sport was before one.

But we did not make a start before 10 a.m., for first

of all the elephants had to be washed like babies. Each was taken down to the river, where, at the orders of its mahout, it lay down in the shallow water, and instead of being soaped, was holy-stoned all over, and then allowed to have a good wallow to wash itself clean. This done, the sun soon dried them, and ornamental fringes were painted with whitening on their foreheads and on their noses, or rather the places where their noses would have been if they had not had trunks instead. At length all was ready, five staunch elephants were chosen, from the rest to carry our howdahs, eight smaller ones were detached to get forage for the rest, and with the remaining thirty-five we formed line, and commenced to crash through the forest.

The trees were tall and the underwood not so very thick at our starting point, so the work was comparatively easy. Almost immediately, a peacock flew up in front of me. I had my ball-gun in my hand, and did not fire, but put it down and took up my shot-gun, when almost directly a beautiful spotted deer went bounding away to my right, and was well out of sight before I had time to pick up my rifle and bring it to bear. This was puzzling, but very exciting, as no one knew what game might be sighted at any moment, from a snipe to a tiger. Presently the jungle got more difficult; and it was then wonderful to see the intelligent manner in which the elephants worked their way through it, and the consideration those which carried howdahs showed for their riders. They would push bodily down small trees, *i.e.*, under thirty feet high, by putting a forefoot against them and swaying backwards and forwards until the trunk yielded to the weighty pressure ; at the command of the mahout they would put their trunks up and break off any branch that would otherwise knock off the head or the hat of the occupant of the howdah ; or, if a mass of creepers clinging to the forest trees barred the way, would stop and patiently pull them down in detail until progress was possible.

All this, of course, rendered it difficult to keep line, and yet considerable abuse fell to the lot of those whom Blake's eye caught lagging behind. He commanded our party, and was himself under the guidance of our "shikarree," a wiry old Nepaulee, whom we all treated with great deference in the hope that civility would induce him to show us an extra tiger or two. The first day's sport resulted in a few deer, jungle fowl, and other small game ; and we sat down to our dinner and a rubber afterwards by no means dissatisfied. For on our return to camp we received information that a cow had been killed by a tiger not very far off, and we hoped to get sight of him on the morrow. Large quantities of cattle are driven into the forest during the dry weather for pasture ; but though they pay nothing for their food the losses by tigers must cost the herdsmen dear.

The next morning the order was, to fire at nothing but tiger ; and rather wearisome work I found it. If the scent were very hot, then it was easy enough to refrain ; but beating as we did for hour after hour through apparently interminable jungle, alternating between tall trees with tangled undergrowth where it was dark at midday, and comparatively open places covered with tall grass from sixteen to twenty feet high, it seemed hopeless to expect to hit upon one particular animal, and the precaution of not firing appeared useless. , And then, too, every other species of game seemed more plentiful than ever, as it always does on these occasions.

At length, after some four hours' hard beating, we had just crashed through a dark bit of forest and were emerging on an open grassy bit of small extent, when my elephant showed signs of uneasiness and gave that shrill scream called "trumpeting," which was taken up by the rest. My mahout pointed silently to the tall grass waving sinuously to my right front and just before Colville, as if some large animal were moving quietly along at the bottom. Colville was peering down as if hard staring would enable him to pierce through the sixteen feet of grass covering, and my chuprassie in the hind seat of the howdah began to cough nervously, and said, " Bagh hoga khudawind." (It will be a tiger, my lord.)

It was very exciting. We all pressed on. Suspicion became certainty, as the sinuous wave became more rapid. And as the grass got thinner on the edge of the trees we were now approaching, on the other side of the open bit, a fine tiger became visible, trotting quietly along; and we all blazed at him, almost simultaneously. He gave no sign, but disappeared in the forest underwood. We all believed, at the moment, that we had hit him. The wish was doubtless father to the thought, and the word to "chase" was given. Our line got much scattered in our eagerness, and I became somewhat separated from the rest.

We went crashing through the thick forest, when suddenly I came upoñ a group of dead trees, and on every tree was a huge serpent, some coiled asleep on a withered branch, and others half hanging down, as if in search of prey. In our excitement we had got amongst them without perceiving it ; and as many of them were on branches just on a level with my howdah, the sensation was not pleasant; in fact it was "creepy," and I felt inclined to compress as much of my person as possible inside my howdah, and I have no doubt my mahout and chuprassie felt the same. I have never seen anything like it since, and we three were the only members of our party who saw it. We stood for a moment until we caught the sounds of the others breaking through the jungle in the distance, and hastened to join them, leaving our serpents *in statu quo.*

On coming up with the others, I tried to get them interested about this ; but they were much too excited about the tiger, and I could command no attention. The serpents were doubtless of the Python species, of which there are a good many in the Terai forests ; but it was very exceptional to see so many collected together and in such positions. It was horribly weird, and the impression it produced on me was lasting.

We went on chasing our tiger for some two hours ; and then gave him up as a bad job. This is a veracious history, and I must admit, that, whether we hit him or not, we did not bag that tiger. Barring the surrounding scenery and the subjective excitement, the incident was tame enough, for the animal trotted as coolly away as if he had been a calf or a donkey, and quite accustomed to the proximity of human beings. It was vexatious to miss him, as both Colville and Blake were good shots, and in this very afternoon I saw Macpherson, who was not a good shot, put a bullet through the neck of a peacock that was sitting on the dead branch of a tree at nearly 100 yards' distance, and shortly after kill at one shot a spotted deer that was bounding along at a great pace, and certainly eighty or ninety yards from him. These were both flukes, doubtless; but we wished that one of them had come off on the tiger.

During the remaining eight days that we shot, we did not see another tiger, though we had plenty of " khabar" (news). Indeed one day a herdsman came running in to tell us that a tiger had just attacked one of his herd, and that he had struck him with a bamboo, and frightened him off. We saw the cow all bleeding from claw wounds, but never got a sight of the tiger. The intrepidity of the herdsman struck me very much ; but I suppose the tiger could not have been very hungry, or he would not have yielded his prey so easily.

One amusing incident was our whole line of forty elephants being put to flight by a small pig scarcely a foot long. We were beating across a wide expanse of open grass, and in very good line, when a shrill grunt was heard, and something seemed to charge our very centre. Blake's elephant turned tail, and a panic seized all the rest ; with some difficulty we got them round and went on again, and the same thing was repeated three times. At length Blake got a sight of the small creature and shot him; and as he was hoisted on to a pad elephant, it seemed too ridiculous that such a thing, not more than a foot long, should three times have put to flight forty elephants and five sahibs with guns and innumerable followers : and it was a good proof of what terribly nervous things elephants can be. Colville moralized in a melancholy way over his death, and regretted bitterly that he had not been allowed to come to maturity in a ridable country.

And now it was time to leave the happy hunting grounds and return to our workaday life. We had had very inferior sport, for the very good reason that we had come up much too early : the grass jungle and underwood was green and thick, and had not been thinned at all by the fires which always occur later on in the season. But we had had a most pleasant ten days, and finished our party in the very sincere hope that we should again join for a similar purpose. The journey back afforded no special excitement ; my obstreperous horses had been replaced by others, and no upsets occurred.

The morning after my return I received a note from Melville, stating that an addition to his family had necessitated his being up all night, and asking me to go to office and take his seat for the day. I was too glad to be of such importance and assumed his place with a certain sense of dignity. Cases already commenced by him had of course to be postponed ; but I ordered the new ones to be brought up, and began to give orders for the issue of summonses, etc. The Sherishtadar here addressed me in an under-tone, and very definitely pointed out that my orders were illegal, as I had not been empowered by Government to receive new complaints, but only to try such cases as were specially made over to me. In fact I was acting altogether without jurisdiction. " Oh," I said, " it's only for to-day." Not a very logical reply ; but he acquiesced with a shrug of the shoulders, which meant to say that he had divested himself of responsibility. Nobody else objected, and no doubt many persons came in on illegal summonses and warrants ; but no harm was done, as no one else appeared to discover the technical flaw.

CHAPTER VII.

ASSISTANT MAGISTRATE IN CHARGE OF DURBHUNGAH.

TAKE OVER CHARGE FROM MY PREDECESSOR.—BUTWARRAS.—A DIFFICULT CASE.—SECOND EXAMINATION.—VOLUNTEER CAVALRY. —PUBLIC MEETING.—" IZZAT" ACCIDENT AT COURT.—INVESTED WITH FULL POWERS.—A NATIVE NOBLEMAN.

HOWEVER my importance became real some few days afterwards, for on the 13th of March I received the official announcement that "His Honour the Lieut.-Governor of Bengal had been pleased to appoint me to the charge of the subdivision of Durbhungah, and had also empowered me to hold the preliminary inquiry into cases triable by the Court of Session, and commit or hold to bail persons to take their trial before such Court, in accordance with Sec. XXXVIII. of the Criminal Procedure Code." This special empowering was rendered necessary by the fact that I was only a subordinate magistrate of the 1st class, and had not been invested with the full powers of a magistrate, as I had not passed my second examination.

It seems odd that an official not ·yet considered fit to take cognizance of all magisterial cases arising within his local jurisdiction, should be appointed the sole criminal authority in charge of an area of over 2,000 square miles in extent; but yet this was by no means unusual, as there was a scarcity of full-power officers to take charge of appointments of this sort, the more so as Government was extending the system, and a great number of new subdivisional jurisdictions were being created in each district. At this time Tirhoot, with its 6,343 square miles, had only one, and all criminal cases had to be instituted here or at the head quarters, which caused great inconvenience to many suitors, in consequence of the long distances they had to come. But five or six years subsequently, this one was multiplied into six, Durbhungah itself being split up into three ;] and I now learn that it has been elevated into a separate district.

The head-quarters of the subdivision were only at this 'moment in course of being established at Durbhungah, for heretofore they had been at a place called Buheyra, some twenty-seven miles further to the south-east ; some official apparently having looked at the map and thought that this spot seemed central. Geographically speaking, it may have been so ; but it was far away from all big towns or even large villages, and consequently nearly all the business transacted in the Court appertained to people who came from a long distance.

When the estate of the Maharajah of Durbhungah came under the management of the Court of Wards, and the European manager came to reside partly at Durbhungah, he found it exceedingly inconvenient to have the Magistrate's Court so far away ; and he was able also truly to represent that Durbhungah was the largest town in the Tirhoot District, and that it was only reasonable the Court should be located there. He was further able to offer a small building as a residence for the Magistrate, and.

another for his Court. Government had just accepted these proposals, and the officer at present in charge was engaged in moving himself and all his paraphernalia of office from Buheyra to Durbhungah.

He was a young fellow,—Lewis by name,—in the uncovenanted service, and had just received an appointment in the new police, which he was most anxious to take up, so he had written and implored me to relieve him as soon as possible. My next examination was to begin on the 6th of April, and Blake suggested that I need not join until after that was over ; but Lewis had to be examined himself, and as we must both be away some third person would have to be in charge during our absence ; and as I was keen to get to more important work, I determined to gratify him and myself, and go there without delay.

My traps were very soon packed, and three ordinary native carts sufficed for their carriage. The furniture was not bulky, and consisted of a bed (which I could carry myself, if necessary), one toilette table (considered a sign of extra refinement), one writing table of antique design, purchased in Mozufferpore, one cane arm-chair and three ordinary chairs, glass, crockery, etc., for about six people, a few sheets and towels, and one book-case, value about eight shillings. My books and a howdah were the heaviest articles to be conveyed.

The distance to Durbhungah was about thirty-five miles, there being four unbridged rivers to cross ; but they gave little trouble in the dry season, though in the rains they increased not only in size, but in number, for they became seven. All things considered, I gave the carts two days' start ; and on the 19th, or six days after I had received the orders, was on the road thither myself.

The new Assistant Superintendent of Police, an Irishman who had found his way out to India, viâ Australia, because he had nothing better to do, and who scarcely knew one word of Hindustani, accompanied me. He was a very good fellow, and very amusing, though it would be some time before he would be of much use. Shortly before reaching Durbhungah we picked up, at short intervals, two pieces of wood, which proved to be the tops of two of my chairs, and this augured badly for the state of my traps ; but on reaching my destination, about 11 a.m., we found nothing lost, though everything was very thoroughly impregnated with dust.

I had ordered my servants to stop at the dâk bungalow, which I found to be of a better class than those ordinarily provided by Government. This had originally been erected by the planters in this portion of the district, or almost entirely at their expense, and had been made over to Government on condition of its being kept in repair. It was consequently on a more liberal scale than usual, and was situated just outside the moat surrounding the Rajah's palace, and well away from the native bazaar, which was a great consideration.

After breakfast, I went through the native town to the residence that had been proposed for me by the manager of the Durbhungah estate ; but it looked so dismal, was so far from the Cutcherry, which was in the palace grounds, and so disagreeably situated, that I determined not to live there, but to get on as best I could in the dâk bungalow, which I found, on inquiry, was nearly always empty, and the rent of which would be only 1 r. per day, equal to £3 a month. Of course I ran the risk of being compelled to turn out if there were a large influx of travellers; but I thought, that was not likely, and at any rate determined not to be anxious about it beforehand. Lewis came in to dinner in the evening. He had only just completed moving the office paraphernalia into Durbhungah, and said he would give over charge the next day. He seemed quite delighted at the prospect of getting away.

The poor policeman was struck down with fever, and could not join us. He had caught it in Assam, and was subject to severe attacks of it. To the east of the dâk bungalow there was a large expanse of low ground, one of the depressions I have spoken of as existing in Tirhoot, which was never entirely free from water, and in the rainy season was covered to the depth of several feet. Poor Doyle (the policeman) had remarked in the morning that it looked "feverish," and his foreboding in his own case proved unfortunately too true. The next morning he was a little better, but very weak, and so strongly of opinion that the place would kill him that he got into a palanquin and went straight back to Mozufferpore. He never returned.

About noon I went over to the building allotted as a Cutcherry by the manager, and found it surrounded by a large crowd outside, and crammed to suffocation within. It consisted of one centre room, about eighteen feet square, and two small closets on each side, about ten and eight feet square respectively. On two sides were verandahs, with slanting roofs of tiled thatch, supported by masonry pillars. The masonry roof was surrounded by an ornamental balustrade, also of masonry. The centre room was, of course, the Court room, and was furnished with a "takhtaposh" (wooden platform), about six inches high, on which was placed a dirty old folding table (commonly called a camp table), and on each side of it a wooden bench for the clerks. The little room, or closet, on the right was called the record room, and the English clerk sat there and prepared the returns and registers, while all round were "almirahs" (cupboards), full of records of cases, etc., in the vernacular, and one containing the papers connected with the English correspondence of the office. The room on the left was màde the Treasury.

At this time much business was not transacted in Subdivisional Treasuries, though a great deal more was soon afterwards thrown upon them, and for the present I had only to take over charge of the stamps, and the money received on account of previous sale of stamps, deposits in rent suits, and criminal fines. All Court fees in India are collected by stamps, the plaints, replies, and other documents being written on paper bearing the stamp of the value required by law. These were sold at my office ; and one of the most wearisome parts of my duty as a subdivisional officer, was counting these when they arrived from head-quarters on my indent ; for supposing any deficiency should occur in the accounts, I was held personally responsible for the difference. On this occasion a new stock had just been received, and it occupied some two hours counting them—Lewis and myself and three clerks and two policemen of the Treasury police guard all counting as hard as we could. The stamps are made up in parcels of 100 at the Government Stationery Office in Calcutta, and were so received by us from the head-quarters at Mozufferpore ; but it was necessary to count each stamp paper, in order to be safe, so we handed them out in similar bundles to each enumerator. The policemen counted slowly and badly, and were constantly arriving at results of ninety-eight, ninety-nine, and 101, instead of the exact 100, which necessitated the recounting of the bundles, with the result always of finding them correct. On one occasion, however, I recollect finding thirty-two stamps, of the value of 4s. each, short ; and the Deputy Collector in charge of the Treasury at Mozufferpore had to make good that amount in money, as he had neglected to see them counted before sending them out to me, though there was no proof that the correct number had ever been received from the head office in Calcutta. These stamp papers were sold to licensed stamp vendors in the town, paid by a discount of four per cent. on their purchases, for whom I opened my stamp shop twice a month, and by them to suitors ; and in order to have some sort of check on their being used for fraudulent purposes, the vendors were required by law to endorse on each paper sold the date of sale and the name of the purchaser. Their books also were liable to inspection on my demand. I also sold postage and receipt stamps.

This over, we went into the record room, where I contented myself with looking into the cupboards and glancing at the so-called library ; and then Lewis and I signed two reports to be sent to Blake, one for the Magisterial and one for the Collectorate side, to the effect that we had respectively received and given over charge of the sub-division of Durbhungah. Lewis then went off to prepare for his departure, and I entered upon the duties of office. My Court establishment, I found, consisted of the following members :—

One English-knowing writer, or sherishtadar, at	. £3	10	monthly.
One clerk, or mohurrir, knowing Hindustani only, at	2	10	,,
One nazir, Treasury officer, etc.	2	0	,,
One clerk, or mohurrir	1	6	,,
Two ditto, ditto	1	0	,,
One potdar, or money-weigher, assistant to nazir	0	12	,,
One duftry chuprassie (pen-mender, etc.)	0	12	,,
One chuprassie	0	10	,,

The second of these was really the most important man in the office, and had been called sherishtadar until the recent change which allowed subdivisional officers English clerks, these latter being fully occupied with English correspon-dence and the preparation of the English registers and returns. The duties of the second clerk were to read over to the Magistrate the reports received daily from all sources in the vernacular, to record his orders, and to make them over to the police court inspector on the Criminal side, and to the nazir on the Collectorate side, for trans-mission, either by post or special messenger, also to bring forward all the cases in their due turn, and to prepare or supervise the keeping up of all the registers and returns not connected with the Treasury, many of which would be afterwards translated into English by the English clerk—

no light work, as on the Collectorate side alone he had to keep up forty-nine registers; and the returns monthly, quarterly, and yearly were even more numerous, to say nothing of those on the Magisterial side. The nazir had charge of the treasury, stamps, etc., and also the issue of summonses and processes in cases on the Collectorate side, and was expected to be generally useful. The other clerks were principally employed in writing, under the supervision of the second clerk.

Lewis had worked well, and left me with a tolerably clear file, so that my first day's business was not very heavy; and as no cases had been fixed for hearing before the following Monday, to avoid inconvenience from any delay in my arrival, this being a Friday, I had two days of comparative leisure. Lewis went off in a palanquin after dinner, and I felt rather deserted in the dâk bungalow all by myself, the only English face within a radius of thirteen or fourteen miles.

The next morning I took a ride through the town, and found it in a beastly state of filth, the thoroughfares covered with refuse, and obstructed by mat erections, verandahs, etc., at the will of individuals. No European official had been stationed here before, so that everything of this nature had been allowed to go on in pure native fashion. This afforded food for reflection; but the question was, how to begin to do any good.

On going to office, the first thing was to listen to the reports of a miscellaneous nature sent through the police, cattle-pound keepers, district postal officials, chowkedarree tax darogahs, etc., on the Magisterial side; and on the Collectorate side the various reports from the nazir and the ameens sent out in cases of settlements and butwarrahs (partitions of estates). The second clerk, Jugdeo Sahai by name, read these out in a glib way ; and though I understood their purport, I found it uncommonly difficult to pass orders on each *sur le champ*, so he (who, of course, knew what a novice I was) suggested the orders to be passed on each. This at first I was inclined to resent, but as I had nothing else to propose, I ended by saying, "Accha" (very well); and he dictated the order to the third clerk, sitting next him, who wrote it on the back of the report, and then it was handed to me for signature. *E.g.*, the pound-keeper of Rowsara sent in a report "that the pound was very much out of repair, and solicited permission to put it in order." I had not the slightest idea what to order; and Jugdeo suggested that the pound-keeper should be ordered to report when the pound had been last repaired, and also to send an estimate of the probable cost of the proposed new repairs. This seemed common sense when suggested, and so did all the other suggestions ; but it was annoying to feel one's ignorance and want of *savoir faire* in the matter, and it took me some little time to obtain the experience necessary to get on without him.

The reports from the chowkedarree tax-darogahs were chiefly with reference to the non-payment of the house-tax, assessed under Act XX. of 1856, the law relating to the appointment and payment of the rural town police. The tax was assessed by a Punchayet, or committee of rate-payers appointed by the Magistrate, and was an assessment, according to the circumstances and the property to be protected, of the persons liable to the same, and not to exceed in the aggregate an average rate of threepence per month per house. In no case was a sum higher than the pay of a chowkeydar, or policeman of the lowest grade, 8s., per month, to be assessed on any one house. Any surplus remaining after payment of the chowkeydar's wages and the salaries of the tax darogahs was to be available for conservancy purposes. There was an appeal to me from the assessments made by the punchayet, and from me to Blake.

When these reports were read, I mentioned to Jugdeo Sahai the filthy state of the town that I had observed in the morning, and asked him if there were any surplus funds that could be made available for its improvement. He said that nothing had ever been done, and that the surplus had been sent to the Treasury at Mozufferpore, where it would be placed to the credit of the town of Durbhungah. "But," he said, "it will be very little. However, now for the first time, an officer of the Covenanted Civil Service has been appointed to this subdivision, bringing with him greater dignity and (as he put it in his high-flown Hindu-stani, or rather Persian) 'splendour of the day' (raunak-af-roz). If your highness will allow me to bring the attention of the rich men of the place to the matter, and then call a meeting, we might get up a subscription." This sounded very sensible, so I assented, and began to understand the potentiality of "moral influence" in such matters.

When the batwarra reports were brought forward, it appeared there was one from the ameen employed in

making the partition of an estate named "Chakka." I
must explain more fully the meaning of the term "batwarra." In Bengal most estates, whether in Hindoo or
Mohammedan families, are held in joint undivided tenancy,
called in the vernacular "ijmali." There being no primo-
geniture, the shares in estates are divided equally as regards
the rental, but no one has any specific portion of land.
The Government revenue also is assessed on the whole
estate, and the shareholders settle among themselves the
method and means of payment of the revenue, as, if not
paid on the due date, the whole estate is put up to auction.
The proprietors, however, retain the right to divide the
estate, and to claim,—each shareholder or group of shareholders,—his or their specific portion of land. But Government also has a voice in the matter, for fear the division
should be collusive; for the law is, that when the estate is
divided, the Government revenue is assessed on each share
proportionately to its value. Now cases did occur in which
by collusion all the bad land was allotted to one shareholder and valued at an altogether false rental. This
share, when separated, would stand in the Government
register of revenue-paying estates as a separate estate,
would be responsible for its own revenue, would not pay it,
and would be put up for sale; the result being, that no one
would bid for it, and Government would lose its revenue.
The remaining shareholders would lose this amount of
land; but they would also be rid of the liability to pay to
Government a sum altogether disproportionate to the
amount of land lost.

To avoid this, therefore, Government, under Regulation

XIX. of 1814, had power to refuse to sanction any batwar-ra, unless satisfied of its being fair and just; and so the actual details of partition were carried out by officers called ameens, under the supervision of the Collector and Deputy Collectors. It continually happened that the shareholders could not agree about the specific portions of land to be allotted to each; and it was sometimes exceedingly difficult, if not impossible, to satisfy them all, and also the require-ments of Government, the chief of which was, that each of the allotments should be compact, with well-defined boundaries. The most important point, then, was to ascertain the actual annual value of each and every piece of land comprised in the estate, and to get all the share-holders to give their signatures to the document setting forth the value so ascertained. This once done, it only remained to apportion a proper amount of land to each; and a recalcitrant shareholder could be compelled to accept an allotment so made.

In this particular case the ameen had drawn up the document above mentioned, called in the vernacular the " rye bundee," and all the shareholders had signed it ex-cept one, the "*objector,*" Jymal Ali by name. I put the "objector" in *italics*, because he was the important person who made all cases easy or difficult, short or long ; and the first question one used to ask in any case of this nature, when brought up by the clerk, was, "Is there an 'objector'?" Jymal Ali was continually before me afterwards, and was one of those litigious persons who are a nuisance to Courts and to everybody connected with them by ties of relation-ship or in business matters.

It appeared that no less than three times had the "rye bundee" been prepared, and three times had Jymal Ali refused his assent. On looking over the objections raised by him, I found there were 603 plots of land or fields in the estate, and that he objected to the rates of value fixed on about half of them. "The only way to settle the matter finally," said Jugdeo Sahai, "is to go to the spot yourself; and what you assert to be right cannot be contradicted. This case has been pending a long time, and if your highness should think fit to go to the spot before the weather gets too hot, and camp there for two or three days, you could get the matter finished before you start for your examination. Besides, there is not a great pressure of cases in Court just now." Sensible advice again, which I thought best to follow. The place was only about fourteen miles from Durbhungah, though, as there were no roads in the vicinity, it was awkward to get at; but I issued notice to all concerned to be there on the following Tuesday, by daybreak.

My first Sunday was lonely and wearisome. Nobody to talk to but native servants; no church nearer than Mozufferpore, thirty-five miles off; no Cutcherry to occupy the time. However, I busied myself in supervising the start of my servants and tent for Chakka. Jugdeo Sahai went on an elephant with the ameen early the next day, and I started in the afternoon to ride half-way, and with an elephant to carry me the last half, where the ground was heavy and swampy.

The next day I was up at 5 a.m., and after a cup of coffee mounted my elephant with my chuprassie behind me with a gun, in case of any game appearing, and Jugdeo and a clerk on another elephant (we had borrowed the two at Durbhungah) ; while Jymal Ali and the other shareholders or their legal representatives were on foot. At 5.45, we commenced operations ; for, the tent being pitched about the centre of the estate, our work lay all around us. It seemed that here the rent was paid in kind, and not in money ; so it was necessary for me to fix, not the money rental, but the actual produce in grain of each field. I felt a little diffident in the matter ; but I recollected Blake's remark, that a Civilian must appear to know everything, and so determined to pronounce my decisions boldly. I had also looked over the papers, and seen the amounts fixed by the ameen, and so had something to go by. Jymal Ali's objections were to the effect that in all the fields allotted to him the ameen had overrated the produce, and underrated it in those allotted to the other shareholders. All I had to do was to make my estimate just on the average.

There was a great wrangle over Plot 1, which the ameen had put down as able to produce seventeen maunds per beegah (local standard of measurement), which Jymal said would only give ten. This was in his allotment. I listened without speaking to the various statements, and then calmly from my elevated seat said "sixteen maunds," and ordered (despite the protestations of Jymal) a move on to the next plot. As the day wore on, he and the others too began to get a little tired ; and every now and then I got him to admit that the rate laid down for one field was applicable to the next ten, and so saved a great deal of time and trouble. By 11 o'clock it was desperately hot, and a terrible west hot dry wind blowing, so we adjourned for breakfast and rest, I to my tent, they to the neighbouring small village. By this time we had accomplished 150 fields.

My tent was miserably hot and uncomfortable, for there were no big trees in the neighbourhood under which to pitch it, and the full glare of the March sun came down upon it; while I was obliged to keep the canvas doors shut to keep out the wind and dust. At 4 o'clock I made another start; but Jymal Ali was much refreshed with his rest, and his objections were more violent and vociferous than ever, so we only got through another 70 fields by sunset. The next morning and afternoon we got through another 220 fields; and in the middle of a wrangle about the rates of one plot bordering on a small piece of water, a flight of teal got up, and I managed to bag a brace, which elicited ejaculations of admiration from the spectators, evinced by shouts of wah! wah! and formed a very pleasant addition to my larder, which had been supplied hitherto with tough and skinny fowls from the neighbouring Mohammedan village.

The next day we came to the close, for which I was truly thankful; and I think even Jymal Ali was glad. Among other things, I had had to estimate the number of mangoes likely to be produced by each and every tree in a grove on the estate. A record of the rates fixed for each plot had been kept by Jugdeo as it had been pronounced by me; and now, in order to prevent any future objections, I called upon the shareholders to sign it on the spot. This they all did willingly enough, except Jymal, who said he would come to Cutcherry and sign it.

After much demur, he took the paper and squatted down in the field to write. He seemed to be a longish time, so ᐧ I made my elephant kneel down, and went up to him, and found that he was adding after his signature, " bamoujib hukum hakim ke " (in accordance with the order of the hakim). I got in a great rage, and I don't recollect what I said ; but it had the effect of making him smudge it out with his finger, and so the matter was settled. Had the words been allowed to remain, it would have given him an opportunity of making objections afterwards, and perhaps rendering of no avail all the time and labour spent on the spot. As it was, I may add here, that this case was now brought to a conclusion without any further trouble ; and the other shareholders were spared any addition to the litigation and expense they had been subjected to for the last five years. It was amusing to think that the *ipse dixit* of so very inexperienced a person as myself should have settled this very complicated matter ; but it serves to show what weight is attached to personal investigation by an English official.

On getting back to my tent, I found the owner of an indigo factory in the neighbourhood, the largest in this part, awaiting me. He was only five miles off, he said, and had he known previously that I was here before, he would have come over sooner to ask me to take up my quarters at his house. The country was ridable ; and would I come over now. It was quite delightful to see a white face again and to talk English ; so I accepted his invitation with pleasure, and we had a refreshing canter over to Kundowl. I could not have gone before, as it would have kept me too late from my work in the morning. There was an artificial lake, called "a tank," here, and we had a long swim before dinner, which was most refreshing after the heat and dust of the day. A cheerful repast and a game of billiards passed the evening pleasantly enough, and it was with regret the next morning that I made an early start for Durbhungah, some thirteen miles distant. There was a road all the way, and my host supplied me with horses and dog-cart to get there.

The dâk bungalow seemed very lonely as I drove up, and the low-lying land in front of it looked dismal. But after breakfast I went to Cutcherry, and found that cases had somewhat accumulated during my three days' absence, and that there was work to occupy me fully until the evening. This state of things lasted till it became time to start for Patna for my examination. A European Deputy Magistrate, Davison by name, was sent out to take charge of the subdivision during my absence. He was old and greyheaded, and told me that as he should not be able to finish any cases before my return, he should only pass the necessary orders to keep things going.

My examination on this occasion afforded no details worthy of record, except that I had to go through a trial in Bengali, in which the Local Committee passed me ; but it appeared doubtful whether the Central Committee would think the papers good enough.

On my return to Mozufferpore, I was delayed four days to take part in a meeting of the Tirhoot Cavalry Volun-

teers. The movement had been set on foot in consequence
of certain rumours about another mutiny,.which never had
any foundation at all ; but it was also recollected that the
Tirhoot officials had been compelled to leave their posts
in the Mutiny, in consequence of the absence of any sort of
force or organization for the protection of the district ; and
it was thought that, in case of future troubles, a body of
volunteer cavalry would be of very real service. The
manager of the Durbhungah estate, Furbelowe, was our
colonel ; Colville and Melville and another planter, Williams, were commissioned officers ; and myself and three
or four others were corporals.

About a hundred names were on the roll altogether ;
but I don't think that on this or any other occasion, as
long as I remained in Tirhoot, we mustered fifty. The
whole thing, indeed, was rather a bore ; but we all went in
for it from a sense of duty. Melville was really the moving spirit ; and I believe that, next to him, I knew my drill
better than anybody. Furbelowe was proud of the honour
of being Colonel, but knew nothing, and could not ride at
any pace beyond a walk. He was useful, however, in
giving big entertainments at Secundrapore. Sometimes
amusing things occurred, as on one occasion one of our
corporals, in the course of a charge on the plain by the
Cutcherries, was seen gradually to emerge from the ranks
and finally disappear at headlong speed down the bazaar,
drawn sword in hand. He did not return for more than
half an hour.

Another time, we carried on our charge farther than
usual, and spread a panic among a crowd of natives look-

ing on. Many of them were well-to-do people, enveloped in rich shawls, who had probably never gone out of a walk in their lives. As we neared them I saw them interchanging looks of doubt and apprehension ; and then came a helter-skelter rush, men tumbling over each other, and heaps of abandoned shoes lying on the ground. Some fled for protection into Percival's Court close by, where he was holding sessions, and begged for mercy and protection. The salient point in our uniform was a rather handsome helmet, with a long crimson plume, made up with a view of striking terror into an enemy ; and we were pleased to find we had such an awful appearance on this occasion.

When I returned to Durbhungah I found that Davison had acted very thoroughly up to his word, for he had literally done nothing. The order on almost everything was, "Let this be brought up when Mr. Gordon returns." The result was, that I was obliged to work very hard for some time to bring up the arrears. To add to my responsibilities, Government had just decided that all rent suits under Act X. of 1859 should be tried in the Collectors' Courts, and not in those of the moonsiffs. The moonsiffs were the local Civil Courts dotted about the district, and under the supervision of the judge on the Civil side, to whom their decisions were appealable. The next grade above them were the sudder ameers, stationed at head quarters, to whom the civil case work, including appeals from the moonsiffs, was distributed by the judge, who could keep on his own file such cases as he chose and had leisure for, his own time being chiefly occupied with criminal appeals and sessions.

Before I had taken over charge, all rent suits in the Durbhungah subdivision had been instituted in the Court of the Moonsiff of Durbhungah and disposed of by him. Then orders had come that the institutions should be made in my Court, and that I might hand half of them over to him for disposal ; and now the rule was that I was to keep the whole on my own file. This made a very great difference in the amount of work I had to get through ; for the Act had given rise to a great deal of litigation between landlord and tenant, and there were generally some hundred institutions monthly. Some of these were very complicated cases and took up a lot of time ; but many were compromised, so that, very fortunately for me, I did not have to adjudicate on the whole.

In my absence Jugdeo had been sowing the good seed, and awakening the minds of the richer residents to the fact that the hakim thought that the dirt of Durbhungah was disgraceful, and that if money were forthcoming, improvements which would conduce very much to their comfort could be made. I was so occupied that it was some time before I had leisure to summon a meeting. But at length an afternoon was fixed, and all the chairs and forms I could muster were placed in two parallel lines in the principal verandah of the dâk bungalow. Jugdeo had written the most flowery letters to the rich commercial residents, inviting them to attend, and he and the nazir had had long consultations as to the order of their sitting ; for any mistake in the matter of precedence might have caused the whole thing to collapse at once.

For myself a chair and table had been placed at one

end, and when they were all assembled, I entered the verandah. They all stood up to receive me, and did not sit until I sat down myself and asked them to do the same. On my right I observed two rich and rival merchants and bankers, named Bunwarree Lall and Nokee Lall. On the left was another man, who was on good terms with everybody, called Dabee Persad. Next to him was a Mohammedan—Wahid Ali Khan, an energetic, pushing person, anxious to become of importance, but not rich. The others were people of somewhat similar station, but of less wealth; and after them came the agents of those who could not or did not care to attend themselves, and some of my own clerks.

I had prepared a little speech in the most high-flown Hindustani I could muster; but when I stood up to address the assembly, they all stood up too, which rather embarrassed me, and I had some difficulty in making them understand that I wished them to remain sitting. This done, I commenced by saying, "I felt much gratification and support in seeing this assemblage of so many noble, so many wise, and so many rich men." They were not noble, for the nobility and gentry had not been asked to attend, as it would have involved a loss of "izzat" to do so in company with the commercial classes. Neither were they wise, nor all rich; but I could see that this exordium was pleasing.

I then went on to dilate on the very dirty state of the town, and said that it was not creditable, and could not be pleasing to the members of such an assemblage to live in such a place, where there were no roads fit for a comfortable vehicle, and where no man could keep his shoes on in wet weather; and I also dwelt on the meaning of the name Durbhungah, which is supposed to be "Door of Bengal," and said that the townsmen of a place holding such a position ought to be zealous for its honour and good repute. Then came the question of funds. The amount of surplus chowkedaree tax standing to the credit of the town was very small; but if properly supplemented by subscriptions, Government would no doubt aid us, and I therefore proposed to open a subscription list at once, and would ask each gentleman present to state what he was willing to give.

Then out spake Bunwarree Lall, and said he would give 100 rupees, upon which Nokee Lall said he would give 110 rupees, and Bunwarree Lall bid 150 rupees; and so it went on like an auction, each wishing to appear more liberal than the other, until they settled to give 350 rupees each. Dabee Persad gave 250 rupees, and the others each something, though smaller sums. On the whole, about 2,000 rupees, or £200, was promised, which result I considered rather successful.

I then wrote letters to the neighbouring nobility, informing them of what had been done, and telling them that I had not invited them to be present at the meeting, as I could not expect them to sit with these people of the commercial caste, and I now asked them to subscribe to the good object. They were no doubt flattered at the distinction thus drawn, and promised altogether another 1,500 rupees, or £150. After this, I sent a report to Government, through Blake, dwelling on the desire of the

Durbhungah people to help themselves; and in due time came a reply, saying that Government was much pleased, and would contribute to the improvement of the town a sum equal to that subscribed by the residents. There was also a sum of about 1,700 rupees (£170) to the credit of the town in the Mozufferpore Treasury, the result of the accumulation of many years' surplus, which nobody before had ever thought of spending; so that altogether we had between £700 and £800 to spend.

It sounds a very small sum to English ears, but was considerable in comparison with the tiny amounts we generally managed to get for local expenditure. A committee was selected, of which I was president, and Dabee Persad, Wahid Ali Khan, and Bunwarree Lall, and one or two others, members. There was some little delay in collecting the amount promised, many of the subscribers being much more ready to promise than to pay.

Among others, Nokee Lall made sundry excuses for not paying up; and finally offered a less sum than he had promised. He was no doubt jealous of Bunwarree Lall being on the committee; and he also repented being led away by his excitement to promise so much at the meeting. He was a man of a sullen and quarrelsome temperament, and it would have been difficult to get him to act in harmony with the others. However, it would not do to let him set an example of not paying; so I thought the best plan would be to shame him into it. Accordingly I let it be known that I intended to pay him a visit on a certain afternoon after office; and on riding down on the day appointed, I found a considerable crowd of curious spectators assembled in the main thoroughfare of the bazaar, on which his house fronted. I sent a chuprassie in to announce my presence, and I sat on horseback outside till he came and stood in his doorway. Then I said, "What is this that I hear, that you refuse to pay the subscription you have promised?"

"Nourisher of the poor," he replied, "I was foolish that day, and I am a poor man. I cannot afford to give that sum; but I offer 150 rupees, if you will take it;" and he stretched out a bag he had in his hand.

"It is not good not to keep promises," I said. But he only repeated what he said before. "Very well," I replied, "each man has given according to his *izzat*, and you, I suppose, are doing the same as the rest. I do not wish that any man should give against his will. Bunwarree Lall, according to his *izzat*, has given willingly 350 rupees. Dabee Persad has given 250 rupees. You appear to consider that yours is worth less. But here are a number of your fellow-townsmen present, and they will know at what you rate your *izzat*, according to the sum you give."

This made him hesitate; he looked at the crowd, who were listening with great interest, and then at me; then went into his house, and returned with a larger bag, which he said contained the amount he had promised. My chuprassie took it, and it was counted, and found to contain 350 rupees. I then thanked him, and complimented him on his liberality, and took my departure. This had a very good effect, and Jugdeo told me that it was the universal topic of conversation in the town; and other lagging contributors hastened to pay up.

The amount of work done with this money was really wonderful, and mostly due to the energy and careful supervision of Wahid Ali Khan. He knew prices of materials and labour exactly, and there were no contractors to make profits. The main thoroughfares were metalled, and provided with masonry drains; they were also widened. Many salient corners of verandahs, and projecting portions of houses being cut down, the owners in most cases being persuaded to allow it to be done without demand for compensation, and any poor people affected receiving small sums. These were all really encroachments on the public thoroughfare, but had been so long in existence that a right to preserve them had been established.

However, I employed most of my leisure in the bazaar, and, by judicious use of "moral influence," overcame the majority of the obstructions without expense. In some cases, too, I was compelled to be severe, and fine people for being a nuisance to their neighbours, under Section 290 of the Penal Code. The fines were, by law, credited to Government in the Judicial Department, so the town got no primary benefit from these. But the spirit of improvement had taken a start. One evening I rather lost my way at the southern end of the town, and came out upon two really beautiful artificial lakes, each a mile or more in circumference, which had been excavated many hundred years before by an old rajah of the neighbourhood. The earth thrown out from the excavations formed a sort of small range of hills, that prettily broke the monotony of the flat surface all round, and trees had grown upon the slopes, among which many small monkeys disported themselves, and enlivened the scene.

It occurred to me that at very little expense a beautiful drive could be made round these; and the next day I took my committee there, who, either from a real impression or a desire to please me, all said it was "a very elegant place" (lutf). Negotiations were entered into with the present owners of the land, who behaved in a most liberal way: gave, free of charge, all the land required for the roadway, permitted any trees to be cut down that offered any obstruction, and allowed me to take for timber, for the construction of the one or two bridges necessary, any of the trees that I could make useful. Wahid Ali Khan showed great energy here also, and in about two months this drive was completed, named after me, and is, I believe, still in good repair.

In about six months I had the satisfaction of seeing Durbhungah quite a different place with reference to roadways and cleanliness, though of course there was still only too much room for improvement; but without money, more could not be done.

The planters who came in used to compliment me on what had been effected; and a rich native banker from Mozufferpore was loud in praise of the improvements. He was named Nundiput, and had received the title of Bahadur for services rendered during the Mutiny. He had a branch business at Durbhungah, and was now building a house there for the use of his agent, a respectable man, who had been selected as one of the members of our committee.

About this time a sort of sub-meeting of volunteers was held at Durbhungah, Furbelowe came over, and naturally the dâk Bungalow was crowded. The sanctity of my bedroom was respected, which was very considerate on the part of the visitors, as they had a right to turn me out altogether if they chose. In a warm climate like India a room at night is not absolutely necessary for sleeping purposes, and some ten planters had beds in the verandah. One night there was heavy rain, and some foolish practical jokers had thrown the beds of two of their number out into the wet. They came into my room and preferred a complaint to me as Magistrate. This was very awkward, but I told them that any complaint must be brought before me in Court the next day; and in the morning I persuaded all parties,—not a very difficult thing,—to settle the matter among themselves. But this and one or two other little occurrences made me feel how awkward it was for me to be subjected to this sort of thing, and to be obliged to depend on the consideration of *bonâ fide* travellers for not being turned out, so I determined to make Nundiput rent me his house above mentioned, when finished.

Government, in the meantime, had issued orders for the building of a sub-divisional residence and Court at Durbhungah, and I had to take action under Act VI. of 1857, (the Expropriation Act), in order to acquire land for the purpose. This gave me infinite trouble; for though I managed to settle the matter without dispute, and satisfy the owners of the land, the drawing up of the report in the form required by the very elaborate rules of the Board of

Revenue was a most difficult task. The fact is, I had dealt with the matter from the paternal government and moral influence point of view, and found it very difficult to make my somewhat irregular proceedings fit into the cut-and-dried red tape form required.

A new Collector had come to Tirhoot, Blake having been appointed to a post in Calcutta which he had long coveted, and at first he was inclined to quash all my proceedings, and this would have involved my taking back money already paid for houses, or rather huts, that had actually been removed. But on understanding my difficulties he did his best to pull me through, and at last the matter was settled; though, in order to do this, I was compelled to have all the parties before me again and formally commence *de novo.* The villagers were much puzzled; but being ignorant and as credulous as Frenchmen about *les formalités*, they were not troublesome.

Jugdeo was pleased at my embarrassment, as, the reports being all done in English, he had no connection with them, and it made it appear that I wasn't yet able to "walk well alone." The sub-divisional residence was to be constructed by the Public Works Department, which was always dilatory in its action, and so was not completed until I left Durbhungah. A circumstance occurred soon after this which made the construction of a Court a serious necessity.

. The rains were very heavy this year; and one day, when my Court was most crowded, and there had been a week's heavy downpour almost without cessation, there came a roar and a crash of falling masonry which made every one think that the whole building was coming down. I was sitting with my back to the window, on the side from which the noise appeared to come. The whole Court was cleared in a twinkling. I was out last, not from any feeling of dignity, but because it was physically impossible for me to get out sooner; and I shall never forget the horrible disgusting feeling I had, that I was about to die like a rat in a hole.

Clerks, suitors in civil cases, prosecutors, accused, and police were all huddled pellmell over each other; and it took a few minutes to ascertain that none of us on this side of the building had received any injury. We then went round to the other side, and found that all the crash had been caused by the fall of a portion of the masonry balustrade of the roof above mentioned. It had come down on the sloping thatched roof of the verandah, breaking this in, and also forcing outwards, two of the masonry pillars supporting it. Here we found three unfortunate persons injured. One was lying with a mass of masonry on his chest, another with his right leg knocked almost off,—it was hanging by a bit of skin only,—and a third inside the verandah shouting and groaning as if in great pain. We turned our attention first to him, for it looked as if the whole bamboo roof had fallen on the top of him. However, it appeared that one of his feet had been caught between two projecting pieces of bamboo, forming a portion of that side of the roof which had fallen to the floor of the verandah, the other side still resting against the pillars which had not been broken. By cutting one of these prongs he was able to extricate his foot; and then it was discovered he had not a scratch.

In the meantime some others had taken the mass of broken masonry off the chest of the other man ; but he lay unable to move. Furbelowe, who lived in a bit of the palace close by, had now come on the scene, imagining from the noise that I must have been killed, and with him the Sub-assistant Surgeon, or native medical officer in charge of the charitable dispensary which he had established with the funds of the estate. He looked at the man with the injured chest, said his case was serious, and he could not recover ; and then at the man with the broken leg, and said it was merely a question of the loss of a leg.

Having no instruments at hand, a carving-knife was sent for from Furbelowe's, and the leg taken off by simply cutting the small piece of skin by which it was hanging. But the unfortunate man fell back in a fainting state, never recovered consciousness, and died that evening. The shock had been too much for his system. It turned out, poor man, that he was a tailor, and had come to demand payment of a small but long-standing debt from one of my clerks, and was waiting for an opportunity of seeing him in the verandah when this crash occurred.

The other man was taken to the hospital attached to the dispensary ; but after two or three days his friends came and stole him away by night ; and this perhaps ensured his recovery, for on making inquiries afterwards, I heard that he had got quite well.

It is a curious fact, that the natives have such a dislike to allowing their relatives to go to hospital, and seldom bring them there voluntarily until it is too late to do anything for them. They fear loss of caste, which is worse

than loss of life. Generally, too, I found them utterly un-
grateful ; and innumerable instances occurred, where, after
being tended with care and their strength restored, patients
ran away before their cases were considered complete, and
took with them the blankets and any other portable hospital
property that had been given to them for use. I can safely
say, however, that this, though somewhat disheartening,
made none of us, either Magistrates or Doctors, relax our
efforts to induce the people to come to our hospitals and
learn to appreciate the benefits of civilized medical treatment. We are doubtless slowly succeeding, and should
have made more rapid progress could we have afforded the
services of more European medical officers ; but I fear the
natives had frequently reason to doubt both the skill and
tenderness of the Sub-assistant Surgeons, and native doctors.
I seldom found instances of these men having any real
sympathy with suffering, but generally a total absence
of it.

I considered it dangerous to use the Court building
again until it had been examined by a competent person ;
and this Furbelowe promised to have done as soon as
possible. In the meantime, there being no other place
available, and tents not being possible in such weather, I
was obliged to hold my Court in the verandah of the dâk
bungalow. It is scarcely necessary to say that this was
very uncomfortable and ill-adapted for the purpose ; but it
is only one among many instances where the representatives of Government in India have been put to such undignified shifts.

But nevertheless, the people seemed to think nothing of

it; and after all it was not so much inconvenience to them as the fact of my not being vested with the "full powers" of a Magistrate. *E.g.*, under the existing law, which has since been altered, I had not power to adjudicate on a charge of "theft in a building;" but I could either commit the accused to the Court of Session or refer the case to the Magistrate of the district for orders. When the property stolen was of very small value, it was a great hardship on the prosecutor and his witnesses to be compelled to go seventy miles into Mozufferpore and back, and cross fourteen streams going and coming, at each of which they would have to pay toll. Such cases frequently occurred, and were all brought under the notice of Melville, to whom they were referred by Blake, or his successor Ellis, for disposal.

At length I was obliged to refer one in which the value of the property was only 4½*d.* ; whereupon Melville was moved to compassion and wrote to Ellis, pointing out the hardships to which the Durbhungah people were subjected in consequence of my limited powers; and also that it was a mere question of routine, as I had passed all my legal examination, and was only prevented from being invested with full powers by my liability to a further examination in Bengali. Both Ellis and Percival, to whom my administration was referred for an opinion, reported me fit for full powers, and Government therefore invested me with them, but without allowing me to draw the extra £60 a year until I should pass my examination in Bengali.

The receipt of this news caused some sensation in

Durbhungah native society, and I had to undergo congratulatory visits from all the native gentlemen of my acquaintance. Among others, came Rajah Ganeshur Singh, brother of the late Rajah of Durbhungah. He had hoped to have the management of the estate after his brother's death; and, when Blake had taken steps to have it brought under the Court of Wards, had united with the Ranee, the widow, to use all efforts in their power to prevent it; and had presented numerous petitions to the Government, accusing Blake of every enormity under the sun. When, however, he found that he could not succeed, and that the Government had finally decided to place the estates under the Court of Wards, he asked leave to call on Blake, and humbled himself, saying that he had been mad, and now hoped to be forgiven. Blake of course forgave him, and I have no doubt had not the slightest personal feeling against him.

Judging from my own experiences afterwards in similar cases, I think I may assert that we civilians showed what may be called a high-minded contempt for the spite and venom showered upon us by those whose personal wishes or interests we were opposing, for their own or the public good.

Ganeshur Singh was now a good boy, and quite willing to admit,—as indeed he could not help doing,—that the management of the Court of Wards had been both considerate and efficient. No caste prejudices had been violated, the two sons of the Rajah were being educated in an enlightened manner, but without any attempt to touch upon religious matters; great improvements had been made in the estate and the buildings; all just debts had been paid; all fraudulent claims had been contested, and generally successfully, in the local Courts; finally, the income was now a clear £120,000 a year, whereas, had the old Rajah lived two years longer, the estate must have been brought to auction for non-payment of arrears of Government revenue.

Ganeshur Singh's own estate was by no means in so flourishing a condition, and he was now anxious to have it also managed by the Court of Wards; but this of course could not be allowed, as the Government did not take upon itself to rescue from ruin all estates of which the proprietors were extravagant or foolish; but merely, as the law on the subject, Reg. x. of 1793 recites, in cases of minors, females (with exceptions), idiots, lunatics, etc., and then only after very careful and complete inquiry.

On this occasion Ganeshur had just returned from his first railway journey from Barh to Patna, the line having been recently opened; and I was anxious to get at his impressions, as a native gentleman, of high family, on the subject. In reply to my first question on the subject, he said, "It makes a great noise." This was discouraging, and I found that he apparently had not taken in any impression of the magnitude of the undertaking or of the great speed attained, and the wonderful difference in the facility of locomotion. His chief idea seemed to be, that it would be very difficult for persons of his high caste to travel at all by such means.

"For instance," he said, "the trains only go at stated times; now I cannot commence a journey except at the minute decided upon by my astrologer as a favourable moment for starting. This makes it very difficult for me to travel at all. To-morrow I have to go to Mozuf-ferpore, and the astrologer has decided that I must start at 1 a.m.

"Now my cousin Gadadhur went by railway the other day with his wife, and daughter of six years old, and a baby. He started at an unfavourable moment. His wife and two children and a maid-servant were put in a palan-quin, which was placed on a truck, which prevented their being seen; and he went in an ordinary carriage. Somehow or other, a spark from the engine flew into the palanquin, and set fire to some of the linen in which the baby was wrapped; and the servant, in her confusion, thinking it was only a bundle of clothes, threw it out. The moment it was done she found out the mistake, and they all shrieked. This was only a mile from the Patna station, and the train soon stopped. The station master was very kind, and did his best; but the palanquin was on fire, and the wife in getting out was seen by many persons. It is not a fit subject even for conversation."

"But what about the baby?" I asked.

"They sent back along the line, and found it still alive; but it died soon afterwards."

It was evident that he thought much more of the wife being seen, than of the death of the child; but this was the result of his training, and that of his an-cestors for generations, so I could not blame him for it.

On going out, he had to pass through my dining room, where the cloth was laid and some knives and forks on the table. "What are those for?" he asked. I explained their use, and hoped to make him understand this small item of Western civilization. "Ah," he remarked, "my caste does not allow me to eat with anything but my fingers." He was proud, rather than impatient, of his caste restraints.

Poor man! he started the next night in torrents of rain, at the favourable hour mentioned by his astrologer, no doubt believing, as members of other religions do under analogous circumstances, that it was "all for the best."

After a few days, the Court building having been pronounced not dangerous, I returned to work there. I had hardly been back two days when a thunderstorm came on which seemed to be exactly over us, the lightning and thunder being simultaneous. There was a crowd of people about the Cutcherry; and suddenly a murmur arose that a man had been struck. I went out to look, and found a man lying dead. He was a rustic, and had no clothing but a waistcloth (dhotee). So there was very little linen to burn; but I examined the corpse for some time before I could find any trace of the stroke. At last I discovered a small piece of singed hair a little on one side of the head. This was evidently the point of entry of the electric fluid, but I could not see any trace of its exit.

The police officer came soon after to hold the inquest, for this is the way these things are done in the Mofussil. In all cases of unnatural death, the police officer holds an inquiry and sends in a report to the Magistrate having jurisdiction, who then passes orders for further investigation or merely for the papers to be filed with the records, as may appear proper. This case illustrated the delay that was brought about through police red-tapeism. As there was no Assistant Superintendent of police at Durbhungah, the formal report had to be sent in to the District Superintendent at Mozufferpore, and from him back again to the Court Inspector, or police officer attached to my Court. Thus, after the lapse of a week, I received the report, stating how the man had been killed, and that his highness Gordon Sahib, the "Ashistant" Magistrate of Durbhungah, had brought the splendour of the day to the spot, and seen the corpse with his own blessed eyes.

CHAPTER VIII.

AT DURBHUNGAH.

NUNDIPUT'S HOUSE.—AN ASSISTANT SUPERINTENDENT OF POLICE.—
SYSTEM OF EXCISE.—FINAL EXAMINATION.—RIOT CASES.—INDIGO
SOWING CASE. — INDIGO PLANTERS. — JUGDEO SUSPECT. — NE-
PAULESE CASE.—A TIGER PARTY.—A NARROW ESCAPE. — NEW
MUNICIPAL ACT.—BUNWARREE LALL AND PUBLIC WORKS DE-
PARTMENT.—APPOINTED TO NUDDEA. — REGRET AT MY DEPAR-
TURE.—AGRICULTURAL SHOW.—GOOD-BYE TO DURBHUNGAH.

NOT long after this, Nundiput's house was finished;
and with some pressure he consented to let me occupy
it. I had to fix my own rent (a matter of very little
importance to him) and the amount of my own chowkedarree, or municipal tax, which I assessed at the maximum. The rent I fixed at what I thought a fair
amount, as he had declined to take anything. The
house was tolerably clear of the Bazaar and with a fair
garden at the back. It consisted of three narrow oblong
rooms running north and south, two very small rooms,
more like closets, at each corner, and two somewhat
larger filling the space between the corners. At the
back was a small square courtyard surrounded by small
rooms intended for the zenana, or women's apartments.
There was a short verandah on three sides, the roof was
supported by masonry pillars ; the walls were thick enough
for those of a fortress, and tended to keep the interior

cool in the very hot weather. On the whole, it was not very suitable for a European's residence, but was better than anything else I could get in Durbhungah. The servants' houses and cookhouse were in separate small buildings outside.

I had scarcely got settled when I received information of the appointment to Durbhungah of an Assistant Superintendent of Police ; and on his arrival I sent to ask him to put up with me, looking forward with some pleasure on my own account to the company of a white face, and not wishing him to be subjected to the same inconveniences as I had undergone myself at the dâk bungalow.

His name was Cookson, and he had been, he told me, in some Highland regiment, but had sold out on his marriage ; and as his father had been in the Indian service had come out to get employment in this country. It was clear enough from his appearance that his mother had been in India too. His wife he had left in Calcutta ; but she was to follow with her baby when he got settled. On the whole, he was scarcely up to what I could have wished, and by no means gave me the idea of being likely to exercise a vigorous control over the police. But we got on amicably enough, and it was a great comfort to get work done more quickly than in the former circuitous manner. We scarcely met on week-days, except at breakfast time and at dinner, so that we had not much leisure for becoming quarrelsome ; at least I had not, for my work was now very hard.

The new Registration Act had now passed, which enacted that every party executing a deed must appear in person and be properly identified before the Registrar, or must be represented by a mookhtyar furnished with a registered power of attorney, to give which the principal must have appeared in person once before the Registrar. Documents so registered were to be received in all the Courts without dispute as legally registered; and this obviated a great amount of litigation about their authenticity, and was an immense improvement on the old system.

The Commissioners and Collectors, having been consulted, had replied that the subdivisional officers could find time to perform the functions of Sub-registrars, but that they ought to receive some small addition to their pay for the, extra work, say £5 a month. Government, as was understood at the time, acceded to this, and in the months of August and September I registered an average of more than 500 deeds per month. This took up a certain amount of time, and involved the keeping up of a number of new and rather elaborate registers, so that there was really a considerable addition to my work. I consoled myself by drawing my extra 50 rs.; but at the end of the two months Government issued a circular stating that they had never authorized this, that it was a misapprehension on the part of the Commissioners, and that all money so drawn must be refunded to the Treasury.

This was thought rather sharp practice by us disappointed ones, for it appeared that the Government had first induced us by promise of extra remuneration to admit that we could do the extra work, and when it found the work was being done had withdrawn the pay. I never quite understood how the blame was to be distributed in the matter, but I did not much care, as my present income was quite sufficient for my present wants.

This was the time too when attention was turned to the development of subdivisional administration, and it was resolved that subdivisional officers should be entrusted with the control of the excise within the limits of their jurisdictions—of course under the supervision of the District Collector.

The object of the system of excise, as stated by the Government, is "to raise as large an amount of revenue from the sale of intoxicating liquors and drugs as is compatible with the greatest possible discouragement of their use. It always appeared to *me* that the great object of the Government was to get a maximum consumption at a maximum rate. In Tirhoot, hitherto, the excise had been under a Deputy-Collector of the uncovenanted service at head-quarters, for most Collectors looked upon this as appertaining to the class of "dirty work," and were glad to get rid of its disagreeable details.

There had been a controversy going on as to the respective merits of the "monthly tax" system, and the "fixed duty" system. Under the former, monthly licences were granted to distillers and retailers at fixed rates; and they could manufacture and sell as much as they pleased. Under the latter, a duty was charged on the actual amount manufactured and sold, and rates also varied with the strength of the spirit. Under this system "public distilleries" were established, as tending to give the authorities greater control.

These were erected at the Government expense, and licensed distillers set up stills therein. Within a certain fixed radius round these, no private stills could be set up, and all retail shops were compelled to get their supplies therefrom. They were under the charge of an officer called a Darogah, whose business it was to tax the amount passed out and to test its strength; also to prevent illicit manufacture, and to look after the licensed shopkeepers who took their spirits from the distillery. These were used of course for the distillation of country spirit only. Imported spirits were treated in a different way.

I don't know who drew up the scheme for the erection of these distilleries in the Durbhungah subdivision; but he had apparently drawn a number of circles on the map, without any consideration of the circumstances of each locality, and said, "There shall be a distillery in the centre of each of the circles." The result was, that at this time came the order that eleven of these distilleries should be erected; and as there was no necessity to ask for the assistance of the Public Works Department, their construction was speedily carried out. Theoretically, the buildings should have been of masonry, and surrounded by a masonry wall. But in Bengal, though the richest province in India, we are seldom allowed any money to do anything on a proper scale; and so the erections were mud walls with tiled roofs, and surrounded by a palisade.

The theory of Government was, that where no legally manufactured spirits were consumed, there must be illicit manufacture. This I firmly believe to be a mistake in the greater part of Bengal known to me. In this subdivision complaints used to reach me now of drunkenness where it was unknown before. Monthly returns from all the distilleries had to be sent by way of my office to head-quarters in Mozufferpore, and as (I am happy to say) many of them did not pay their expenses, I was constantly harassed to report reasons for their not doing so. The simple reason was, that they were not required in their neighbourhood ; which answer, however, my superiors declined for some time to receive as conclusive. Finally, however, some three or four of them were abolished.

It was my duty to visit these distilleries as often as opportunity occurred, and to examine the Darogah's accounts, test the quantity of the spirits in store, and also its strength with the hydrometer. All this was very disagreeable. The buildings were make-shift and dirty ; the smell was abominable, and the very nature of their duties seemed to have a demoralizing effect on the Darogah and his subordinates.

I also had to keep an opium shop at my treasury, and sell the drug,—supplied to me from head-quarters,—to the licensed vendors, who generally united this trade with the sale of stamps. Dealing with this, however, was better than with country spirits.

But the most harmful drug is " ganja," a preparation of hemp. The use, or rather abuse, of this did not come much under my notice until I was transferred to Eastern Bengal, so I will not remark upon it here.

Apropos of the above, I may relate, that I was one day driving through the town in my buggy with Cookson when we came upon a drunken chowkeydar (policeman). In this drunken state he did not perceive who I was, and, irritated at being ordered to get out of the way, he struck at me with his latti (bamboo stick). So I pulled up, got out, and tackled him. He was too drunk to be a formidable opponent; but it was unseemly for me to be seen struggling with him, so I called out, "Will no one come to assist the hakim?"· Two or three men came rushing up, in the twinkling of an eye undid his turban, bound his arms with it, and at my orders led him away to the police station. Cookson all this time did nothing; but I suppose he thought it best to keep hold of the reins. The news of this event spread rapidly through the town, and the next morning the crowd at my Court, to see me sit in judgment on the man who had assaulted me, was very great. I believe the uninitiated thought in a vague kind of way that nothing short of the extreme penalty of the law would be considered sufficient punishment. Among others, his mother was there, and flung herself down before me in an agony of supplication. The wretched man was so frightened that he could scarcely speak. However, he admitted he had been drunk, and said he did not know what he was doing. I read him a lecture on the disgrace attaching to him as a guardian of the public peace, and fined him eight annas, equal to one shilling, saying, that no doubt the Police Superintendent would dismiss him. He was so relieved at finding nothing worse was to happen to him, that I am afraid the sentence had very little effect on him. I may add here, as a somewhat curious fact, that natives, when accused of being drunk, always admitted the fact.

My work now was very hard, and I could only keep pace with it by working double tides, that is, by holding Court twice a day. I would commence in the morning at 6.30 a.m., first do the registration work, hear the various police reports, and try the criminal cases, which would occupy me till 12. Then return to my house to bath and breakfast, be back in office at 1.30, and work away at batwarras, excise, and rent suits, till 6 or 6.30; so that by the end of the day I was pretty well done up, and had very little time for outdoor investigations. In the midst of all this, I was supposed to be preparing for my examination in Bengali, not a word of which was spoken in the district.

At length the time arrived, and Davidson once more came to act for me. A rule had been promulgated that the examination of two Commissioners' divisions should be taken together, at the head-quarters of each alternately; so on this occasion I had to go all the way to Bhaugulpore, four days' hard travelling there and back, in order to undergo one day's examination. But travelling expenses were allowed by Government, and I felt more like a schoolboy going out for a holiday, than a hard-worked administrator going up for examination. It is not necessary to go into detail about this journey; but it will suffice to say that I did very badly, but was allowed to ·pass in consideration of the small opportunity I had had for study; and I enjoyed the society of white faces there very much. My pay was now increased to 500 rupees a month, or £600 a year.

It was late in November when I returned, and I

found that a serious case had occurred in my absence, which Davidson had abstained from touching in anticipation of my return, though it had required prompt action. Two indigo planters, Arkell and Ball, had visited a village which had been leased to them, with a view to collecting rents in arrears, and had been seriously assaulted; and further, their tent, pitched in the neighbourhood, had been destroyed, their tent furniture broken or carried off, and the provisions they had brought with them thrown into a stream in the vicinity.

This really was a quarrel, not about the cultivation of indigo, but about the payment of rent. The villagers were known stubborn characters, who had given their own native zemindar great trouble about their rent; and he in despair had leased the village to Arkell, who had at first taken it with the view of getting indigo cultivated; but had at length given up the idea.

The term village includes, of course, the lands surrounding the habitations of the villagers, and cultivated by them. On this occasion, after many fruitless missions of subordinate *employés*, he had gone in person, with his assistant, Ball, to endeavour to hold a friendly conference with the villagers; it having been suggested by one or two of the more reasonable of them that he should do so. Expecting to stay two or three days, they had sent their tent to be pitched near; and Ball had taken his gun with him in the hope of sport. From their evidence, and that of their grooms, it appeared they had ridden into the village, and gone to the cutcherry,—the term used for the office in every village where all the landlord's or lessee's business with the villagers is carried on,—and that almost immediately they were surrounded, abused, and threatened ; and finally assaulted, though not hurt seriously. They both lost their hats, and got to their horses with difficulty. I adjourned the case, to get independent evidence if possible ; and as in the meantime it became necessary for me to go to a distant town, called Rowsara, to revise the assessments of the town-tax made by the town council, I appointed my camp there as the place for finally hearing the case, and directed the accused persons to have all the evidence for their defence ready.

Arkell and Ball had some twenty-five miles to come to my tent. There was no means of getting anything to eat and drink, except with me, so I felt constrained to offer them breakfast ; but this made me very careful to finish the case, if possible, without going back to my tent at all. The complainants' evidence was clear ; that for the defence absurd. They admitted there was a quarrel about the rent ; but said that the two sahibs had come into the village cutcherry, and fired off the gun at the villagers, inside the building. No one had been hit, and no one could give any account of where the charge had struck, or whether it was shot or ball. Further, Arkell and Ball both swore that the gun had never been loaded at all ; and their statement was reliable ; for though European planters do condescend to allow false evidence to be given in cases in which they are interested, they do not give false evidence themselves.

The case took a long time, and at the end I had to write my grounds of judgment, as well as pronounce sentence, which also was a long business, as I had to take notice of all the evidence, which was very voluminous. I just had daylight enough, sitting under a big mango tree, to do it. There had clearly been a riot, and the two complainants had been maltreated in attempting what they had a legal right to do. The rioting made the matter serious, so I gave the ringleaders nine months each, and a fine of fifty rupees; some others, lighter punishments. The ink on my paper was scarcely dry, when both parties filed petitions for copies. As I came tired into my tent, I met Arkell just about to start on his dark ride home.

"I've often said that you civilians are overpaid," he said; "but I'll never say it again. I would not go through the labour you have gone through to-day for £5,000 a year. I could no more have written my judgment sitting there, all at once, as you did, than I could have jumped over the moon."

"And now," I said, "tell me about your beard," which I had observed very much thinner and shorter than I had known it.

"Oh," he replied, "they pulled a lot of that out in the row; but my mookhtyar advised me to say nothing about it, as it would so lower my status with the natives to make it public in Court."

This showed that native public opinion was worth something in his eyes.

I had to make a separate case of the plunder of the tent, for that was testified to by other witnesses. Davidson's delay in taking action, had given them facilities for disposing of the stolen property. At length the police found a knife and fork in the house of a Mohammedan woman of bad fame, and, following up the clue, found in two Mohammedan houses, some seven or eight miles distant from the spot, several pieces of canvas, tent-ropes, and other European articles; and I was able to indict the householders as "receivers." As this was a case of plunder, with violence, by more than five persons, the case came under the technical definition of dacoity, and I was obliged to commit it for trial to the Sessions Court, over which Percival presided.

Now, in the first case, he had upheld my decision, when an appeal was preferred to him; but in this case, he acquitted the accused, on what appeared to me very unsatisfactory grounds. Section 125 of the Criminal Procedure Code enacts that the search of any house by the police shall be conducted in the presence of two or more respectable inhabitants of the place in which the house searched is situate. The police officer in this case, knowing all the inhabitants of this village to be hostile to the discovery of the truth, had conducted the search in the presence of two persons from a neighbouring village. This might have been of importance if the accused had denied that the articles had been found in their houses, or asserted that the police had put them there (as is often done); but they admitted that they had been found there, and said they had found some, and purchased some. However, the Judge acquitted them on the ground of the above technical informality.

This was matter for regret, as it tended to the triumph of the wrong side; but we Magistrates generally found that when ,we decided ourselves, our orders were very seldom upset on appeal ; but that in cases committed for trial to the Sessions Courts, it was just a toss up which way they would go. In India there are many causes to bring this about. It is so easy to get at witnesses between the magisterial inquiry and the Sessions trial—at poor men by bribes, at any of the better class by saying, " Why should you condemn a poor man to prison or death by your evidence ? You can so easily make a little discrepancy before the Judge, and so on." This argument has an extraordinary effect on witnesses who don't happen to have any personal spite against the accused. In some cases, I have known bribed witnesses deliberately deny before the Sessions Judge facts to which they had deposed before the Magistrate, and submit to be tried and punished for perjury in consequence ; and I have ascertained afterwards that the bribers persuaded them to do so, by assuring them that the Judge would not give them more than three years for perjury, and that in the meantime their families would be well cared for. In the case just mentioned, however, nothing of this sort occurred.

My revision of the assessment at Rowsara took me some three days' morning and evening work, the middle of the day being occupied by Court work, done under the tree above mentioned. While there, a man came in with a complaint that an European planter, whose factory was near his village, had forcibly dispossessed him of a lot of his land, and sown it with indigo. Under the existing law, Sec. 318 of the Criminal Procedure Code, we Magistrates had powers, in case of such disputes, to confirm the party actually in possession, without reference to right or title. We generally tried, however, to keep in possession the party whose claim appeared the best, and so throw the onus of proof in the Civil Court on the wrongful claimant. This is analogous to the spirit of our procedure on the Collectorate side, in the "dakhil kharij" cases mentioned above ; but, as Magistrates, our chief object was to prevent all chance of a riot.

The scene of this complaint was about fifteen miles from my tent, so I determined to go there by night in a palki, inspect the ground in the morning, and get back to my tent by mid-day, in time for some Court work. It was rather comfortless ; but I took some bread and a teapot with me, and managed to get some hot water from the village (with great difficulty), made my tea, and commenced my inspection about 6.30. The planter was there, and pressed me to accept the hospitality of his bungalow close by ; but under the circumstances I did not like to. I told the complainant, Juggoo Tewarree, to point out the plots of which he alleged himself to have been dispossessed, and he proceeded to point out every plot sown with indigo, but in most of these, when they came to be measured, his statements were found to be wrong ; in fact, he bungled his case altogether, and I did not see that I had any legal ground for ousting the planter from the land he had already sown with indigo. However, I reserved my decision, declining again to go to the planter's house, as I thought I should have to decide in his favour, though I felt certain that the villagers would not willingly have let him have all the land.

On reaching my tent I found news that Ellis was coming out from Mozufferpore the next day but one, to inspect me, that is, my office, work, etc., etc., so that I had to get back to Durbhungah as quickly as possible. When Ellis came I mentioned this case to him, and said I was afraid to pass orders which might oppress an injured party. He was a brusque-mannered man, with lots of energy, and a good deal of impatience of any technicalities which seemed to hamper justice.

" I'll take up the case myself," he said, "and decide it while I'm here." He had power by law to transfer any case from my file to his own. He went vigorously into the matter, and managed to come to a decision ousting the planter from a great deal of the land he had occupied.

I read his order, and I pointed out that the planter was in possession ; that by the law that was all he had to look to, and though it might be just, I did not understand his decision to be legal.

"Never mind," he said, "justice first, and dovetail in the law afterwards."

The planter appealed to the High Court in Calcutta, and Ellis's order was upset. The result was, that the unfortunate Juggoo had to go into the Civil Court to get back his own, after having spent a lot of money in defending the appeal before the High Court. About a year after this, as I was about to leave Tirhoot for good, I asked this planter what the real truth was. " Simply," he said, "that Juggoo had leased me a certain amount of land, and I had taken a great deal more. Juggoo wanted to get not only this back, but also some of that he had leased to me, and so made those confused statements which puzzled you. When we went into the Civil Court we made a compromise which gave me a good deal the best of it." A transaction not creditable to either party, certainly not so to the planter.

The cultivation of indigo is, beyond a doubt, unwelcome to the native cultivator. In Lower Bengal the power of the indigo planters had been broken up by the very strong measures of the Lieutenant-Governor. In Tirhoot there had been no general disturbance, but an increase of rate had been conceded to the cultivators. The cultivation of indigo in this part is of two kinds, that called the "zeraat," or land cultivated by the planter with hired labour, and that called "ryotwarree," cultivated by the small peasant farmer. If the planter could get land enough for his purpose to cultivate on the zeraat system, there would be no objection to the thing; but, in the first place, it would be exceedingly difficult to do this, and in the next place he does not wish it, as this system is so much more expensive than the ryotwarree.

It is very seldom that a planter can get the ryots to cultivate indigo for him, unless he is lessee of the village from the zemindar, or landholder, or unless he happens to be himself the proprietor; for all the land is held by these small peasant farmers, either by prescriptive right or by lease. They object to cultivate indigo, as it is a very troublesome and not a profitable crop. The land takes a great deal of preparation, and there is a great deal of weeding to be done. Further, he much prefers a food crop; and indigo comes into antagonism with all such in

Behar, except rice. But the ryots are proverbially improvident, and find it difficult to resist the temptation of a money advance from the planter, on consideration of their contracting to grow a certain amount of indigo. At the time I was there the rate was, I believe, 7 rs. a Tirhoot beegah ; equal to about two-thirds of an English acre ; but out of this the ryot had to pay the price of the indigo seed supplied by the planter.

The advance once accepted, the ryot becomes liable to much bullying until the crop is actually cut. The planter keeps servants who go round to see that the land is properly prepared, and the crop kept weeded. These men, knowing they have European influence at their back, are often very oppressive, and by threatening to complain to the planter or his head man, induce the ryots to bribe them into friendship. Otherwise they would continually be summoned in to the planter's cutcherry, and if they refused to go, taken there by force, men called peons being kept expressly for this purpose. But about indigo oppression I will speak further in my next chapter.

The profits from indigo in a good year in Behar were very great. I have known a case where an outlay of £30,000 has brought in at the end of the year a return of over £100,000. On the other hand, in a bad year, from drought, rain at the wrong time, or the ravages of the beetle, the result might be a considerable loss. The planters, too, in times of distress were kind to the ryots ; they were of great assistance in the construction of roads, and, as a general rule, if the ryots behaved well about the indigo, did not bother them much about their rent, which was really a secondary consideration. Some, however, more greedy for gain, would sublet the villages to their own native headmen, and then the unfortunate ryots had not only to grow indigo, but pay the uttermost farthing extracted by the grasping native.

Planters, too, made the district much more pleasant for the European official when moving about in camp; but the former was always obliged to be on his guard against creating wrong impressions in the minds of the natives; and it was only in very few cases that friendship could be free and unrestrained. One young planter said to me one day, " What a lot of money we should make, if you fellows were not here !" And no doubt the planters' impression is that we act as very troublesome buffers. On the other hand, the natives continually accuse us of partiality for our European brethren; so that, on the whole, we may, perhaps, lay the flattering unction to our souls that we administer tolerably even justice.

But there was an instance near Durbhungah of indigo cultivation being carried on with good feeling on both sides, and respect on the part of the native for the planter. The latter was a Scotchman, of patriarchal aspect and habits. He was thought wanting in enterprise by his neighbours; but though his profits were not colossal in good years, his losses were small in bad, and everything that the natives did for him was done willingly. He was an Honorary Magistrate, a post equivalent to our J.P., and though his decisions were not based on the strict rules of evidence, they were, what is much better, substantially just. They were seldom appealed against. Such a thing as a complaint against him or any of his servants never occurred; an official could accept his hospitality with a perfectly secure mind, and I spent some happy days with him.

Ellis pronounced himself satisfied with his inspection of my office, the manner in which the work appeared to be done and routine details attended to; but, to my sorrow, he didn't like Jugdeo.

"He wears too swell a puggree (turban)," he said, "and makes himself of too much importance. You ought to snub him publicly."

This annoyed me all the more that I felt there was some truth in it. The man was really a good and clever ministerial servant, and I did not like to snub him. All this time I had only had to find fault with him on one occasion, and that was so truly characteristic of the native way of doing things, that it is worth mentioning.

Among the many criminal returns we had to forward monthly to the District Magistrate, was a statement showing the number of witnesses summoned, the number whose evidence was recorded, and the number heard on the first, second, third, fourth, or fifth day of attendance. This was intended, of course, as a check on unnecessary delay in the hearing of witnesses. On looking over my returns, after I had been some three months at Durbhungah, I found that all the witnesses examined had been entered as heard on the first day of their attendance. I knew that this could not be the fact, as it was impossible for me to complete on each day all the cases coming in on that day. So I asked Jugdeo, who prepared the return, what it meant.

" I never enter the witnesses as present," he said, "until your highness is ready to take up the case. If I enter them as having been three or four days in attendance, then it is necessary to send an explanation to the Magistrate, and the return does not look so *thêk*" (a word expressing all excellence).

Of course I put a stop to this; but it is a type of the way in which a native, to avoid a little present labour, will roll up any amount of future trouble for himself.

Another thing now came to my mind that made me think he must be looked after. A petition had been presented to me by the proprietors of a certain estate near Durbhungah, that the neighbouring proprietor, who was my landlord, Nundiput, was constructing a heavy embankment on the border of the two estates, which would stop the water way in the rainy season, and subject the whole neighbourhood to the risk of an inundation. Nundiput rejoined that he was making a road to connect a certain place called Bhowareh with Durbhungah, and that it would be a great public convenience. I went out to the spot myself, and saw that the road would be a good thing, but the embankment would probably cause an inundation. So I told Nundiput he must make a bridge at a particular spot. He agreed to do this, and I therefore passed orders that it was not necessary to interfere with the embankment ; and this being what was called a " miscellaneous " case, I told Jugdeo to embody my order in a " roobekarree " or " proceeding," drawn up in the vernacular. This was done, and he produced it before me for signature one day when I was very busy, and I signed it, trusting to him.

Some two months afterwards another petition was pre-sented, to the effect that the opening for the bridge had been made in the wrong place. I went again to the spot, and found this to be fact, so ordered an opening to be made in the embankment at the proper place at once. Nundiput now appealed to the Judge, who called upon me for a report on the matter; and I then, in looking through the papers, read through the above-mentioned roobe-karree, which I found contained a most fulsome eulogium on Nundiput, and made out that he had shown the greatest public spirit in wishing to construct this road at his own expense, and that it ought by no means to be interfered with. I now, of course, had to neutralize the effect of this roobekarree, and finally the Judge upheld my orders in the matter. The embankment was broken through, the bridge was never made, nor the road completed.

Nundiput told Furbelowe that he thought I had treated him very badly, that he had let me have his house, had subscribed to my town improvement fund, and done all he could to please me; and yet that I had decided against him—typical of the native line of thought. Jugdeo, how-ever, I felt certain knew as well as possible that the con-struction of the road was all humbug; that the embank-ment was only intended to protect Nundiput from inunda-tion at the expense of his neighbours; and must have had some consideration from him for writing the roobekarree. I did not believe in the road myself; but if it were to do no harm, there was no necessity for interference on my part.

As the cold weather progressed, and the cutting of the rice crop began, various riot cases occurred. In cases of murder or accidental death, if the corpses were not too much decomposed for transmission, they were sent in for *post-mortem* examination by the Sub-assistant Surgeon ; and in murder cases I used to view the body myself. One morning I was told that the body of a man killed in a riot case was awaiting my inspection. I went out and found the corpse of a splendid-looking fellow cleft from the shoulder down to the middle. It was an awful wound. Little Cookson went out to the spot to hold a local inquiry, and I remained behind, thinking that I ought not to go out, but wait to hold the preliminary magisterial inquiry.

In due course a report came in, to the effect that the deceased, Sriram Thakoor, with some of his relatives and labourers, had gone to cut his rice crop, when the Rajah of Begumpoor had come on an elephant, with a number of followers, armed with swords, spears, and clubs, and some with reaping hooks, and had ordered them to cut what was left of the crop and carry off that portion already cut ; that the Thakoors had remonstrated, and shouted out, " duhai " (justice). The Rajah had said, " Maro," and then one of his followers, Sheik Lallun, had cut down Sriram with a sword, and that others had wounded many of the Thakoors with spears and clubs. Some four wounded men were sent in as complainants, who gave evidence to this effect, and ten or twelve very respectable-looking witnesses, who said that they were working in their fields in the neighbourhood, and had seen all the above details, and further, that all the crop was looted and carried off.

I issued warrants for the arrest of the Rajah and awaited

further details. At the end of a week I was thunderstruck at receiving through the Magistrate a most tremendous wigging from the Commissioner, Coldham. He scolded everybody all round; said the police had been slow, and their report was most unsatisfactory; that I had been most apathetic in not proceeding at once to the spot myself; that the Magistrate was to blame for not telling me to go; that I was to go there now at once, and explain why I had not gone before.

I should explain here, that in all heinous cases an English report, prepared by the District Superintendent, was sent to the Magistrate of the district, who forwarded it to the Commissioner, with his remarks and orders to the police; so that the Commissioner was kept *au courant* of all such matters.

I was indignant at the wigging, and said so to Jugdeo, intimating that I did not think any good would be done by my going out, especially as I had so much heavy work in office. He replied with his usual good sense, that "the first thing to be done was to obey orders." So I sent my tent off to the spot, some twenty miles off, and started myself the next day, having first given as my reason for not going before, that I thought that the presence of the Assistant Superintendent of Police on the spot rendered mine not only unnecessary but unadvisable.

I had not gone a mile before I met the accused Rajah coming in in a palanquin. He rolled out when he saw my buggy coming, explaining that he had rheumatism and could scarcely stand. I had ordered him to be admitted to bail of 10,000 rs., and told him so. This appeared a great relief to him, and he salaamed to the ground. He vociferated that he had nothing to do with the riot; he had been ill in bed; that the land was his, but he had leased it to another, and in the lease was a special clause to the effect that the responsibility of all criminal affairs rested with the lessee; and he held out a document, a copy of the lease. I took it from him, though it was somewhat an irregular mode of filing a proof, and went on my way, saying I would send for him if I wanted him.

On reaching the spot, I examined the locality, and found the field in dispute was situated within a dried-up tank or reservoir about two miles in length, excavated by some old Hindoo king, and was approached by a sort of lane cut through the embanking walls. Here I got hold of one or two men actually working in the fields adjoining, and took their evidence as to what they had seen. To my surprise, they told a totally different story. They said that Sriram Thakoor and his party had come in the early morning with a crowd of followers and actually reaped the crop; that they were engaged in carrying it off, when in the lane they met the opposite party under the Rajah's lessee, who opposed their progress. Some abuse took place, and then Sriram Thakoor, who was a great athlete and clubman, stepped forward and hit Sheikh Lallun, who appeared to be the hired champion of the other side, a tremendous blow with his "latti;" that Sheikh Lallun then cut him down himself with his sword, some few others joined in the fray, and some were wounded on both sides. The Rajah was not there at all.

This made me suspect that the evidence of the witnesses

first taken was all false. I had ordered them to be on the spot, and the next day examined them as to the fields in which they had been working. Each man pointed out his field, but when taken to the tent could not state its dimensions; and on inquiry I found these men had no cultivation in this village at all, that their names were not on the rent roll, and in fact that their statement was altogether false.

By degrees I elicited the real facts. The Rajah, who was the landed proprietor, had had a long-standing dispute with the Thakoors about rent. Finally he had got tired of it, and leased the land to a stubborn Mohammedan, Ameer Ali, on condition that he would bring these recalcitrant Thakoors to reason. He had got a decree against them in the Civil Court on some ground or other; and in execution thereof had got their crops attached. Two peons (sheriff's officers) of the Civil Court had been sent down to go through the legal form of attaching the crops; but the Thakoors had bribed them to put off execution of process for one day. In the meantime they had got a large party together and cut the crop; but were met as described by the witnesses above, the peons being with the lessee, Ameer Ali's party, and on their way to attach the crop. Ameer Ali was prepared for resistance; but the other party were the aggressors, and the whole case was reversed.

I afterwards asked Cookson how it was that he had been so easily taken in by the witnesses he had sent in, and he told me that on arriving on the spot he had found them actually in the fields in the vicinity, and that they had pretended to run away, as if unwilling to be asked to give evidence in the matter. He had ordered them to be caught ; and as they deposed before him in a very reluctant manner, he thought they were all the more likely to be speaking the truth. Of course it was a pity that he had not made them point out which were their fields.

In due course I committed all this batch of witnesses to the Sessions Court for trial for perjury; but Percival acquitted them all on what seemed to me to be very insufficient grounds.

I also committed some of the rioters on the Thakoor's side ; but they too were acquitted, the Judge remarking that it was a very confused case. Sheikh Lallun evaded justice for a long time, but he was at length caught, and I committed him for trial for the homicide of Sriram Thakoor ; but the Judge admitted his plea that he was exercising the right of self-defence, and acquitted him also. I thought that, as he had gone to the spot armed for a battle, he ought not to have been let off. There is no doubt that he suffered severely from the effects of Sriram's blow. The Rajah of course I set at liberty; but as he was legally bound as land-owner to have used every effort to prevent the riot, and also to have informed me of it,—and as it was proved that he was cognizant of it,—I fined him 500 rs., or £50, under Sec. 154 of the Penal Code ; which sum he promptly paid, without even appealing against the order. The sheriff's officers were dismissed, on my report of their conduct.

Just as the case was concluded, I received an anonymous letter, saying that Jugdeo had taken a bribe of 5,000 rs. from the Rajah for his good services in the matter, and that the current report was, that I also had received a similar amount, and that Jugdeo was telling everybody that he could do what he liked with me. The report, possibly, was based on the fact that the Rajah had paid his bail of 10,000 rs. in cash into my treasury; and it may have been stated that it was so divided. I don't think the natives really believed that I personally had taken any money, but very likely they thought Jugdeo had ; and perhaps he had.

However, on the top of this, came a note from Coldham enclosing a similar petition, which had been sent to the Lieutenant-Governor, and which had been forwarded by him to Coldham "for disposal." This meant, to take any or no steps, as he might think fit. His note to me was, "Tear this up, after perusal."

However, it all annoyed me very much ; and the next morning, when I went to Court and Jugdeo began to read the reports, I told him to hold his tongue, and to hand them over to the Nazir to read. I never saw a man look so crushed, but it was the only way I could see of snubbing him in public, as Ellis had advised ; and I had no proof against him of bad conduct.

Wahid Ali Khan was a great friend of his, and came to me privately, on hearing of his disgrace, to intercede for him ; whereupon I snubbed him too, and told him he had very much lowered himself in my estimation by interfering in matters which did not concern him. He went away sorrowing, but I forgave him in a week or so.

Poor Jugdeo asked for a fortnight's leave, and I gave it him very willingly. In his absence a very untoward thing occurred. Some of the Nepaulese chieftains who lived on the border had taken leases of certain villages in the Durbhungah estate ; and one of them, Roopun Singh by name, had fallen into arrears with his rent. A decree for ejectment had been obtained against him ; and he had come across the border with a small band of followers and some elephants, and carried off the two village accountants (patwarrees) with all their papers. I had heard nothing of this ; but presently an order came from the Magistrate, asking for further information, and I replied that I had received no report from the police. Whereupon the police were called upon for an explanation as to why no information had been sent to me, though the Magistrate of the district had received it. It turned out on inquiry, that information had been sent to me, but that it was contained in three lines at the end of a long report devoted to other matters, such as pounds and roads. Wuzeer Ali, the Nazir, had read it out in the usual sing-song way ; but probably had not thought it worth while to read the last three lines ; and my order, recorded on the back of the report, only referred to the first portion. Just at this crisis, Jugdeo returned. It was of course a sort of satisfaction to him that this had happened in his absence. I had to eat humble pie ; but the police caught it from the Commissioner for putting such an important matter in the fag-end of a report.

Jugdeo was equal to the occasion. He knew all about the treaty with Nepaul, framed to meet such cases ; and I prepared a case with much care for submission to the Governor General through the Foreign Office. Negotiations were entered into with promptitude ; and Roopun Singh was ordered by Jung Bahadur, nominally prime minister, but really king of Nepaul, to give up the patwarrees, and pay a fine of 500 rs., or £50, which Jung wished to make over to the aggrieved parties ; and the offender was to be punished by six months' imprisonment *in his own house.* The fact was, that he was a friend, if not a connection, of Jung Bahadur's, and at first he was inclined to be recalcitrant and actually defeated a small band of men that Jung sent for his arrest. However, he thought better of it, and made haste into Katmandou, to make due submission, and was sentenced as above. Our Government refused to allow the patwarrees to receive the 500 rs.; but they came to me and thanked me in the most touching way for their restoration to freedom and their native country. They had not been badly treated, but very much frightened.

After this I allowed Jugdeo to perform his usual duties, but I thought it advisable always to treat him with considerable reserve.

Another annoying thing took place about this time. Two brothers had had a quarrel, and the one had struck the other and killed him on the spot. The deceased had an enlarged spleen, which had been ruptured by the blow and caused instantaneous death, a very common thing in India. There was no doubt about the case; but as the place of occurrence was only six miles off, I rode out in the morning, telling the head constable who had charge of the case to meet me on the spot. The father of the deceased was a poor peasant, and after I had finished my inquiry, which disclosed no new facts, he came to me with a propitiatory offering of 1 rupee (2s.) in his hand. The

head constable,—whose own salary, by the way, was only
14s. a month,—intervened, saying, "No; you are a poor
man, the hakim will not take anything from you."

If I could have killed him with a look, I suppose I
should have done so. But the harm was done, no amount
of explanation would have made the rustic understand
that we officials thought it wrong to take presents. He
would only have been frightened, and thought that he
ought to have offered more. As for the policeman, he
naturally would have taken a bribe willingly offered, and
would probably have demanded it if it had not been. I
scolded him to the best of my ability; but I knew he was
no worse than his compeers.

Curiously enough, on my return I found another body
awaiting my inspection—that of a beautiful Mohammedan
girl, about seventeen years of age. She had a deep wound
behind one ear, and the mark of a cord round her neck.
The story of this case is best told in the confession of one
of the murderers, or rather murderesses, of the deceased.

"My name is Sukee, and my husband and I had been
married twenty years. We have two children, one my
daughter (about eighteen) who killed the deceased with
me, and my son married who lives in another village.
A year ago my husband married this other wife (the
deceased). I am old and I am no longer pretty, but I
have worked for my husband and brought up our children.
When he married this other wife he neglected me; he
spent all his money on her, and gave her new dresses and
the key of the rice store. To us, my daughter and me,
he gave nothing. She used to mock us and laugh at us,

and dance before us in her new dresses; and often we had nothing to eat when my husband was away from home, as she would give us nothing.

"The other day, when my husband was away, my son had come over to visit me. He had come a long way, and he was tired and hungry. I wanted to give him a meal, but I had nothing, and I humbled myself before the new wife and asked her for a little rice; but she refused, and mocked me and abused me, and my son was obliged to go away without food. Then my daughter and myself consulted, and we said we must kill her, otherwise our life is nothing. So we waited until she had gone to sleep that night, and I strangled her with a string, and my daughter beat her head with a curry stone" (used for grinding curry powder).

The daughter confirmed this story. She was a widow altogether dependent on her father. I felt sorry for them, very; but I was obliged to commit them for trial to the Sessions Court, and Percival sentenced them to death, considering, that though they had had great provocation, as several hours had elapsed, and the murder had been committed with deliberation, this could not be taken into account. I informed them of the sentence, which they received with apathy. But in these cases the confirmation of the High Court is necessary, and the Judge in Calcutta to whom this happened to be referred commuted the sentence to transportation for life, on the curious ground that there was no "dole," or deceit, in the matter.

When I informed the women of this, they were in despair. They begged to be hung instead; and it was necessary to keep a careful watch over them to prevent their committing suicide. Prisoners under sentence of transportation are sent to the Andaman Islands in the Bay of Bengal; and the natives of India, who have a religious dread of the sea and an undefined fear of the nature of the savage inhabitants of these islands,—indeed a very vague idea of the whole thing,—would much prefer death to this exile.

At length, on the Collectorate side, I came into antagonism with Furbelowe, as Manager under the Court of Wards. He had ejected, for arrears of rent, a certain lessee, without bringing a case in Court. The ejected party sued for recovery of possession, under the provisions of Act X. of 1859, alleging that his ejectment was illegal. Both parties filed the lease, in which it was agreed that the lessee, if in arrears, should be liable to ejectment without being sued in Court. I held that the lease was illegal, and contrary to the provisions of Act X. of 1859, and that I could not recognise it; that such leases were intended to make the Court of Wards judge and plaintiff in its own case; and that whenever the other party did not acquiesce in all its proceedings, the tendency would be to create disturbance. Supposing, for instance, that a lessee, whose ejectment was sought under these conditions, should resist, and the Court of Wards were to apply to the magisterial authorities for assistance, they would be bound, according to the law, not to interfere with the party already in possession, and to refuse the application. I therefore considered that the plaintiff in this case had been illegally ejected, and gave him a decree for recovery of possession.

This created a great sensation, as nearly all the Durbhungah leases had been framed on these principles; and Furbelowe told me afterwards that I had taken upon myself a grave responsibility, as both Blake and Coldham had approved this form of lease. I could only reply that I had, as a judicial officer, decided as I thought right, according to the best of my ability. The result, however, proved that I was right; for this case was never appealed. The Lieutenant-Governor himself had the matter under consideration, and the form of lease was altered.

I may mention that shortly before this Cookson's wife had arrived, and they were continuing to put up with me. She had brought her baby with her, a pretty little child of three months old, and Cookson had gone into Mozufferpore to meet her, and drive her out in his buggy. Seven horses were considered necessary for this journey, and animals had been borrowed for all the stages but one, which had to be accomplished by Cookson's own quadruped, a wretched little beast, furnished with very old rickety harness. At first it refused to start, and then dashed forward with a bound; the harness all fell to pieces like tow, down came the shafts on the ground, both breaking, while the horse disappeared in the distance. They were obliged to re-harness the horse just taken out, after making jury-shafts with a couple of bamboos, and arrived some two hours late for dinner, just as I had given up expecting them, and was preparing for bed. It was a startling introduction to Mofussil life for a young mother and baby.

Poor young baby! my acquaintance with it was short;

for less than a month afterwards, it fell ill of dysentery, and died after three days' suffering. The loss of a child is always a touching thing, but in this out-of-the-way place the anguish was doubly felt; the more so as, I think, we were all conscious that the little one might have been saved, had European medical assistance been promptly available. The Native Sub-assistant Surgeon had done his best, according to his lights; but he had never treated an European child before. I was at office when the sad news reached me in the afternoon. Burial follows so quickly on death in India, that the first thing to be done was to make the necessary preparations for conveying the little corpse the thirty-five miles into Mozufferpore. I went over to Furbelowe, who happened to be at Durbhungah. He was most kind, and sent a mounted messenger into Mozufferpore to give orders that the grave should be dug, ordered his carpenter to make a small coffin, and had dâks laid for a barouche for the next morning. The poor parents were completely overcome, and I ordered myself to be called the next morning when the coffin should be ready. It came about four o'clock, and I called Cookson out, and asked if he would like to do what was necessary; but both he and his poor wife were too prostrate with grief to do anything. So upon me devolved the inexpressibly sad office of nailing down the little clumsy case, made in native fashion. I recollect taking it out into the verandah, that they might not hear the sound of the hammer. As they drove off, about an hour afterwards, *vis-à-vis* to their mournful burden, the assembled servants raised a wail of lamentation; and it was a relief

to me that my work in office was heavy enough to turn
my thoughts from the sad scene.

They were away three days or so, and as (it being now
about the end of March) a tiger party in the adjoining
district of Bhaugulpore was about to make a start, and I
had received an invitation to join it, I thought it a good
opportunity to let them be alone in the house for a day or
two on their return. There were also some native holidays
coming in most conveniently, so the day before their return, on going into Court, I ordered all the mookhtyars
and legal agents present to come in, and I said, "Now I
have worked very hard for a long time, and I am going
away for three or four days' 'shikar' (sport), and I shall
expect you all to behave well, and to have no riots or
heavy cases in my absence. If any of your principals
have any such case, I shall look upon their mookhtyars
as bad men."

They all promised to be good, just like children; and as
I knew most of them would be glad to visit their friends
and relatives in my absence, I felt pretty confident.

That night I started in a palanquin, and the next day
reached an outlying indigo factory, where I found a
friendly planter, with an elephant ready to go on. After
a couple of hours' rest, for bath and breakfast, we started,
and had a long and weary night on the back of the
elephant. It was not possible to sleep for one second, for
fear of falling off, as we had only a "guddee," or cushion,
no "howdah" (framed seat). It was very tedious, and we
talked "de omnibus rebus et quibusdam aliis," about land
tenure, indigo-planting, law of evidence, native marriages,

sudder distilleries, on which point he quite agreed with me, etc., etc. My companion was very intelligent, and I got a good deal of information from him. At length, about 5 a.m., we saw the white tents of the encampment, on the borders of the broad stream of the Coosee river, and in an hour and a half, refreshed by a cheery welcome and a cup of coffee, we were on our way to shoot.

The Coosee runs down from Nepaul, and is bordered on its northern bank by the primeval forest of the Terai; on the other bank, the land is cleared and cultivated, while in the stream itself are numerous islands, covered with long grass, to which thousands of cattle are swum across for pasture. The tigers swim across from the other side to feed upon the cattle, and the annual loss to the herdsmen is very great. To the sportsman, however, the place is a paradise. There are plenty of deer, florican, and partridge, with an occasional rhinoceros. Our party was a large one, and included several ladies, who, after we had forded the river and formed line, were placed in the centre, on two of the steadiest elephants.

The first day we got some deer, and I shot my first florican—a beautiful bird, and very good eating. We saw traces of rhinoceros, but did not come across the animals themselves. On our return, we found a crowd of Brahmins feasting at the approach to the only practicable ford, and as the feast was spread on the ground, we could not pass through without disturbing them. We did our best, but some of the rice got scattered, and an elephant or two took a mouthful; and I heard the Brahmins cursing us and our female relatives as we moved off, and praying their gods to give us bad sport. We dined in a large tent, and the ladies sang, and made the evening pleasant; though I am not sure that my bed was not the sweetest thing to me.

The next day we visited another island, and had not been beating for more than an hour, when (despite the Brahmins' curse) the sportsman next to me in the line shouted, "Tiger!" and fired. I just caught a glimpse of some red and black stripes disappearing through the long grass, and fired also. The order to chase was then given, and the whole line moved on as rapidly as possible, the elephants all trumpeting, and everybody peering into the grass in front in a state of keen excitement. Presently, at a small open space, we came on some spots of blood, and while deliberating in which direction to go, I became sensible of a roaring, crackling sound behind. But the roar was not that of an animal; and looking round, I saw a vast sheet of flame and smoke advancing towards us with the rapidity of the wind. "To the river," shouted our leader—planter and sportsman of old-standing; and away we went at right angles to the fire, the island, fortunately, being very narrow, and stood in the shallow water, while the flame rushed over the spot we had recently been beating. There was a strong west wind blowing, the dry wind of this season; and the grass, set on fire probably by some herdsman's pipe at the other end of the island, had ignited like tow all along. It was exciting to see the cattle all rushing into the water; but I was surprised to observe no wild animals, except one or two deer.

In about half an hour the fire had ceased, dying out as rapidly as it had blazed up, and we returned to our sport. We found several green patches which had not been burned, and here doubtless any animals that might have been on the island had taken refuge. Among others, our tiger. We beat all these without success; but on emerging from the last, we saw him in the distance, crawling with difficulty over the ground, where the burnt grass was still smoking. He was evidently badly wounded, and we soon came up to him, and finished him. Then one of the elephants was made to kick the body, to see that no life was left in him,—for practically dead tigers have occasionally killed over-rash sportsmen,—and finally we descended from our positions of safety and examined our prey. He proved to be a fair-sized tiger, and I was pleased to have assisted at his death; though it was not admitted that I had been the first to wound him, so I did not get the skin. He had not shown fight at all; but yet it was something to bag a tiger, and this was the first I had seen killed. With much jabbering and hauling he was got on the back of one of the guddee elephants; and as the day was now well spent, we returned to camp.

The Brahmins, who were now in their temple, which we had to pass on our way, looked sullen at the inefficacy of their curse. Before dinner, I saw the tiger skinned. It was a curious sight, and the muscular arrangements of the fore-arm and shoulder showed an astonishing power. One blow from a tiger's paw is enough to smash in the skull of a man.

The next day we tried yet another island, and had

a long beat without getting any sport. It was fearfully hot, and the ladies were much done up. Suddenly my elephant, who was on the extreme right of the line, began to trumpet and show signs of alarm. It was a small animal, and not really fit to carry a howdah ; but I had been unable to get a better, and as it· was known to be timid, its behaviour was not thought of much consequence. We were just commencing to descend a slope with grass some sixteen feet high all about us, so that it was not possible to see much, when the elephant on my left also began to trumpet. "What is all that row about ?" said our leader. He had scarcely uttered the words when there came a roar like many claps of thunder, and there was a tiger on the head of my elephant. He had got right on his head, and the mahout sitting on the neck was completely under his belly. The elephant was shaking his very best to get the brute off, which of course had the effect of very nearly shaking me out of the howdah. I felt myself holding on with one hand to the framework of the howdah, and trying to hold my gun straight with the other, while I was actually looking down the roaring animal's throat. I did pull the trigger ; but with the gun wobbling so it was just a chance where the bullet went, and it certainly did not hit the tiger. At the same moment he fell off, unable to retain his hold, and my elephant ran away. This takes longer to narrate than it did to take place.

There were no trees, so there was no danger ; but the shaking was awful, and myself, my guns, and my servant behind were rolled about like peas in a frying-pan. I cast a helpless glance back, and saw that the tiger had broken through the line of elephants, and was bounding away to the rear with his tail up, roaring as he went. A straight shot from some one bowled him over; but it was evidently not a vital wound, for he stood up, having got into a place where the jungle was lighter, and looked at the line of elephants now advancing towards him. My mahout, who was really a plucky fellow, had now turned my elephant, and was with difficulty inducing it to follow the rest. The tiger now came charging down at the line and singled out the elephant of my friend with whom I had travelled. He was a magnificent sight, roaring and tearing up the grass as he came, with his bristles all erect and his tail lashing his sides; but my friend hit him in the foot with a bullet which completely rolled him over. He was up again directly and charged all round till other wounds made him weaker and weaker; and at length I managed, having now come up nearer, to send a bullet into his mouth.

On measurement he was found to be ten feet six, a young tiger, and well marked. He was a grand animal, and had certainly done his best to give us the sensation we sought, for he had attacked us without being touched, and fought gamely to the end. Our captain told me he had never seen a narrower escape, as the brute's paw must just have shaved my face; a few inches would have made all the difference in the result. One of the ladies told me she had got into a drowsy state from the heat, and was roused by the roar to see the spectacle of the animal on my elephant with his head close to mine.

On taking stock of damages, I found that the mahout had had a great gout of flesh taken out of his left arm, and that there were some severe claw wounds in the elephant's forehead. These were, I expect, caused by the claws of the hind feet, which must have been expanded to their utmost, for I could scarcely span with one hand the space between the scratches. I had some brandy and water in the howdah, and washed the mahout's wound, which must have made him smart; but he seemed much more concerned that his "chapkan," or jacket, was torn. This was a matter easily settled, and he pluckily consented to go on beating, though my elephant was very fidgety and timid for the rest of the day, and anything but comfortable.

We rather hoped to get the female of our dead tiger; and in about half an hour after the above, being again in very thick jungle, some animal was observed moving the grass in front of us. We formed a widish circle, and commenced closing in with a keen sensation of excitement, when the animal made a rush out between two elephants, and proved to be an ordinary-sized hog deer. This caused a great revulsion of feeling, and nobody thought of firing at him. After this we took to small game, and finished the day pleasantly enough. The tiger skin was awarded to me on a consideration of all the circumstances, and I was very pleased to get it. The next day being Sunday, I made a start in the evening of this eventful day, and by travelling a weary forty hours in a palanquin got back to Durbhungah in time to hold Court in the afternoon of Monday. Nothing troublesome had occurred, but orders had been received that the new Municipal Act III. of 1864 had been extended to the town of Durbhungah.

The intention of the Act was to commence the instruction of the native community in the mysteries of local self-government. It gave me a great deal of trouble. Firstly, it was necessary to select persons to be recommended through the Magistrate and Commissioner to Government for appointment as municipal commissioners. I sent up the names of my honorary committee, with one or two others, all of whom were approved. The Magistrate of the district was *ex-officio* Chairman, and myself Vice-chairman. The Commissioner, Coldham, was an *ex-officio* commissioner, to give him the right to attend meetings if necessary, and the Public Works official, called the Executive Engineer, attached to the district, was also a member of the body, as an expert to be consulted.

The scheme of assessment was changed, and the tax was to be an assessment not exceeding 7½ per cent. on the rental of houses and lands situate within municipal limits. The circumstances of the persons liable to the tax were no longer to be taken into consideration, and there was no power to exempt any one from payment on the ground of poverty. As a very large number of houses, or rather huts, in Durbhungah were let for 8*d.* or 1*s.* per annum, it will easily be understood that the collection of 7½ per cent. on this sum in four

quarterly instalments could not result in much profit
to the Commissioners. Indeed, it was clear that the
proceeds of the tax, at the maximum rate of 7½ per
cent., which was at once and unanimously decided upon
by the commissioners, would be less than those under
the old law. The new Act gave us power to spend
all surplus receipts on hospitals, schools, and various
other improvements; but as it appeared probable that
the payment of the municipal police, which was to be a
first charge on our revenues, would absorb all but a few
shillings annually, we found it scarcely necessary to frame
any scheme for these purposes.

The first thing we had to do was to reassess the
whole town, which cost money and labour, for the result
was 7,000 appeals, each of which must be decided by
at least three commissioners. There were nine of us
actually working members, and we divided ourselves into
three parties, and so only had some 2,300 each to do;
but it was weary work, and a heavy addition to my
other duties. Just at this time, too, occurred one of the
fires usual in Durbhungah at this season, when everything is rendered as inflammable as touchwood by the dry
west wind. I had previously issued orders in my capacity
as magistrate, that all thatched houses in Durbhungah
should be tiled, and no fires lighted between 8 a.m.
and 6 p.m. The legality of these orders was more than
doubtful, and I did not exact strict obedience to them;
but I hoped it would make the inhabitants generally
careful. On this ocasion 700 habitations were burned
down. The fire originated in a small thatched hut which

had not been tiled, and which leaned against a rather pretentious tiled mansion. When I went to view the scene of the conflagration, the owner of this latter assailed me with loud lamentations, saying, " What is the use of my obeying your orders, when the owner of this wretched little hut ruins us all by not attending to them." The owner was a poor old woman, who certainly had no money to spend on tiles, so I could say nothing in reply.

However, all the burnt-out people now petitioned for remission of their tax until their houses should be rebuilt, and this necessitated 700 more inquiries and decisions. We all worked hard, none more so than Bunwarree Lall, mentioned above as having opened the bidding for subscriptions at the meeting called by me soon after my arrival at Durbhungah. I was much pleased with him, as he showed more energy and spirit than is usually found in natives of his class.

He had, too, offered to spend 50,000 rs. in building a bridge over the river Bhagmatty, a narrow and deep stream about two miles outside Durbhungah, on the Mo-zufferpore road. His object was to built a temple on the other side of the stream, and make it easy of access by means of the proposed bridge. All he demanded of Government was, that the Public Works Department should supply him with a plan of the work ; but he in-sisted on keeping its construction under his own control, as he had dealings with Nepaul, and could get stone and timber down the river of good quality and at small ex-pense. His further object was to avoid waste of money by the Public Works officials. He had very good grounds for this, and I supported his request to the best of my ability. The Public Works Department, however, refused to supply a plan unless allowed to carry it out themselves, and held their own ; for as far as I know, the bridge is not yet·built, and this great convenience lost to a large number of travellers.

In the middle of all this, a heavy charge of rioting was brought against him. He had some land some few miles out of Durbhungah, and a boundary dispute had arisen between him and the owner of the neighbouring estate. Both parties had turned out in force, and blows had been interchanged, and one or two tolerably severe wounds inflicted. It was not asserted that he was present in person, but as the inquiry proceeded evidence was forthcoming that he had instigated the rioters on his side. It was a complicated and difficult case ; but so far I had not found it necessary to compel his attendance in Court in person, when I received official information that I was appointed to officiate as Joint Magistrate and Deputy Collector of Nuddea, a district some 400 miles distant. I was inclined to think that I could leave this case for disposal by my successor.

He was not to arrive for a fortnight ; but there were so many witnesses, and the defence was such a long affair, and some of the leaders of the riot on both sides had not yet been arrested, so that it was not probable it would be ripe for final orders before the expiration of that time.

I was as much surprised as pleased to find the genuine

(at least I believed it so) regret expressed at my departure
Cookson was naturally sorry. Nundiput had told him that
he could not let any successor of mine have his house.
He was entitled by the Government orders to one room
in the new subdivisional residence. But the new subdivisional residence, built on the model plan by the P.W.D.,
contained only three rooms, two bath rooms, and a verandah. The amount allowed for the purpose by a Government in this respect parsimonious in the extreme, was
small, and the P.W.D. were not good hands at making
small amounts go far. My successor was a married man ;
and the problem of two married couples living in three
rooms, of which the largest was only 20 ft. by 16 ft., was
not to be solved. So he and his wife sought the shelter
of the dâk bungalow, and I persuaded Nundiput to let
my successor have his house until the subdivisional
buildings were completed. One of my clerks, I recollect,
—having, I suppose, his own ideas of what the residence
of a ruler should be,—asked me if the partially-erected
residence was not the cookhouse (baworchi khana). I
felt somewhat ashamed in telling him the truth ; though
perhaps I ought to have been proud to think that the
ruling nation was so careful of expenditure in such a
matter.

But I really believe that my native friends were as sorry
as Cookson. I was the first hakim who had been settled
at Durbhungah ; and though I have been obliged, through
fear of being prolix, to omit many details illustrative of
the fact, I was on terms of genuine friendliness with all the
leading native gentry in the neighbourhood,—such friend-

liness, I mean, as caste restrictions and national characteristics would permit. I had always been specially careful to conform, as far as my knowledge allowed me, to their notions of courtesy; and, to the best of my recollection, had never wilfully hurt the feelings of any of them. As regards my Court work, I had honestly done my best for the convenience of suitors; and, being a tolerably quick worker, had avoided vexatious delays. There were some, of course, who disliked me. For instance, I don't think Nokee Lall was sorry to see me go; and the younger brother of Ganeshur Singh, the young Rajah's uncle, Mitreshur, probably disliked me, as I had endeavoured to bring him to terms with his brother, with whom he was quarrelling about their ancestral property, and whom I believed to be in the right. My moral influence was, I consider, worth something.

I have omitted to mention that in the cold season just past, an Agricultural Exhibition had been held in Mozufferpore. The new Lieutenant-Governor was desirous of introducing a series of these, and hoped to accustom the mind of the native cultivator to some new ideas about husbandry (at present the same implements are in use as those of the time of the flood, or antecedent to it) and breeding cattle, etc., etc. Upon me devolved the task of stirring up the landholders in the Durbhungah jurisdiction to exert themselves to assist in contributing to the forthcoming show. It was only through them that the small peasant farmers could be got at.

I held an open-air meeting, at which some of the landowners and a good many of their agents attended, and placing the former on my right hand and the latter on my left, I adjured them, in the best Hindustani I could command, to be zealous for the credit of the district of their birth, and not to allow it to be surpassed by the contributions of outsiders. The landlords I addressed as "ap log," the honorific title given to an equal in conversation, and begged them to bestir *themselves*; the agents, as "tum," the term given to inferiors, and begged them to stir up their principals. My planter friend, the patriarch above mentioned, was present, and complimented me on the manner in which the proceedings had been conducted. As a result, the Durbhungah subdivision was really well represented at the Show.

I was ordered in there, to assist during the week that it lasted, and held my Court in a tent pitched in Ellis's compound. The Show grounds were down by the Race Course in a grove of trees. I was deputed, with one or two others, to receive or reject objects brought for exhibition.

Among other things that I was compelled to reject, were a spotted deer, a peculiar kind of crane, a puppy with five legs, and a he-goat that gave milk.

The populace, too, had curious rumours about the purpose of the Exhibition, which had to be contradicted. There were seven gates to the grounds, and most of the samples of grain were exhibited in very small earthenware platters, ranged on wooden shelves. One rumour was to the effect that cannon were to be planted at each of these gates; that when a large crowd of people were assembled inside, at a given signal they were all to be ordered to eat out of these platters, and so lose their caste. Those who refused were to be blown away from the guns.

I also had to act as judge in awarding prizes for grain exhibited from the neighbouring district of Sarun; but I managed to get an intelligent native gentleman to go round with me, and with his advice I managed to give tolerable satisfaction.

On the whole, it was a very jolly time, for a great number of Europeans were assembled, and only suitors with real grievances took the trouble to come all the way in from Durbhungah to prosecute their cases, so that my Court work was light, and I had a little leisure to enjoy myself.

Ellis was a good deal worried with arrangements and correspondence; and when I afterwards became a full-blown Collector I was able to appreciate the enormous additional work that these extra things threw on an officer in that position. On such occasions a Collector may truly say, with the Psalmist, " Lord, how are they increased that trouble me !"

I was complimented on the result of the influence I had exercised ; and now I was to leave the place where I had employed nearly two years in creating that influence, and go among a people who knew me not. And yet I could not say that I should have wished it otherwise, for the move was promotion to me. I should draw an extra £240 a year, should be stationed at the head-quarters of the district as the Magistrate's first lieutenant, and lead a much less lonely life. And yet I was really and truly sorry to say good-bye to my Tirhoot friends, and would much have preferred that my promotion had been to the post held by Melville in Mozufferpore. He was just appointed to act as Civil Officer with the column about to invade Bhootan. Cookson I never saw again. The number of Assistant Superintendents of Police was not long after much reduced ; and he was one of those whose services were dispensed with, and who received a small compensation.

Nearly all my furniture was eagerly bought up by my native friends,—I mean chairs, tables, dog-cart, lamps. They would probably none of them ever be used, but kept in a special room, "dekhne ke waste" (to be looked at). On leaving a district, civilians are allowed to dispose of their goods and chattels in this way, as it is not supposed that the natives will be anxious to curry favour with them any longer, and no suspicion can attach to the transactions. Yet many of my Durbhungah friends continued to correspond with me for a long time ; and I received a letter from one only the other day, after the lapse of a dozen years from the date of my last seeing him.

At length the day of departure arrived. I had made over charge to my successor ; I had given so many certificates of character to clerks, police officers, chuprassies, tax darogahs, distillery darogahs, and every other person who had served under me, that I was weary of writing the words, "performed his duties to my entire satisfaction." These certificates are most eagerly sought after, and in more advanced districts the natives have all they get printed, and bound up into little books. Some of those who are intimately connected with me had gone as far as

the river which Bunwarree Lall had wis
there I found him and Wahid Ali Kha
say a last good word for his bridge in
was quite relieved at length to find
my groom.